Night of Reunion

Also by Michael Allegretto

Death on the Rocks
Blood Stone
The Dead of Winter

MICHAEL ALLEGRETTO

Night of Reunion

CHARLES SCRIBNER'S SONS
New York

Charles Scribner's Sons
Macmillan Publishing Company
866 Third Avenue, New York, NY 10022
Collier Macmillan Canada, Inc.

This is a work of fiction. Names, characters, places, and incidents either are the product of the author's imagination or are used fictitiously. Any resemblance to actual events or persons, living or dead, is entirely coincidental.

Library of Congress Cataloging-in-Publication Data

Allegretto, Michael.
Night of reunion/by Michael Allegretto.
p. cm.
ISBN 0-684-19133-4
I. Title.
PS3551.L385N5 1990 89-27233 CIP
813'.54—dc20

Design by Ellen Sasahara

10 9 8 7 6 5 4 3 2 1

Printed in the United States of America

For Linda

I wish to thank both Dominick Abel for pointing the way toward this book and Susanne Kirk for helping me get there.

Special thanks to Pamela Allegretto Franz, co-owner of Custom Hair, for her patience and expertise. Any errors are, of course, mine.

Night of Reunion

1

SHE STEERED THE CAR STEADILY westward through the winter night.

She was alone on this long, flat stretch of highway, and her headlight beams knifed quickly through the darkness, illuminating swirling flakes of snow. The dashboard lights painted her hands and face a sickly green.

She drove in silence, the radio off. The only sound was the hum of the tires on the cold black asphalt.

She'd been on the road for several days, sleeping where she could, eating only when she had to. Her money was almost gone. She couldn't afford to stay in motels or dine in roadside restaurants. She could barely afford the cheap, greasy take-out food she forced herself to eat.

Gasoline. That's where the last few dollars had to go.

And so she ignored the rumblings in her empty belly from too little food and the ache in her back and legs from sleeping in the car. She could even ignore the fact that she hadn't bathed in days, although her body odor seemed to grow thicker by the hour within the confines of the car.

But she could not ignore the cold. It numbed her feet and hands and made her hunch forward over the wheel, shivering.

She swore at the car's heater. It seemed to have a mind of its own. Sometimes it gave forth warm, welcome air, enough to take away the chill, at least briefly. But most of the time it was silent and cold.

The car's previous owner hadn't had time to tell her about the heater. She'd had to find that out on her own. And really, it wouldn't be so bad if the clothes she'd borrowed were better. Oh, they were pretty clothes, and they were almost exactly the right size, but they weren't warm enough, not if you were driving with no heater.

She tried not to think about the cold. Instead, she thought about pleasant things. Leaving the hospital, for example. And speaking by telephone to the nice man at Alex Whitaker's old school. He'd told her that Alex no longer taught there; he'd accepted a post in Colorado Springs. The man had even given her a home address, although he hadn't known if it was current.

"It doesn't matter," she'd told the man. "I'll find him."

And she knew that she would, even if she had to track him clear across the country. She'd find him because she had to. Finding him was all she had left. That and her hate.

And now her headlights splashed across a sign on the side of the road. She grinned and read it aloud.

"Welcome to Colorful Colorado."

She drove through the black-and-white landscape, ignoring the cold. Her fingers on the steering wheel were as stiff and hard as the talons of a bird of prey.

2

SARAH WHITAKER TOOK THE mail from the box, barely looking at it.

She unlocked the front door, stepped into the foyer, and dumped the mail—two magazines and a handful of envelopes—on the small table. Then she peeled off her gloves, shook herself out of her coat, and hung it in the hall closet.

When she turned around, she nearly tripped over the cat.

"Hey, Patches, what's going on?" She squatted down and rubbed the big orange-and-white cat behind the ears. He bumped his thick head into her leg and purred hard enough to be heard. Then he circled Sarah with his tail erect and his body leaning against her. She noticed that his left ear was smudged with dirt.

"What've you been doing? Chasing phantom mice?"

Patches meowed.

"That's what I thought," she said, and stood.

Sarah crossed the foyer to the foot of the stairs, the cat at her heels. She turned the thermostat up to seventy-two. Then she remembered last month's bill from Colorado Springs Utility, swore under her breath, and turned it down to sixty-eight. She heard the muffled roar of the gas furnace kicking on in the basement and, almost immediately afterward, the soft ticking of warm water flowing through the pipes along the baseboards.

That was the first improvement she and Alex had made right after moving in last June—installing hot-water heat. They'd abandoned the forced-air furnace, which they both knew would cause uneven heating, drafts, and faint black streaks on the walls above the registers. But even with their new, efficient heating system, they were apprehensive about the cost of keeping a house this size comfortable. Especially through Colorado's winter months.

Actually, the house had more space than they'd ever need. But soon after Sarah and Alex first met, they'd learned that they'd been sharing a dream—to live in a large, old home. And just before they were married, this one had come on the market. It seemed perfect. And since the housing market here was somewhat depressed, the house had been perfectly priced for their combined incomes.

"Besides," Alex had said, "look at that backyard!"

Sarah had to agree that the two acres of wooded ground behind the house would be a wonderful place for her son to play and explore. In fact, what six-and-a-half year-old boy wouldn't want a backyard the size of a small park?

Sarah smiled to herself, climbed the curving staircase, and walked down the hallway to the master bedroom.

She pulled off her jeans, which were a bit too tight. Because they'd shrunk, she told herself, *not* because she was "bulking up for the winter," as her partner at the shop liked to say. Her shirt smelled faintly of perm solution. She tossed it in the hamper along with her panties and bra, then climbed into the shower. This was another improvement that Alex had made to the old house—hanging a shower curtain around the bathtub and installing a spray head. Sarah let the hot needle-spray massage the stiffness out of her neck and shoulders.

When she was finished, she toweled herself off, then stood naked in front of the mirror and blow-dried her hair. It was black and silky and shoulder length. She'd had it cut in a simple style, which made it easier to take care of—a small relief after spending the day taking care of *other* people's hair.

She put aside the brush and drier and leaned forward, examining her face in the mirror.

Sarah had even features and a "cute" nose, which she hated, even though she knew women who'd paid thousands of dollars to get one just like it. Maybe that's why she didn't like it. She thought her best feature was her eyes, which were wide set and deep blue. She didn't think of herself as pretty, although she'd been called that often enough. She did, however, think of herself as "young," even though last week she'd found her first gray hair.

The sight of it had stopped her brush hand in mid-stroke. She'd plucked out the pale offender, betrayer of age, and carefully dropped it in the wastebasket, trying not to feel old.

I'm months away from my twenty-ninth birthday, she thought. Hardly old. That hair had been a premature aberration, not a harbinger of age.

She examined herself in the mirror, turning slowly, raising her arms, looking for dreaded wrinkles or sags but feeling confident about not finding any. Everything looked and felt smooth and firm—arms and legs, breasts and stomach, buttocks and thighs.

Best of all, she felt great. So what are you worried about? she thought.

Thirty, she knew.

She was closing in on it, and there was something about that number. In her twenties, she'd considered anyone over thirty to be old and not entirely to be trusted. Of course, in high school she'd thought the same of anyone over twenty.

Okay, she admonished herself, so it's all relative.

Still, there had been that gray hair.

Half an hour later, Sarah, now dressed in yellow sweatpants and matching sweatshirt, was in the big, old-fashioned kitchen, with its hanging pots, wide counters, and ceiling-high cupboards. The radio on the countertop was tuned to a Golden Oldies station. Sarah shook chicken breasts and drumsticks in a sack filled with crumbs and spices and kept time to Aretha Franklin singing "Respect." When the song ended, she began arranging the breaded chicken pieces on a baking tray.

She heard the front door open, and a moment later Brian burst into the kitchen, still wearing his parka and wool cap and waving a sheet of paper.

"Hey, Mom! I got a silver star!"

Sarah smiled down at the black-haired, blue-eyed ball of energy. "Hiya, kiddo. A silver star? Let me see. Wait a minute."

She rinsed her hands in the sink, dried them on a dish towel, then took the paper from her son. It was thick brown drawing paper on which he'd rendered an ominous-looking figure with a white face, a black cape, and a yellow sticklike object from which emanated red rays. A silver star had been glued to the upper right-hand corner.

"It's Lord Doom," he said, looking at the tray of coated chicken pieces. "What's that?"

"Lord Doom? It's dinner."

"Yeah, but what *is* it?"

"Brian, come on, it's chicken."

"Oh."

"You love chicken, remember?"

"I guess." He sounded uncertain.

"It'll look a lot better after it's baked. Trust me."

"Okay, Mom." He started to leave.

"Hey, do you want your picture?"

"Oh, yeah." He came back for it.

"So who's Lord Doom?"

"You know, on the Saturday cartoons. Lord Doom and the Sword of Power."

Sarah bumped her forehead with the heel of her hand in an exaggerated manner. "Oh, *that* Lord Doom."

"Mom," Brian said, smiling, his head cocked to the side, "there's only one."

Sarah smiled back. "Well, I think it's neat that you got a silver star."

He beamed, then lowered his eyes. "Lots of the other kids got one, too."

"Even so, I'm proud of you. That's the best picture of Lord Doom I've ever seen."

"Really?"

"Really."

"All right!"

He spun toward the doorway, nearly colliding with Alex.

"Hey, slow down."

"Sorry, Dad," Brian said, and he was gone.

Alex took Sarah in his arms. He was a few inches shy of six feet, which made him half a head taller than Sarah. His light brown hair looked the way it usually did, as if he'd just run his fingers through it, and there was a familiar sparkle in his greenish-brown eyes.

"Hi," he said, and they kissed. "How was your day?"

Sarah hugged him, and the wool of his sweater-vest tickled her nose. "Busy, as usual."

"Good," he said. "It'll keep you out of trouble."

She gave him a playful punch in the ribs. "I'll give you all the trouble you can handle, buster."

He laughed.

"And how are things at Jefferson High?" Sarah asked, turning back to the platter of chicken. "Are your students brimming with more historical knowledge tonight than they were this morning?"

"This close to vacation? Are you kidding? They're thinking

more about Christmas purchases than the Louisiana Purchase. Can I help with dinner?"

"Everything's under control."

"Okay," he said, tugging at his tie. "Then I'm going to get washed up and dressed down."

"We'll eat in an hour."

"Great." He patted her on the backside and started toward the door, then stopped.

"Did we get any mail?" he asked.

"It's by the front door. Looks like mostly junk and maybe a bill or two."

"No use ruining my appetite now," he said, and walked out.

Sarah put the oven on "bake" and turned the dial to four hundred. She pulled open the refrigerator and got out a head of lettuce, a red onion, a small can of black olives, and a thin wedge of feta cheese. While she made the salad, she heard muffled noises from upstairs—the clomping of feet and a faint, high-pitched scream followed by laughter. Sarah pictured Alex chasing Brian down the hallway, and she smiled.

She knew how fortunate she was to have them both. And how fortunate that they got along so well. She'd heard of more than one divorced woman who'd remarried, only to find that her child and her new husband were not compatible.

But not me, she thought, and knocked her knuckles twice on the wooden cutting board.

Brian and Alex had hit it off from the start, and for the past eighteen months—seven of which they'd spent under the same roof—their respect and fondness for each other had grown. It matched the love that Sarah felt for them both. She knew that at last she was exactly where she belonged.

And this is where the chicken belongs, she thought, smiling to herself and sliding the tray into the oven.

Later, while they ate dinner at the big table in the kitchen, they discussed where they should put the Christmas tree. After all, it was their first Christmas in this house.

During Christmases past, when Sarah had lived in the small house across town—first as a mother and a wife, later as a single parent—there had been no question about where the tree should go: the only available corner of the tiny living room. Of course, Brian had come into the world after the tree's location had been determined, so he'd had no say in the matter. And Alex had never had a tree before. At least not in the apartment he'd lived in when Sarah first met him. Before that, when he'd been with his first wife in New York, Sarah couldn't say.

The three of them quickly dismissed the dining room as the place for the tree, and just as quickly, the music room. That left the family room and the living room.

Alex opted for the former, because it was the largest room in the house.

"More room for a tree," he said.

Brian immediately scrambled out of his chair.

"Brian, where—"

"I'll be right back," he said, and ran out of the room.

Alex looked at Sarah and shrugged. A few moments later Brian returned.

"The family room is a *great* place for the Christmas tree," he said. "We can put it in the corner next to the TV."

"Good idea," Alex said. "Now how about sitting back down and finishing your dinner."

As soon as Brian was reseated and had picked up his half-eaten drumstick, Sarah said she preferred the living room.

"If we put the tree in the bay window," she said, "you could see it from the street."

Brian's chicken leg hit the plate, and he was up and out of the kitchen door in a flash. Sarah looked at Alex.

"We don't have a third choice for a room, do we?"

"If we think of one, let's wait until after dinner."

"Good plan."

Brian came back.

"The big window is a *perfect* place for the tree," he said.

"Hey, what about *my* idea?"

"It's good, too, Dad."

"See," Alex said to Sarah.

"So, can we have two trees?" Brian wanted to know.

"Nice try, Brian," Sarah said. "Now get back up here and finish your dinner, okay?"

They decided on the living room, mostly because of the fireplaces. They'd yet to use the one in the living room, but they'd already burned a half-dozen fires in the family room, and the combination of heat and dry air was sure to quickly dry out a pine tree.

After dinner Brian went up to his room, and Alex helped Sarah clear the table and wash the dishes.

"Would you like tea?" Sarah said.

"Sounds good."

Sarah put the kettle on the stove. Alex left the kitchen and returned in a few minutes with the mail. He was sorting through it as he sat down.

"Junk, junk, phone bill, junk, bi—"

He stopped, and Sarah looked at him. He was frowning at the plain white envelope in his hand.

"What is it?"

Alex shook his head. "It's . . . odd, that's all."

He slit open the envelope with his thumbnail and removed a single page folded in thirds. As he unfolded it, a small newspaper clipping fell to the tabletop. Alex glanced at it, then sucked in his breath and snatched up the newsprint.

"Oh, my God," he said, his eyes scanning the item. He held it between his thumb and forefinger, and Sarah could see that he was squeezing so tightly his fingernail was white.

"Alex, what?"

He acted as if he hadn't heard her, quickly reading the handwritten letter. Then he reread the news item.

"Alex?"

Sarah stepped toward him, and his head jerked up as if he'd forgotten that she was in the room. For a brief moment she saw something in his eyes that she'd never seen there before—fear. And then it was gone.

He stood awkwardly, pushing the chair back with his legs, making it screech on the floor.

"Honey, what is it?"

Alex shook his head no, looking down, avoiding her eyes.

"Nothing," he said, "it's . . ."

He shook his head again and walked from the room.

3

SARAH STARED AT THE EMPTY kitchen doorway.

Alex's footsteps faded into another part of the house. Sarah had never seen him so upset. She hesitated about going after him. She wanted to know what was wrong. Also, she wanted to assure him that whatever it was, he could tell her about it. She'd listen. She'd help if she could. After all, they were together now, for better or for worse.

The kettle began to whistle behind her. Sarah switched off the stove and moved the kettle to a cold electric burner.

Don't crowd him, she thought.

She opened a cupboard and took down a tin of tea, then placed one bag in a white mug painted with small purple flowers. She poured in steaming water, then put away the tea tin.

When she brought her mug to the table, she noticed the envelope.

Alex had taken the letter and the news clipping with him, but he'd left the envelope behind. It lay facedown, a stark white rectangle with one jagged edge. Sarah hesitated for a moment, then sat down and turned over the envelope.

It was addressed to Alex in blue ink in a shaky script. The return address was that of Joseph Pomeroy of Albany, New York.

The name Pomeroy was familiar to Sarah, but it took her a minute to place it. And then she had it: It was the maiden name of Alex's first wife. Deceased wife, Sarah corrected herself. She knew little about her, for Alex had always been understandably reluctant to dwell on the tragedy of his past, but she did know that Laura Pomeroy had had only one living relative: her father.

Sarah set down the envelope and sipped her tea.

She remembered that soon after they'd first met Alex had told her about his recent past, how he'd lived and taught in Albany and how four years ago his wife and their adopted son had been killed in a terrible automobile accident near their home. Alex admitted that he'd become severely depressed and decided to leave New York behind and try for a fresh start in life in a new location. He'd accepted a teaching post in a high school in Colorado Springs. And after living and teaching here for several years, he'd met Sarah and Brian.

Sarah carried her empty mug to the sink, washed it, and set it in the drainer to dry. She picked up the envelope, considered tossing it in the trash, then placed it on the countertop. She thought Alex might want it, perhaps for the return address.

Sarah couldn't imagine what Joseph Pomeroy could say that would so upset Alex. She assumed that Alex would tell her when Brian was asleep in bed.

But after she'd tucked her son under the covers, kissed him good night, and rejoined Alex in the family room to watch *Masterpiece Theater*, he'd said nothing about the letter. He'd regained his composure and acted as if nothing had happened. However, Sarah could see that his eyes were focused sometimes on the carpet, sometimes on the wall, but rarely on the TV screen.

They'd gone to bed with no mention of the letter.

† † †

The next morning, Sarah had a nine o'clock appointment, so Brian left the house with her.

Whenever Sarah's first customer was scheduled later than nine, Alex took Brian to school, because the timing was better for them all. And Alex always picked him up in the afternoon. First, because they got out at the same time. And second, because Will Rogers Elementary School was almost in a direct line from the Whitakers' house to Jefferson High, where Alex taught world history to struggling sophomores and American history to all three upper grades.

Sarah and Brian, bundled in coats and neck scarves and gloves, followed the flagstone path around the south side of the house to the garage. The sky was clear and blue, but the air was very cold. Last night the local TV weatherman had predicted an overnight low of fifteen degrees and a high today of thirty-six.

A veritable heat wave, Sarah thought grimly.

She unlocked the side door of the garage. Neither she nor Alex had mentioned the letter this morning. Now, as she followed Brian inside, she tried to push it from her mind.

It was cold in the garage, but not nearly as cold as outside. The overhead heater roared on now and then to keep the temperature from dipping below fifty—warm enough to ensure that the aging Jeep Wagoneer and the two-year-old Toyota Celica would both start.

The best part about the garage, Sarah thought, remembering those years without one, was that there was never a need to scrape frost from the windshield.

She flipped a switch on the wall. A motor clicked on. One of the garage's two big doors rolled up, curling over the decade-old Jeep Wagoneer. Sarah and Brian climbed in, and after they'd fastened their seat belts, Sarah started the engine. She let it run for a minute before she backed out of the garage.

Brian opened the glove box, removed the garage-door remote control, and pointed it through the windshield. He made a noise with his mouth that Sarah supposed was the exact sound of an interstellar laser weapon, and the garage door slid closed.

Sarah backed the Jeep up the curving drive and into the street. The foothills to her right were still white from last week's snowfall. The streets had been plowed clear of snow, but there were numerous patches of ice where the plowed snow had melted and flowed over the asphalt during the day and then frozen at night.

Sarah drove with care.

She crossed Pikes Peak Avenue and turned left on Colorado Avenue. They drove eastward past a little-used parking lot that had recently been converted into a Christmas-tree lot.

"Is that where we're going to get our tree, Mom?"

Brian's finger was pushed against the side window.

"Maybe so. I think it's the closest."

"When?"

"I don't know. Pretty soon."

"Tonight?"

"I suppose we could, but—"

"All right!"

"But we'll talk it over with your dad first, okay?"

"Okay, I guess. But we didn't last year, did we?"

"No, because last Christmas your dad and I weren't married yet, remember? We weren't all living together then."

"Oh, yeah."

One block from the school Sarah waited at a stop sign as a crossing guard, holding high her own stop sign, led a group of children across the street.

"Mom?"

"What, hon?"

"Do you like Dad better than you liked Daddy? I mean, you're not going to get a divorce, are you?"

"No, honey, of course not."

Sarah was taken aback by the question. She was also surprised by Brian's comparison: "Daddy" was his natural father, Ted Saunders, and "Dad" was Alex.

She remembered the first time Brian had called Alex "Dad," some months after she and Alex were married. That had been a significant moment for Sarah, symbolizing for her Brian's acceptance of his new father. It had been particularly satisfying because Brian's natural father had abandoned them. Well, perhaps "abandoned" was too strong. Ted hadn't *exactly* done that. But after the divorce he'd moved to Seattle and Sarah had rarely seen him—him *or* his alimony and child-support checks. That was okay with her, though. Ted had never been close to Brian, even during the marriage. He'd seemed to resent Sarah's dividing her attention between two males, and he'd turned much of that resentment toward his son.

Better that he's gone, Sarah remembered thinking. Besides, she had a good job, and she and Brian could get along just fine, thank you, without any help from an ex-husband.

However, the divorce had made Sarah cautious—perhaps too cautious—in her relationships with men. In fact, during the two years plus between her divorce from Ted and her chance meeting with Alex, she could count on her fingers the number of dates she'd accepted. When Alex had come along, though, she'd known immediately that he was someone special.

They'd gone together for nine months before they'd married. Everything had seemed so easy and natural between them, as if they'd been meant for each other. Just as important to Sarah, Brian and Alex got along well. And thankfully for all of them, Ted Saunders had not stood in the way of Alex's adopting Brian.

The adoption had been six months ago, and since then Brian had rarely mentioned his "daddy" and had not once spoken of the divorce.

Sarah looked at her son, but he was staring through the windshield.

"Why did you ask me that, Brian?"

"Just because."

"Because why?"

He shrugged, still staring straight ahead.

"I guess because I really like Dad and I don't want you to get a divorce from him like you did from Daddy."

"Oh, Brian, I love your dad." She gave his leg a gentle squeeze. "I love him a whole lot, just like I love you a whole lot. You know?" She squeezed his leg near his knee, making him giggle. "You know?"

"Yeah."

"The three of us will be together for a long, long time."

"Promise?"

"Promise," Sarah said.

She let Brian out in front of his school and watched him run up the sidewalk to join a group of children entering the red-brick building. Then she headed toward North Nevada Avenue, turned right, and drove south for two miles to the shopping center. She cruised through the huge, mostly empty parking lot to the far end of the shops. Hair Today was the second from the end, tucked between a fabric store and a State Farm Insurance office.

Sarah parked the Wagoneer in one of the many empty slots. She unlocked the heavy glass door and pushed through into her shop—actually, hers and Kay Nealy's.

Nine years ago, when Sarah had graduated from junior college in Cedar Falls, Iowa, she never imagined that she'd eventually co-own a business. Actually, she hadn't been at all certain just what she wanted to do.

She'd studied art in school, and she'd shown some talent, although not enough, she felt, to ever consider making her living as an artist. After graduation she'd worked for a time in an arts-and-crafts store, but the pay had been practically negligible. She found herself waiting tables at a family restaurant to pay the rent on her new apartment. She liked the people contact but not the job.

Then she'd met Ted Saunders and they'd fallen in love. He'd told her that there could never be another woman in his life, and so they were married. A few months later, Ted's employer, a sporting-goods manufacturer, transferred him to Colorado, requiring Sarah to leave behind her family, friends, and job.

After the move, Sarah began to change her aspirations from "job" to "career." A friend of hers in Iowa ran a hair boutique, so Sarah was acquainted with the business. She knew, for instance, that her friend earned a lot more money than *she* ever had waiting tables.

For the next ten months Sarah worked part-time as a waitress in Colorado Springs and attended school full-time, learning about cuts and styles, tints and perms. Soon after her graduation, she was styling hair in a beauty shop near the center of town.

Sarah liked what she was doing. She enjoyed the company of her customers, and she found satisfaction in her work, which, after all, contained elements of her first love, artistry.

Then she'd gotten pregnant with Brian and eventually was forced to quit her job. By the time Brian was two, Sarah had decided two things: He was old enough for a day-care center, and she was more than ready to go back to work.

Those had been days of mixed emotions. She was delighted to be working for her new employer, Kay, with whom she was quickly becoming fast friends. On the other hand, her marriage was in jeopardy. Before Brian turned three, Sarah and Ted had divorced.

Sarah overcame the trauma of separation by focusing her attention on her son and her work.

After a year or so, Sarah had built up a large enough clientele to justify opening her own shop. She hadn't said anything to Kay, but Kay knew exactly what was on her mind: You could make a much better living owning a shop than working for someone else on a percentage basis. And the best way to own a shop was to work for someone for a while and then leave and take your customers with you. Kay knew all about that. After all, that's how *she'd* gotten started.

So before Sarah had made the big move, Kay had offered her a proposition. For ten thousand dollars Sarah could become her equal partner, splitting the expenses and keeping separate the profits from her own customers. That way they'd both benefit. Even though Kay would take in less money each month, she'd cut her expenses in half, substantially reduce her paperwork as an employer, and she could put the ten grand down on a almost-new Porsche she'd been eyeing. Best of all, she wouldn't have to start searching for a suitable replacement. Sarah would be out ten thousand, but that was a much smaller investment than if she opened her own shop. Plus she'd be half owner of a business, and her profits would start going up immediately.

Sarah borrowed the money from her parents.

She'd paid them back after only one year of becoming a co-owner.

Sarah removed her coat and hung it on the hall tree near the door. Then she switched on the track lighting, which was adjusted to surround the stations with even light. Comfortable chairs were arranged around this end of the room and partway along the front wall. There were large potted plants and a wicker basket filled with magazines.

Sarah and Kay's stations were at the far end of the room. Each station consisted of a leather-and-chrome hydraulic chair and a large mirror over a shelf and cabinet. Hanging from one end of each shelf was a large hand mirror, and attached to the other end was a holder for curling irons and a hair drier. The top of each shelf held a small basket filled with assorted hair clips, a bottle of Barbacide to hold the combs, a covered basket of clean brushes, a basket with various types of scissors, a spray bottle filled with water, a jar of styling gel, a can of mousse, a pump bottle of hair spray, and an ashtray.

The latter was for some of their customers, since neither Sarah nor Kay smoked.

Sarah opened the Levolor blinds on the front window, then crossed the room to the desk, which was backed up to the chest-high divider that separated the front room from the back. She pulled open the bottom drawer and stuffed in her purse and her empty "cash box"—a cigar box she used to hold cash, checks, and credit-card vouchers.

She phoned their answering service, but there had been no messages last night, no last-minute cancellations.

Then she turned her attention to the large, well-used appointment book that lay open on the desk. Sarah shuddered to think of what would happen if it were ever lost—absolute chaos and confusion for at least eight weeks, because that's how far in advance some customers scheduled themselves.

Sarah ran her finger down her column of today's page, Thursday, December 3. On some days the pages had gaps here and there, hours in which no one had made an appointment. This was not one of those days—Sarah was booked solid from nine until seven tonight. She saw that Kay would be nearly as busy but wouldn't start until ten.

Sarah rechecked her first customer—9:00 A.M., Veronica Santori, cut only—then went to the back room. She paused just past the doorway to turn the thermostat up to seventy-five.

What the hell, she thought, the heat is included in the rent.

The back room was furnished more for function than for comfort, and Sarah and Kay had softened its look as much as possible with hanging plants and pastel-toned prints in chrome frames.

On the right was a hydraulic chair that was used for perm and color applications. It faced a large mirror over one end of a countertop that ran the entire length of the room. The cabinets below the counter were stocked with baskets filled with assorted perm rods. Halfway down the counter were a pair of hydraulic chairs tilted back and fitted under porcelain shampoo bowls. At the far end of the counter was a sink, a Mr. Coffee machine, and a stack of cups.

Across from the counter were a pair of straight-backed chairs that sat beneath beehive-shaped hair driers. Beside them was a closet filled with towels and assorted cleaning supplies. On the other side of the closet was a cabinet filled mostly with chemicals for perms and hair coloring.

And lastly, on Sarah's left was a small refrigerator that presently contained two apples, an orange, celery sticks in a plastic bag, a bottle of Evian, four cans of Diet Pepsi, some concentrated lemon juice in a small yellow plastic lemon with a green screw top, and three-quarters of a jug of Carlo Rossi Chablis.

Sarah plugged in the coffee machine, poured in water, and switched it on without adding coffee, since some of their customers preferred decaf or tea. She walked out to the front just as Veronica Santori came through the door.

4

"Hi," Sarah said.

"Am I late?" Veronica was a small, meek-looking woman, and, Sarah now recalled, she always seemed to feel guilty about something.

"You're right on time."

"Are you sure?" Veronica checked her watch, then looked at the clock on the wall to be certain.

"I just got here myself," Sarah told her. "Come on back and we'll get started."

She shampooed Veronica's hair, which was black and streaked with gray. Thus far, Veronica had turned aside Sarah's suggestions that they color it. Sarah rinsed her hair, massaged in a conditioner, then rinsed it again and wrapped it in a towel. Then she led Veronica out to her station. While the woman got settled in the chair, Sarah turned to the stereo. It was tuned to an FM jazz station. She didn't know whether Veronica liked jazz or not—probably not—so she kept the volume low.

While Sarah combed and cut her hair, Veronica explained to her in detail how miserable her life was. Too many bills, too many kids, too many aches and pains. Sarah tossed in an occasional "No kidding" and "I know what you mean."

By ten Sarah had finished Veronica's hair, accepted her thanks and her check, and swept the floor. Her next customer and Kay's first of the day were waiting quietly, leafing through magazines. Then Kay walked in—burst in might be a better way of putting it, Sarah thought—and the atmosphere in the shop immediately changed.

Kay Nealy was an attractive woman in her "dirty thirties" with blond hair so curly it was almost kinky, plump thighs, and heavy breasts. "I was built for comfort, babe," she liked to say, "not for speed." She had an abundance of energy, an overdeveloped set of vocal cords, and a strong sense of self. In other words, she was active and loud, and she knew it. She'd come from a large family—two sisters, four brothers—and she'd told Sarah that if you didn't speak up or push your way into line, you got lost in the crowd.

"Good morning!" she said, bustling in, tossing her coat on the rack. "Hi, Sarah. Hi, Linda. Hi," she said to Veronica, whose name she didn't know. "God, I need some coffee. Sarah, wait till I tell you what happened last night at the house. It was like a fu— Oops," she said, touching her fingers to her lips and glancing at Veronica. "I mean, it was like a gosh-damn Three Stooges movie. Come on, Linda, and we'll get you shampooed."

Kay flounced toward the back, clicking and clattering her numerous colorful bracelets. She paused at the stereo only long enough to turn up the volume three or four notches.

After Kay returned to the front and sat her customer before the mirror, she told Sarah what had happened last night.

"Katie, my oldest, had a boy over from school—Wayne or Dwayne Somebody—so she could help him with his algebra for a big test they've got tomorrow, and she's probably the smartest one in the family, so it's no wonder other kids want her help. Rick's out in the living room with me, and he's saying probably what the kid wants is to get into Katie's panties, which is ridiculous, but that's Rick. Anyhow, they were in the kitchen at the table with their schoolbooks and Cokes (thank God they're still drinking it and not snorting it) and some cake when Mr. Moto, our black lab, strolls in and decides he's so fond of this boy, Wayne or Dwayne Whatever, that he pees all over the poor kid's pant leg. Well, Katie starts screaming at the dog and throws her glass of pop at him, and Rick hears her screaming and thinks the kid has finally begun to molest her, so he goes charging in, steps on an ice cube from Katie's drink, and slips and falls right down on his ass right onto a big hunk of broken glass. He starts yelling bloody murder and the dog is barking and Katie's boyfriend is standing there with dog pee on his pants and he doesn't know whether to faint or run for his life. Meanwhile, Rick is bleeding like a bastard, and I ended up driving him to the hospital, and all the way he's pissing and moaning and trying to sit on his side. What really got him going, though, was they had to shave some of the hair off his butt to get him patched up. All the way home he's cussing about Wayne or Dwayne, about how it was *his* fault that the whole thing happened. I go, 'Rick, do you think that poor kid *wanted* Mr. Moto to pee on him?' and he goes, 'Some kids are like that, Kay, and you can bet I'm going to ask him about it the next time he walks into my kitchen,' as if the poor kid will ever come within a mile of our house again. Plus, he's probably flunking his algebra test even as I speak."

Sarah had to wipe the tears of laughter from her eyes before she could continue cutting her customer's hair.

"So anyway, Sarah," Kay said, "what's new with you?"

"Nothing much." Then Sarah remembered the letter from Joseph Pomeroy. "Nothing's new," she said.

Sarah steered the Wagoneer down the quiet, dark street.

She was getting home later than she'd expected, because King Soopers had been packed with people. It had looked as if everyone in town had chosen this evening to nudge their overflowing food baskets through the checkout lines.

The streetlights cast impenetrable black shadows behind every tree and bush. The neighborhood would have looked forbidding except that every house Sarah glimpsed through the trees seemed alive with warm yellow window light. She noted with pleasure that a few of her neighbors had already hung strings of colored lights on their shrubbery. It reminded her that Christmas was barely three weeks away. It also reminded her that this morning in the car she and Brian had discussed buying a Christmas tree. Had she promised him they'd buy it tonight? She hoped not, because it had been a long day, and she wanted nothing more than an evening of doing nothing.

She unlocked the front door, a bag of groceries tucked under her left arm. She'd barely closed the door behind her when Brian came down the stairs and ran into the foyer, his cheeks flushed, his eyes aglow.

"Hi, pumpkin," she said.

"Dad says we can get our Christmas tree tonight, Mom!"

"He did?"

Alex entered the foyer from the kitchen hallway.

"Yeah!" Brian said. "So can we?"

"Well . . ."

"Your mother looks kind of tired," Alex said, rescuing her. He gave Sarah a kiss on the forehead, took the grocery bag from her, then looked down at Brian. "Maybe we should wait till tomorrow."

Brian's face fell. "Tomorrow?"

"I promise there'll be a perfect tree just waiting for us. Okay?"

"I guess," Brian said, scuffing the toe of his shoe on the tile floor.

"Well, wait," Sarah said, unable to resist the downcast look on her son's face. "How about if you give me an hour to get my second wind and then we can go."

"Really?"

"Sure, why not?" she said, answering Brian but looking at Alex. "You've heard of Supermom, haven't you?"

"Isn't she on TV on Saturdays right after Lord Doom?" Alex asked, then said, "Look, if you'd rather not do it, just Brian and I could go."

"Are you kidding?" Sarah gave him a look of exaggerated shock. "You think I'd trust you two alone with something this important?"

"Silly of me," he said. "However, I take it that even Supermom requires nourishment."

"She does."

"Well, soup's on."

"You have dinner waiting for me?"

"Of course."

"What a guy. What are we having?"

"Like I said. Soup."

Alex carried in the rest of the groceries and helped Sarah put them away. He'd already set out a pair of place mats with plates and bowls, napkins and silverware. He'd also reheated the remainder of the vegetable soup that they'd made and frozen last Sunday.

Sarah sat at the table while Alex warmed some sourdough rolls in the microwave oven. She could hear Brian thumping around upstairs.

Alex glanced at the ceiling. "I already fed him."

Sarah smiled briefly, searching the countertop with her eyes. She noticed that the envelope from Joseph Pomeroy was no longer where she'd put it. Alex was watching her, and he apparently guessed what she was thinking.

"We need to talk about that," he said.

"I know. Even though I don't know what it's all about."

Alex nodded. "It's . . . complicated. Some of it I should have told you before, but—"

They both heard Brian clomping down the stairs.

"Later," he said quietly.

After Sarah and Alex had eaten and Brian had sat fidgeting at the table, barely able to contain his excitement, they all went out to get a tree.

Alex drove them to a lot near the north end of town, just off Fillmore Street. The lot was surrounded by a tall, temporary wire fence that sagged between wooden posts and threatened to collapse at the first loud sneeze. Inside the enclosure, which was strung with bright, naked light bulbs, were scores of evergreens nailed to crude wooden stands. They stood crookedly at attention like poorly trained soldiers in uneven ranks. Brian went on an immediate and thorough inspection tour.

Naturally, he was looking for the largest tree on the lot, regardless of its shape or fullness. Alex trailed behind him, scrutinizing each tree. He seemed more concerned with symmetry than size.

It took nearly an hour for Brian and Alex to systematically examine every last tree. Sarah was stamping her feet from the cold and beginning to wonder if Christmas would come and go before a decision was made.

Finally, Brian announced his choice—a lopsided giant that Sarah doubted would fit under their ceiling. And Alex proclaimed his—a perfectly shaped beauty not much taller than himself.

Sarah tried arbitration to no avail.

The lot owner, a big-bellied man wearing a peacoat and an orange ski cap with "Denver Broncos" stitched across the front, suggested with a grin that they could purchase *both* trees. Sarah gave him a look. He stepped back, held up his mittened hands, and cleared his throat.

Then he pointed out to Brian that although his giant tree *appeared* to be the biggest around, the trunk would probably need several feet cut from it because it was so crooked. In addition, some of the branches needed trimming because they stuck out too far, and there was a large bare area on one side, so when you got right down to it, it wasn't so big, after all. But right over *here* was a fine tree, nearly as big as his first choice, with a much better shape.

Then he pointed out to Alex that although *his* tree appeared to be perfect, in fact it was noticeably thicker on one side. In addition, a tree this size looked best in a small apartment, not a house, and for almost the same price you could get a much larger tree with the same shape.

"For instance," the lot owner said, "that one over there. The one your son's looking at."

Brian was standing before a seven-foot pine, as wide as it was tall, with evenly spaced branches thick with soft needles.

"What about *this* one, Dad?"

"Good choice," he said.

Alex and the lot owner carried the tree to the Wagoneer, hoisted it on top with the tree trunk pointing forward, then secured it with some lengths of old clothesline. Alex paid the man and climbed in the vehicle with Brian. Sarah hung back for a moment, then slipped the lot man an extra ten-dollar bill.

"What's this for?"

"For keeping me from freezing to death out here," she said. "Merry Christmas."

When they got home, Alex parked the Wagoneer in the driveway. Then all three wrestled the big tree off the roof, dragged it along the stone walk to the front of the house, and pulled it onto the porch, leaving behind a scattering of pine needles.

"Can we get it through the door?" Brian asked somewhat fearfully.

"No problem. But do we want to do it tonight?" He was looking at Sarah.

"Yes!" Brian said.

"What do you think?" Alex asked Sarah.

"I think, number one, I'm pooped, and number two, it's too close to bedtime for school-age children."

"Aw, Mom."

"Your mother's right, Brian. Besides, I'll need time to cut a bit off the bottom of the trunk to square it up. And we'll have to buy a tree stand, won't we?"

"We've got one," Sarah said. "That is, I think we do. We may have to search the basement."

She remembered that when they'd moved in they'd let the movers haul a lot of things through the side door into the basement. And there had been a lot. "Junk grows," her mother had once told her, "and if you don't believe me, wait until you have to move it." Sarah hadn't thought that she and Brian could have accumulated so much stuff. However, they were both the types who would shove something in the back of a closet before they'd think of tossing it out. Sarah knew that she still had things from her early days of marriage to Ted, from before she'd gotten pregnant with Brian. And she was fairly certain they had some of Ted's old stuff, packed in cardboard boxes and sealed with tape.

When Alex had moved into Sarah and Brian's small house right after their marriage, he'd kept his apartment as a place to store all of his "dear junk." A month later, when the big house was ready for them to move into, he'd had everything hauled over, along with all of Sarah and Brian's things.

Maybe if the house weren't so big, Sarah thought, they'd have held a garage sale before the move or given things to Goodwill. As it was, they had more room than they needed, and perhaps they'd felt obligated to fill up all that empty space. In fact, they'd been "forced" to buy a few more roomfuls of furniture for the big house.

Yes, she thought, and smiled to herself, the tree stand was most probably in the basement. There might be a problem finding it, though.

They laid the tree against the house next to the front door. Then Alex parked the Wagoneer in the garage, and Sarah took Brian upstairs and tucked him in bed. While she was still in the bedroom, Alex came in to say good night, with Patches trailing behind.

Sarah left them all together and went down to the family room.

Although it was a large room, it usually felt cozy to Sarah, with its stone fireplace, thick carpeting, and comfortably overstuffed couch and chairs. But now the room seemed bleak and cold. The picture window, which during daylight gave a sweeping view of the backyard and trees and the mountains beyond, was now black and featureless.

Sarah sat on the couch and waited for Alex.

When he walked into the room, she saw that he had the envelope with him.

5

ALEX SAT BESIDE SARAH ON THE couch. He held the envelope on his knee, away from her. He looked at it and said, "Brian's so excited about the tree. Was he like this last year?"

Sarah shook her head no and smiled briefly. "Last year he didn't get to help pick it out."

Alex nodded, his eyes still on the envelope. They sat for a few moments in relative silence, the only sounds being the occasional creak and groan of the old house settling in for the night. Sarah started to reach for Alex's hand, then stopped when he spoke.

"This is difficult, Sarah." His voice was strained. "It . . ." He shook his head as if to clear it. Then he took a deep breath and began again.

"I'm afraid I haven't been completely honest with you."

Sarah opened her mouth to speak, then closed it. She was remembering several years ago when Ted had spoken those words, or ones quite similar. He'd gone on to say that he was in love with another woman and that if Sarah wanted a divorce he would oblige. Sarah had known, or at least strongly suspected, that Ted was seeing someone, and when he'd finally admitted it, it had been more of a relief than a numbing blow. But Sarah felt numb now. And she was fairly certain that whatever Alex was about to tell her had nothing to do with infidelity. But he was speaking, his voice low, and she'd missed his last words.

"I'm sorry, what did you say?"

"I said, I lied when I told you that my first wife and our son died in an automobile accident."

"What?"

He nodded.

"How did—"

"It wasn't a car accident, Sarah. It was . . . more terrible than that."

Sarah held her breath.

"They were murdered," he said. "Butchered."

Sarah felt a chill go through her.

"My God."

"I know I should have told you the truth long ago, but it was something I'd been trying to forget, trying to put behind me." His words came in a rush. "I wanted to start over, to make a new life, and when I met you, I knew we were meant to be together, and I didn't want to have anything bad between us, so I lied. It was the wrong thing to do, I know, and I'm sorry." He reached for her hand. "I swear to you, Sarah, I've never lied about anything else, and I never will again."

"It's all right," she said softly, although she was shocked by Alex's words. "I trust you, Alex. I love you."

And she did, more than anything or anyone in the world. She loved him as much as she loved Brian. And she could understand why he'd lied to her. It didn't matter; it changed nothing between them. However, she knew that he wasn't finished. There was more.

Alex looked in her eyes. "I love you, too, Sarah, so very much."

Then his eyes moved away from hers and fell again on the envelope.

"I have to tell you how they died," he said.

"Alex, you don't—"

"No, I do. For you to understand, especially about Christine."

"Who?"

"Christine Helstrum, the . . . psychopath who murdered them."

Sarah felt another chill. She'd expected him to say that his family had been killed by a man, possibly a mugger or a burglar, or even a street gang, but not a woman.

"It was about five years ago," Alex began, "when Laura and I were married. When we learned that she couldn't have children, we decided to adopt."

Alex and Laura found one-year-old Timothy at a state agency in Albany and immediately fell in love with him. They were told, however, that Timothy would probably have to overcome emotional problems, because he'd been abandoned by his father and physically abused by his mother. Alex and Laura were prepared to deal with that. They were prepared to give Timothy a safe, secure, and loving home.

Unknown to Alex and Laura at that time—but all too well known to them later—Timothy's natural mother, Christine Helstrum, had been convicted of felony child abuse and sent to prison for a year, with psychiatric treatment recommended. After her release, she began looking for her son. When the adoption agency refused to give her the name of Timothy's new parents, Christine returned to the agency at night, broke into the building, and ransacked the files.

The next day, she confronted Alex on his own doorstep. She was screaming that he'd stolen her son and that she'd come to take him back.

When he told her to leave, she knocked him aside and charged into the house, searching for Timothy. Alex grabbed her from behind, fought with her, and physically threw her out of the house while Laura phoned the police.

Christine was arrested. She was charged with assault and felony menacing, then, mistakenly, released on bond. That she was on parole had somehow escaped the attention of the authorities, or she would have been held until her court appearance and then, most probably, returned to prison. Of course, a spokesman for the city said, in defense of the system, that a return to prison might have delayed Christine's act but wouldn't have prevented it.

In any case, the mistake had been made.

That night, while Alex was away from home playing poker with friends, Christine broke into the house.

Laura was in the living room watching television, and Timothy was upstairs, asleep in his crib. When Laura heard a noise in the kitchen and went to investigate, she found Christine standing before an open window, a butcher knife in her hand.

Before Laura could think or act, Christine attacked her, stabbing and slashing her. Laura tried to get away, but Christine grabbed her by the hair and stabbed her repeatedly from behind. Laura fell, bleeding from numerous wounds. Christine left her on the kitchen floor and went upstairs. Laura was in shock and extreme pain, but she was conscious. She knew what was happening. She struggled to her feet, her hands slippery with her own blood, and stumbled to the stairs. She left her blood on the walls and the carpeted steps and the banister. When she finally reached the top of the stairs, Christine was coming down the hall with Timothy under her arm.

The boy was in hysterics, and his cries drove Laura to fight.

But Christine had the advantage in size and weight—and she still had the knife. She seemed unmindful now of the child's flailing to break free from under her arm. She stabbed at Laura, who grabbed her, and they struggled in a dance of death at the top of the stairs. Suddenly, Timothy fell from Christine's arm and tumbled down the stairs.

Laura screamed and started down, but Christine yanked her back. Then she ran down the stairs, scooped up her son, and bolted from the house.

When Alex returned home, he found rooms smeared with blood and his wife lying near death in the upstairs hallway.

He frantically called for an ambulance. While he waited for it to arrive, he held Laura's head and watched the lifeblood seep from her body. She described what had happened, her voice barely a whisper.

Laura died in the ambulance on the way to the hospital.

The police found Christine Helstrum that night at her apartment. Timothy was snugly tucked in her bed, dead, his neck broken from the fall down the stairs. Christine calmly, almost gaily, explained to them that she'd only done what any other mother in her situation would do: taken back her son. The police led her away in restraints.

Christine Helstrum stood trial for the murders of Laura and Timothy Whitaker. She interrupted the proceedings several times, screaming obscenities at the judge and the jury, and especially at Alex, whom she somehow blamed for the death of her son. As she was being removed from the courtroom, she yelled in Alex's face that she would get even with him if it was the last thing she ever did.

Christine was found innocent by reason of insanity. She was committed to the Wycroff State Mental Hospital for the Criminally Insane near Albany, New York.

"That was four years ago," Alex said.

Sarah sat perfectly still, stunned by what she'd heard.

"It took me months to get over the pain and the nightmares. Eventually, I pushed it all down, buried it in some corner of my mind, and after a while I almost believed that it hadn't really happened, not to me, to someone else, perhaps, but not to me. Until yesterday."

Alex held the envelope in both hands as if he were reading the shaky blue script.

"Do you know who Joseph Pomeroy is?"

"Laura's father," Sarah said. Her voice sounded hollow, a stranger's voice.

Alex nodded. He took the letter and the clipping from the envelope and handed them to Sarah. She read the letter first.

> Dear Alex:
> I hesitate to send you this because I know it will be upsetting to you. It was for me. Still, I think you should know. I'll write again if I learn more.
>
> Sincerely,
> Joseph Pomeroy

Sarah picked up the flimsy clipping. It had been cut from a New York newspaper and was dated Thursday, November 26, exactly one week ago.

> Albany, NY—Christine Helstrum, an inmate at the Wycroff State Mental Hospital, escaped sometime yesterday afternoon or last night, according to authorities there. No details were given on how she was able to leave the facility, which is said to be highly secure. State and local police have launched a statewide search for Helstrum, who is said to be extremely dangerous.

Sarah put down the clipping.

"She's free, Sarah, and she'll try to find me. Us. She wants her revenge."

"But why? You didn't do anything."

"She blames me for Timothy's death."

"But that's . . ."

"Insane," Alex finished for her. "I know. But to her it's real. And now she's out there somewhere. She's coming for me."

"Alex . . ." She held his hand, not knowing what to say.

He pulled gently away from her and stood, then walked to the picture window and looked out at the darkness. Sarah could see one small light shining weakly through the blackness of the trees that surrounded the backyard. She could not believe that someone was stalking Alex. She *would* not believe it. She reread the letter and the news clipping, looking for something, anything, to grab on to.

"This clipping—" Sarah said. "It's a week old. Maybe Christine has already been captured."

Alex turned from the window to face her across the room.

"No," he said. "I'd hoped for that, too. But I spent most of this morning on the phone."

He came back and sat near her on the couch.

"First I talked to Joseph, but he could tell me nothing. He's an old man and he's been sick lately, and he confessed that he had not kept up with the local news. So I called the hospital."

"Wycroff?"

Alex nodded. "They gave me the runaround for nearly an hour. I must have talked to six different people. I explained who I was, that Christine had threatened *me*, that she'd murdered *my* wife and—" He took a deep breath, then let his shoulders sag. "In any case, they kept telling me that all information concerning hospital patients was confidential. Finally, though, I spoke to a Dr. Fulbright. He at least admitted that Christine was a patient there and that she had escaped. Although he called it 'an unauthorized departure.' He said that the Albany police department and the New York state police had both been notified but that Christine had not yet been returned to them." Alex smiled sardonically. "He told me not to worry about anything, that Christine would 'turn up' sooner or later. His main concern was that she might hurt herself while she was 'absent from their care.' "

"What are the police doing to find her? Did he say?"

"I called them myself—both the city and state cops—and neither of them were too open with me on the phone. I asked to speak to Lieutenant O'Hara, but he's retired now. The only thing I could find out for sure was that the police had been notified of the escape and that there was an APB out on Christine Helstrum."

"An APB?"

"It means that there's an alert out for her, but no one has been specifically assigned to track her down."

There was a bitterness in Alex's voice that Sarah had not heard before. It angered her that a woman whom she'd never met or even seen, and in fact before today had never even heard of, a woman who was two thousand miles away and four years buried in her husband's past, could have such a negative effect on him. On them.

"Who's the man you mentioned? Lieutenant O'Hara?"

"Frank O'Hara," Alex said. "He's the homicide lieutenant who led the murder investigation. He was a great help to me back then, very kind and considerate. I'm certain he'd tell me exactly what's going on now."

"But you said he's retired."

"Even so, he might have been able to help. But the Albany police wouldn't give me his home phone—departmental policy. I asked if they'd give him *my* number and then ask him to call, and the cop I spoke to said he would, but who knows if he'll bother? After I talked to him, I called long-distance information. There's no listing for a Frank O'Hara." Alex took the clipping and the letter from Sarah, folded them, and stuck them in the envelope. "It probably doesn't matter," he said. "He probably couldn't tell me anything, anyway."

Sarah opened her mouth, then closed it. She had an idea about how to get Frank O'Hara's telephone number, but she decided not to say anything now.

"Maybe he'll call you," she said, trying to sound hopeful.

"Maybe."

Sarah put her hand on the back of his neck. She could feel the muscles there, bunched like ropes.

"Let's go to bed," she said.

Alex nodded. "You go on up," he said. "I'll check the . . . doors."

Their eyes met, and understanding passed between them. Every night, one or the other of them would check to see that the doors were shut and locked. But tonight that simple act seemed to have greater significance.

And for how many more nights? Sarah wondered.

6

THE NEXT MORNING—BEFORE they left for work—neither Sarah nor Alex mentioned their talk last night. This was partly because they'd both overslept and were rushed to get to work. But mainly they'd kept quiet because Brian was awake and within hearing. Without verbalizing, they'd seemed to agree that it would be better not to talk about Christine Helstrum in his presence. Besides, what could they say to him? Or to each other, for that matter?

During the morning Sarah tried to concentrate on cuts and perms and tints while attempting to digest all that Alex had revealed. His first wife and adopted child brutally murdered. The murders committed by the child's natural mother. Her oath of revenge. Her confinement. Her escape.

It was nearly too much for Sarah to accept, much less to keep inside. More than once that morning she'd stopped herself from telling Kay everything. It had been difficult not to confide in her, because Sarah thought of Kay as a sister. She trusted her implicitly, and there were no secrets between them. That is, there hadn't been until now.

But this is different, Sarah thought. It's just too involved. Too . . . personal.

So as Sarah shampooed and trimmed her customers' hair, she

kept her thoughts to herself and her feelings hidden—especially her growing feeling of fear.

What if Christine finds us? What if she finds Alex?

She fought her fear with reason. There were two significant factors in their favor, she knew. Time and distance.

Four years had passed since Christine had been committed to a mental hospital—four years of treatment and care. Surely by now she'd changed, softened. Of course, there had been that phrase in the news clipping, ". . . said to be extremely dangerous." But perhaps she'd forgotten about Alex. After all, four years was a long time.

And then there was the distance. If Christine had escaped from the Colorado state hospital in Pueblo, Sarah knew that she would have been more concerned, for Pueblo was less than fifty miles away, almost walking distance. But Christine was two thousand miles away, probably without money or suitable clothing. Did they let inmates in an asylum keep money on hand? Sarah wondered. If they did, she guessed, it probably wasn't much—certainly not enough to buy traveling clothes and an airline ticket to Denver or Colorado Springs.

But reason or not, the fear remained. And it was made worse by not knowing, first, if Christine were still free, and second, if she was, what steps were being taken to apprehend her.

And so when Sarah took her lunch break from one until two, she went home not merely to eat but to use the telephone in private.

Sarah made a sandwich with tuna salad and lettuce on thin-sliced whole wheat bread. Patches circled her feet, begging, brushing her leg with his tail. Sarah smiled, then dished up a few spoonfuls of tuna into the cat's dish. He went after it with enthusiasm. After Sarah's first bite of the sandwich and her first sip of lemon-lime soda, she got out the phone book. She dialed the number of AT&T's long-distance information service. Eventually, she got a New York operator on the line, and soon after that she was dialing headquarters of the Albany police department.

Sarah remembered what Alex had said: The police department wouldn't give out home phone numbers. So when a man answered with "Albany police," Sarah was prepared to lie.

"I'm trying to find the number of a retired Albany policeman. He was a lieutenant. Frank O'Hara. He's my cousin and . . ."

"Hold on, please."

After a few minutes another man came on the line and asked Sarah if he could help her. She repeated what she'd said.

"What's your name, ma'am?"

"Sarah O'Hara," Sarah said before she realized how funny that sounded. "I'm Frank's cousin and our Uncle Ted just died and it's important that I talk to Frank."

"I'm sorry, we don't give out the private phone numbers of our officers."

"But he's retired, isn't he?"

"Even so. If you'd like to leave a message, then I . . ."

"I need to call him right away, don't you see?" Sarah said, trying to sound anxious. And, in fact, she was. "The funeral is tomorrow, and I'm just at my wit's end. Frank should be there, he'd *want* to be there, and I've been trying to reach him for several days. He's apparently changed his number sometime during the past eight years, which is how long it's been since I've talked to him, but I know that Frank was a favorite of Uncle Ted's, and I know for certain that Ted left something for Frank in his will. If Frank doesn't hear of this until *after* the funeral, he'll feel just terrible, I know, and he might blame me, although he's such a kind man that—"

"Okay, okay, lady," the man said in exasperation. "Hang on a minute."

Sarah closed her eyes and crossed her fingers.

In half a minute the man came back on the line and said, "I'm not supposed to do this, but here's the number."

Sarah wrote it down. "Thank you so much," she said, and hung up the phone.

She felt a bit guilty for having lied to get what she wanted. But she also felt more than a little pleased for having gotten it. She dialed the number, then listened to the phone ring three times before a man answered.

"Hello?"

"Hello, is this Frank O'Hara?"

"Yes?"

"Mr. O'Hara, you don't know me, but my name is Sarah Whitaker. I'm calling long—"

"If you're selling something, lady, I'm not interested. And by the way, how'd you get this number? It's unlisted."

O'Hara's voice was slightly hoarse. Sarah wondered if he smoked too much.

"I'm not selling anything," she said, "and I got your number from the Albany police. I'm afraid I lied to them in order to get it, but it's important that I talk to you."

"What's your name, again?"

"Sarah Whitaker."

"Whitaker . . ." he said, trying to remember.

"Four years ago you investigated the murders of Laura and Timothy Whitaker."

O'Hara was silent for a moment, then said, "Yes, I remember. Laura and Timothy, and the husband's name was Alex, I believe. You're a relative?"

"I'm married to Alex," Sarah said.

"I see."

"My husband just learned that Christine Helstrum escaped from the Wycroff State Mental Hospital. She was the one who—"

"I know who she is," O'Hara said. "And I read about her escape. But that was over a week ago, so I would assume by now she's been caught. The crazy ones usually don't get very far."

"I'm afraid this one has," Sarah said.

"Come again?"

"My husband phoned the hospital yesterday and was told that Christine Helstrum was still free. Mr. O'Hara, I don't know whether you remember, but at her trial that woman threatened my husband."

Sarah waited for a reply, but all she heard was the soft hiss of the phone lines.

"Mr. O'Hara?"

"Yes, I'm here. I was just thinking. I remember Helstrum's threats at the trial, and I can understand your husband's concern, and yours, too. Truly, though, you shouldn't be too worried. Those kinds of threats are common enough, and nothing usually comes of them. I must say, though, that I'm a little surprised Helstrum hasn't been caught yet. Who told your husband that, anyway?"

"A Dr. Fulbright," she said. "We were wondering . . ."

"Yes?"

"We were wondering—*hoping*, actually—if maybe you could check on what's being done to find her. That is, on what the police are doing."

"Mrs. Whitaker, I'm retired, or didn't the Albany policeman you lied to tell you that?"

"Yes, I know, but, well, no one seems to be willing to talk to us about this, and Alex told me that you were very considerate to him during the trial and all. And, well . . ."

She heard O'Hara sigh uncomfortably.

"Mr. O'Hara," she said, "this is difficult for me. I have a hard time asking people for favors, particularly strangers. Although I almost feel as if I know you. In any case, I am asking you this favor. Will you please check with the Albany police about what's being done to apprehend Christine Helstrum? It would mean a lot to Alex. He's . . . well, both of us are . . . concerned."

"You shouldn't be, honestly." His voice sounded strained.

"But we are. And not just for us. For our son, as well."

"Mrs. Whitaker . . ."

Sarah said nothing. She heard O'Hara sigh again.

"Okay, I'll see what I can find out," he said, a note of resignation in his voice. "But," he added quickly, "it may be nothing."

"Thank you so much. Anything you can tell us would mean a lot to both of us."

"Right," O'Hara said. "What's your number there?"

Sarah gave it to him.

"I'll call you in a day or two."

"Good-bye, and thanks again."

O'Hara hung up.

Sarah put the receiver in the cradle. It rang at once, startling her. She picked it up, thinking it was probably O'Hara calling back to ask her something.

"Hello?"

Silence.

Sarah listened for a moment.

"Mr. O'Hara?" she asked.

A pause.

"No."

A dial tone.

Sarah stared at the handset. There had been just that one word, "No." But the voice had belonged to a woman.

Brian heard the first bell ring, meaning that the lunch hour was almost over and, further, that he had fifteen minutes to come in from the school yard, walk partway down the long hall to his homeroom, hang up his coat on a hook in the rear of the room, go to his seat (last row on the right, third desk from the front), and sit. But he made no move toward the building.

"And *I* got to pick out the tree," he said.

"They don't let kids do that," Eddy Teesdale said.

Brian and Eddy were standing near the tall cyclone fence that encircled the school grounds. They shuffled their hiking boots in the wet gravel and watched most of the other kids start to drift toward the building.

"They do so," Brian said.

"Do not."

"Do so."

Eddy snuffled and rubbed his freckled nose with the back of his glove. Then he pulled up the zipper of his ski parka from halfway to three-quarters. Brian adjusted his coat's zipper accordingly, since, after all, they were best friends.

"So, did you get a Christmas tree yet?"

"Not yet," Eddy said. "This weekend, I think."

"Will your mom and dad let you pick out which one?"

"No way, José," Eddy said. "You know what?"

"What?"

"Tommy Akins told me that his brother told him that there's no such person as Sanny Claus."

"Tommy Akins eats boogers, too," Brian said, and they both giggled.

"But his brother said so."

"So?"

"His brother's a fifth-grader."

"So?"

Eddy wiped his nose again.

"So what if there *isn't* a Sanny Claus."

"*Course* there is."

"But what if there isn't?"

"Who do you think brings you presents on Christmas?" Brian demanded.

"Tommy Akins' brother said it's your parents that do it."

"*Course* they do. But so does Santa."

"Tommy Akins' brother says your parents give you *all* the

presents and they wait until you're asleep and then they put them under the Christmas tree and they write, 'From Sanny Claus,' on them."

"That's *dumb*."

"But he's in the fifth grade."

"So?"

"So, fifth-graders are supposed to know a lot."

"So, I bet he eats boogers, too."

They both giggled again.

"So, what are you gonna ask Santa for Christmas?" Brian asked.

"A radio-controlled truck and a pocket knife and a Lord Doom Sword of Power and I don't know what else yet."

"They *have* those now?" Brian asked.

"What?"

"A Sword of Power."

"I don't think so."

"Well, how can you ask for one, then?"

"Maybe they'll have them before Christmas."

"Maybe," Brian said, discouraged, then, "Maybe you could make one."

"You could not."

"Could so."

"Could not."

The school yard was mostly empty except for some of the fifth- and sixth-graders who were hanging around near the asphalt-covered basketball courts. They, like Brian and Eddy, were waiting for the second bell.

"Is that your mom?" Eddy was looking over Brian's shoulder.

Brian turned around and stared through the chain-link fence. A woman was standing on the sidewalk across the street. She wore a long dark coat and a plaid scarf that was wrapped over her head and ears and tucked under her chin.

"*Course* that's not my mom," Brian said.

"Well, she sure is staring at you."

"She's not staring at *me*. She's staring at *you*."

"She is not."

"Is so."

"Is not."

The second bell rang, warning them that they had five minutes to get to their desks.

"Race you to the door!"

They ran off side by side, just as they always did, toward the warmth and safety of the school building. But today they ran a bit faster.

They ran as if Lord Doom himself was after them.

7

SHE STOOD IN THE MOTTLED sunlight beneath a leafless sycamore and stared at the house. It was much larger than she'd expected. Apparently, Alex had taken a step upward since moving out of his apartment.

She'd gone to the apartment this morning. In fact, it was the first stop she'd made after arriving in Colorado Springs. Certainly she'd been disappointed that his name was not listed in the directory by the outside phone. Disappointed but not surprised— people moved.

And the manager had been most helpful.

When she'd told him that she was an old friend of Alex's, he'd invited her in and even poured her a cup of coffee. Perhaps because he's old, she'd thought, and needed someone to talk to. In any case, he'd been extremely pleased with Alex as a tenant, and he spoke freely about him. Yes, he knew his new address and where he worked and even where his wife, Sarah, worked.

"She was married before," he'd said, "and has the cutest little boy. Brian, I think. He's in the first grade."

She'd left Alex's ex-landlord rinsing out coffee cups in the sink and had driven to the house. She hadn't stopped, though. Instead, she'd driven throughout Alex's neighborhood, searching for the nearest elementary school.

It was Brian who interested her now.

When she'd left New York, she hadn't considered the idea that Alex might have remarried, much less have a son. That changed everything. In fact, it made it perfect. A son for a son.

She'd found the school; it had to be the right one, she felt, for it was only a few miles from the house. She'd parked the car and climbed out before she'd realized that she didn't know what she was going to do. She couldn't simply walk in and start asking the teachers which child was Brian Whitaker.

So she'd stood there for several minutes, trying to sort out her thoughts, staring across the street at the school yard. Two little boys stared back at her. For a moment she'd considered walking over and asking them if they knew Brian. But then the bell had rung, and they'd scampered across the gravel yard and into the building. So she'd driven back to the house and left the car parked safely a few blocks away.

Now she left the shade of the sycamore tree and walked down the driveway and across the walk to the front porch. Obviously, no one was home. She wasted no time in taking out her crude picks and going to work on the front-door lock.

She grinned.

At least I learned *something* at Wycroff, she thought.

But after several minutes of concentrated effort, she had not opened the lock. After several minutes more, she was nearly angry enough to break the picks in half and hurl the pieces across the porch.

She stomped around the side of the house.

The garage was on this side, twenty feet from the house. She could see from here that the lock on *that* door would be a cinch to open. But it wasn't the garage that interested her; it was the house. She saw two doors on this side. One was up half a dozen redwood steps and apparently opened into the kitchen. The other door was down half a dozen concrete steps and led to the basement.

Neither lock would budge under her picks.

She walked around to the rear of the house and then along the north side, her shoes breaking noisily through the thin, crusty snow. She looked up at the windows. Too high to reach. She looked down at the basement windows. They were all alike: square wooden frames holding four panes of glass. She knelt beside a window and rubbed dirt from a flimsy pane. The basement was uniformly dark. The weak, indirect sunlight illuminated nothing more than the inside of the window frame.

And the simple latch that held it shut.

8

SARAH PULLED INTO THE DRIVEway just as Alex and Brian were coming out the side door of the garage. They waited for her to park the Wagoneer, then walked together around the house to the front.

"All right!" Brian said when he saw the tree lying by the front door. "Can we take it in now?"

"I need to trim up the bottom first," Alex said, unlocking the door.

"And we have to change out of our school clothes," Sarah said, ruffling Brian's hair.

Sarah followed Alex up the stairs to the master bedroom. He removed his houndstooth coat and hung it in the closet. She watched Brian, who was followed closely by Patches, hurry to his room, out of hearing.

"I talked to Frank O'Hara today," she said.

Alex turned, a look of surprise on his face. "When did he call?"

"I called him."

"What?"

Sarah explained how she'd gotten O'Hara's number.

"What did he say the police are doing about Christine?"

"He knew less than we did. He'd assumed that she'd already

been caught. But he's going to check into things and call us back in a day or two. He said we shouldn't worry."

"Right." There was sarcasm in his voice.

Sarah sat beside him. "Should we be worried?"

"I . . . I don't know, Sarah," he said, and put his hand on her knee. "Maybe not. Maybe she's forgotten all about me."

"You don't believe that, though, do you?"

He paused. "No."

"But she doesn't know where we are," Sarah said hopefully.

"I've considered that, too. But there are a number of people in Albany who know I'm out here. It wouldn't be too difficult for her to learn that much. And once she knows which city we're in . . ." He shrugged and looked at Sarah as if to apologize.

"But, really, how could she get here?" Sarah said. "I mean, she probably has nothing but the clothes on her back, no money, no transportation. I'm sure the police have been watching the bus stations and—"

"She could hitchhike, Sarah, or, or whatever. She could find a way." His chest rose and fell in a sigh, and Sarah thought she'd never seen him so depressed. "She could do it," he said. "And if she does . . ." He stood and stepped away from the bed, then spoke with his back to Sarah. "If she does, I'll do whatever I have to do to protect you and Brian. I'll . . . I'll kill her if I have to."

"My God, Alex," Sarah said, coming off the bed. She stood behind him, her arms around his waist, her head on his back. "Please, don't even talk like that."

He said nothing.

"Maybe O'Hara will call with good news," Sarah said. "Maybe they've already caught her."

Alex nodded. "I'd better get busy if we're going to get the tree up tonight."

Sarah changed into faded blue jeans and a baggy forest-green sweater, trying all the while to push Christine from her mind. She went downstairs and surveyed the living room.

The room had a slightly formal air to it. But not *too* formal, Sarah thought. She'd spent a lot of time making certain that everything was just right. The carpet was a tight weave of light gray with a rose undertone, and the same shade of rose was present in the delicate floral design on the couch and chairs, and again in the floor-length drapes.

Sarah stood in the doorway and pictured the tree standing in the bay window. Nestled there now were a small cherry-wood table and two matching chairs. They have to be moved, Sarah thought, and since there's no room for them in here . . . She carried one of the chairs out of the living room, down the hall past the dining room, and into the family room. She looked around the room, frowning, then carried the chair back to the dining room.

During the six months that they'd lived in the house, they'd used the dining room sparingly. It was a sizable room, with windows along the north wall. They overlooked the side yard, with its pair of huge sycamore trees and a copse of Russian olives, all leafless and bleak looking in the dying winter light. A large fireplace was centered in the west wall, back-to-back with the one in the family room. The two remaining walls were painted robin's-egg blue with white trim and were hung with several framed prints. The center of the room was dominated by a dark polished wood table that could comfortably seat eight. Four chairs had been pushed up to the table and four more placed against the walls.

A bit excessive, Sarah had always thought, but what the heck, you can't have an empty room.

She pushed together two of the dining-room chairs against the wall to make room for the chair she'd carried in. She knew the extra furniture in here would look out of place, but at least it wouldn't be in the way.

Alex came down the stairs as she passed by on her way to the living room. He'd changed into a plaid flannel shirt and heavy corduroy pants that were tucked into high-topped leather-and-rubber boots.

"You look like Jacques the Lumberjack," Sarah said good-naturedly, hoping to lighten both of their moods.

Alex attempted a smile, and when he spoke, it was with a fake French-Canadian accent.

"You want trees to be chopped down, *ma chèrie*? You come to Jacques." He poked his thumb in his chest.

Sarah laughed. "Okay, but help me move the table out of here first. Then we'd better eat something before we turn you loose with a saw."

After they'd moved the furniture, they all agreed that they were more anxious than hungry, so they had sandwiches for dinner. Then they paraded out to the garage. Sarah and Brian picked up opposite ends of a sawhorse and followed Alex, who carried a crosscut saw back to the front porch. Alex lifted the trunk of the pine tree onto the sawhorse, squinted at it under the yellow glow of the porch light, then raised the saw and drew it across the bark.

"Aren't you supposed to draw a pencil line first?" Sarah asked.

"Jacques need no line," Alex said, and began sawing three inches off the trunk.

Sawdust sifted down, and Sarah could smell the fresh-cut wood. Then a round plug of pine, thicker on one end than the other, hit the porch with a solid thunk. Brian ran over and grabbed it up with both hands.

"Hey, cool! Can I keep this?"

"For what, Brian?"

"Um, I don't know. Maybe to make the handle for Lord Doom's Sword of Power."

"I wish Lord Doom was here to help us get this baby inside," Alex said.

It took all three of them to drag the tree through the front door, across the foyer, and into the living room. It looked decidedly out of place on the carpet—a huge blue-green mound. Its soft-needled branches reached like tendrils toward the feet of the surrounding furniture.

Patches crept into the room. The big cat sniffed the very tip of the treetop, then moved away and eyed it suspiciously.

"The tree stand?" Alex asked.

"In the basement," Sarah said. "I just hope we can *find* the darn thing. Plus all the ornaments."

Sarah and Brian followed Alex through the foyer, down the short hall to the kitchen, then through to the laundry room. It was crowded with a new washer, a new drier, and an old, deep-bellied cast-iron sink. There were small-paned windows set in the south and west walls. During the day they looked out over the driveway and the garage to the south and the sprawling backyard to the west. But now they stared blankly into darkness.

Alex stepped to the door that was set in the east wall, a dozen feet from the doorway they'd just come through. Sarah always thought that it gave the illusion of leading back into the kitchen. Of course, she knew it was a step or two north of the refrigerator and the north kitchen wall.

The door was equipped with a sliding-bolt lock that was nearly a foot long and as thick as Sarah's thumb. It rested impotently in the stout guides fastened to the door.

"Don't we keep this locked?" Alex asked.

"Not usually."

"Maybe we should from now on."

"But the outside basement door's locked, isn't it?"

"Even so. Let's keep this locked, too."

"Why, Dad?" Brian asked.

Sarah glanced at Alex.

"Just for safety," Alex said.

He opened the door, stepped onto the small wooden landing,

then turned back and fumbled with the light switch. The dusty bulb above his head remained dead, but a light had come on at the bottom of the stairs. It lit Alex's face from below and from the side, giving him a ghoulish appearance.

"Let's go," he said. "Be careful on the stairs." He took one step down, then stopped and looked around. "Brian, maybe you'd better stay up here."

"I'm not scared," Brian said, sounding scared.

Sarah smiled. "That's not what Dad meant, hon. You can come down, but stay right behind me and hold on to the banister, okay?"

"Okay."

Sarah looked at Alex. "We'll be careful, Dad," she said, "we promise."

Patches meowed at their feet.

"That doesn't include you," Sarah said, gently pushing the cat away from the door.

She closed the door behind them, and then she and Brian followed Alex down the dusty wooden steps. Brian stayed close to Sarah, giving her the feeling that he liked the basement even less than she did.

Sarah had been down here only once, and that was when the real estate agent had shown them the house. She hated to admit it, even to herself, but she felt uneasy. The basement was the largest she'd ever been in, much less owned. It was large enough to live in. In fact, it had been lived in by servants sometime in the past.

When they reached the foot of the stairs, they were facing a long, narrow hallway with faded wallpaper and a low, roughly plastered ceiling. There were two doors on the right and three on the left. Sarah hugged herself and rubbed her arms.

"It's cold down here."

Alex opened the first door on the right. It was pitch-black inside. He found a light switch just inside the door and clicked it on. A harsh, bare bulb lit up the large room, which was dominated by an immense furnace. Its cylindrical body was fully six feet in diameter and stood nearly as high as the ceiling. It spread its thick, round ducts upward like the legs of a gigantic spider.

"Not in here," Alex said.

"What's *that*?" Brian asked with more than a trace of fear in his voice.

"The old furnace," Alex said.

He led them into the room, which was slightly warmer than the hallway.

"Back in the old days," Alex told Brian, "when this house was first built, the people who lived here burned coal in that furnace to heat the house. Later on they fixed it so it would burn natural gas."

"Which do we burn?"

"Gas. But over there."

Alex pointed to a small gas heater—ridiculously small, it seemed—that squatted in the corner near the hot-water heater and was connected to an array of copper pipes. There were several wooden crates lined up on the floor between the door and the heaters. Alex lifted the lid on the nearest one, sending up a cloud of dust.

"Is that something of ours?" Sarah asked.

Alex turned his head and sneezed loudly, making Brian giggle.

"It is now," Alex said. "A lot of junk that's been down here forever."

They left the room, and Alex closed the door. He stepped across the hall and opened another door, revealing another totally dark room. When he worked the light switch, nothing happened.

"We need a flashlight," he said, and turned toward the stairs.

"I thought we knew where the movers put everything."

"I guess not," Alex said, smiling. "I was upstairs with you, making sure they put the furniture in the right rooms without breaking anything. I'll be right back."

He climbed the stairs. Sarah and Brian stood alone in the hallway, saying nothing. Sarah heard Alex's footsteps on the floor above them.

"Mom, I'm scared down here."

"There's nothing to be fri—"

Suddenly, a muffled roar erupted from the furnace room. Brian launched himself against Sarah's leg and hung on with both arms.

"It's just the furnace, honey," Sarah said, putting her hand on his head. But she'd jumped at the noise, too.

Sarah heard Alex on the landing and saw that he was replacing the bulb at the top of the stairs. When he came down, he brought a flashlight and a paper sack that tinkled faintly with light bulbs. He followed his flashlight beam into the dark room and put a new bulb in the ceiling socket.

Sarah clicked on the light.

The room's walls were lined with vacant, dusty shelves that had apparently been used to hold jars of preserves. A few empty jars were scattered about as reminders of times past.

They moved down the hall to the next room on the left: the kitchen. Everything in here wore a fine coat of dust—the linoleum floor, the sink, and the countertop, even the drab curtains over the windows. The cupboard doors stood open, displaying bare shelves. There was an old stove and a refrigerator, both of which had been pulled away from the wall and disconnected. Four wooden chairs had been placed upside down on the scarred, white-painted wooden table.

Sarah pictured the warm, clean house above them and tried to guess which room they were under. The family room, she thought, or possibly the dining room.

"Did somebody *live* down here?" Brian asked.

"Sure," Alex said. "Probably in the old days the rich people lived upstairs and their maid and butler or maybe the gardener lived down here."

"Are we rich, Dad?"

"Not hardly."

"So there's no one down here now, is there?"

"No, Brian. Just us."

The room next to the kitchen was the bathroom. There was a yellow-stained porcelain sink, a toilet, a bathtub that stood on metal feet, and an empty medicine cabinet with a foggy, cracked mirror.

They stepped across the hall to the bedroom. Alex clicked on the light to reveal a bare mattress and box springs, a battered wooden dresser, and a wooden wardrobe, which stood against the back wall.

Sarah walked into the room. It felt cold and musty. She drew her fingers through the thin film of dust on the closed door of the wardrobe.

"I didn't know this was down here, did you?"

Alex shrugged.

"This is cedar," Sarah said. "You know, this would go well in our bedroom."

"You want to drag that thing upstairs?" Alex groaned.

"I don't mean now. . . ." She tried to tug open the door, but it seemed to be stuck. She brushed dust from her fingers. "Sometime, though."

"Sometime," Alex said.

They left the bedroom and walked down the hallway, which made a sharp turn to the left—into darkness.

Alex walked ahead of them, lighting the way with his flashlight. He stopped partway down the hall and changed a light bulb in the ceiling. His flashlight showed a door on the right and another at the end of the hall. The far door led to the outside. Alex walked to it, found the light switch, and turned on the hall light. Then he checked the lock on the door.

"Is anything wrong?" Sarah asked.

"No," Alex said.

There was a window in the door partly covered by a heavy

curtain. Alex shone his light through the window, faintly illuminating concrete steps leading up to ground level; then he pulled the curtain all the way closed.

"I remember now, the movers used this door," he said. "So I guess they put everything in the living room."

The living room was the last room in the basement and the one nearest to the outside door. The room was long and narrow, extending under the entire front of the house. Cardboard boxes were stacked three high along the east wall. Most of them had been marked with a black felt-tip pen: "Basement."

"I didn't know we had so much stuff down here," Alex said.

He tried to open the nearest box, but it was sealed with fiber tape.

"This would be a lot easier if we'd have marked the Christmas boxes."

"Next time," Sarah said.

"Right. I'll need a knife." He started out the door, saying, "I saw something in the furnace room."

Alex returned in a few minutes with a box cutter. Its thick handle was dented and pitted with rust. Alex loosened the screw, slid the rusty single-edged razor blade forward, then retightened the screw.

"Hey, that's neat," Brian said. "Can I see it?"

"This isn't a toy, Brian," Alex said, and he slit open the first box. "What is this stuff?"

Sarah leaned over his arm. "Oh, I think those were Ted's."

Alex gave her a look.

"Okay, okay," she said, feigning defense. "I'll get rid of everything this spring. We'll have a big yard sale, okay?"

Alex spread his hands in a mock-defensive gesture of his own. "Hey, I didn't say a word."

"You didn't have to," she said, and gave him a playful punch in the arm.

Alex opened nearly every box before they found the ornaments and the tree stand. Sarah stacked two boxes onto his arms, picked up one herself, and followed him into the hallway. Brian lingered behind, then came hurrying after them. They carried everything upstairs to the living room.

"Did we get the door?" Alex asked.

"I'll do it."

Sarah set down her box, walked back to the laundry room, and started to close the basement door. Then she stopped, listening, her head turned sideways to the dark landing.

There was no sound.

But she'd heard something before, a muffled noise from below.

She listened for a few more moments, then shrugged, shut the door, and slid the thick bolt into its metal socket in the doorframe. She gave the bolt a half twist, setting it solidly in place.

It was probably only the furnace, she thought.

She hurried back to the warm, secure living room.

9

ALEX SET THE DEEP METAL BOWL of the tree stand near the bay window. He secured the four legs so that they were parallel to the floor, then loosened the four screw clamps inside the bowl.

It took all three of them to right the tree with its trunk in the metal bowl.

Alex lay on the floor, reached under the lower branches, and tightened the four clamps around the base of the tree. His job was made harder by Patches, who thought Alex was playing a new game and crawled under the tree, tickling Alex's nose with his tail. Sarah and Brian tried not to laugh at his awkward predicament while they told him to "tip the tree this way some, now back the other way a little bit" until it was exactly vertical. Sarah brought a pitcher of water from the kitchen, and Alex emptied it into the stand.

Brian had already searched through the cardboard boxes and found the fluffy cotton sheet of "snow." He helped Alex position it on the floor around the legs of the tree stand.

Then all three laid out the strings of colored lights on the carpet, plugged the strings together, and plugged the end one into the nearest electrical outlet. The dark strands jumped alive with bright, elongated globes of green and red and blue and yellow and white.

"Hey, cool!" Brian said.

Sarah didn't think it was cool enough, and she was anxious to get the lights off her carpet. They checked for dud bulbs, replaced the few they found with good ones, and unplugged the lights.

"I need something to stand on," Alex said, eyeing the top of the tree.

Sarah got the step stool from the kitchen. Then Alex stood on it and began placing the strings of lights on the tree, starting at the top and wrapping them spirally downward. When he was finished, Sarah stuck the end into the wall socket, and the tree burst into multicolored lights.

"All *right!*" Brian exclaimed.

"Looking good," Alex said.

"We missed a spot," Sarah put in.

"It doesn't have to be perfect, you know."

"Yes, it does."

"It does?"

"Of course. Doesn't it, Brian?"

"Yeah."

"See?"

"Okay, okay," Alex said, smiling.

Sarah pointed out the few "dark spots," and Alex adjusted the lights accordingly. Then Sarah turned out the tree lights, and they began removing the square, flat boxes of ornaments from the cardboard cartons, handling each box as carefully as if it contained eggs.

Sarah and Brian had accumulated enough ornaments to decorate the tree several times over. There were shiny colored-glass globes, tiny wooden toys, and hollow spheres with miniature scenes inside. There were stars, Santas, angels, and animals.

There were a few homemade ornaments and a few with a history—"Remember *this* one, Mom?"—some fancy, some plain, and some so ugly they were cute. Brian showed one to Alex that made him laugh out loud.

When they were satisfied that the tree was hung with just the right number of ornaments, they began draping on the tinsel. They did this carefully, a few strands at a time, so that it hung freely—enough to add sparkle to the tree but not so much that it looked messy.

Patches sniffed at the tinsel, then batted one of the lower ornaments with a padded paw.

"Is that going to be a problem?" Alex asked Sarah, nodding toward the big cat.

"It hasn't been before," Sarah said.

As if to confirm that fact, Patches meowed once and ambled out of the room.

Now Alex stood on the step stool and placed the star-shaped ornament on the very top. He stepped down and was about to turn on the tree lights when Sarah stopped him.

"What for?" he asked, bewildered and amused.

"Yeah, Mom, why?"

"Because this is our first Christmas tree together and our first tree in our new house and it deserves something special, so you guys just wait for a few minutes."

Alex and Brian looked at each other and shrugged. Sarah spent the next quarter hour making hot chocolate in the kitchen. Alex used the time to carry the empty boxes and leftover ornaments down to the basement, setting them in the storage room rather than carrying them all the way back to the basement's living room. By the time he was finished, Sarah was filling three big mugs with hot chocolate and topping off each one with a marshmallow.

They carried their mugs out to the living room, and Alex

plugged in the lights. The tree came alive with bright colors, which were multiplied by the shiny ornaments and tinsel. Now they toasted the tree with raised mugs; then they sat cross-legged on the floor and sipped their drinks and admired their beautiful work.

Later, Sarah took Brian upstairs and tucked him in bed.

She kissed him on the forehead. "Good night, pumpkin. Sweet dreams."

"Good night, Mom." Then, "Mom?"

"What, hon?"

"I really like our Christmas tree."

"Me, too."

"I think it's the best one ever."

Sarah smiled. "Me, too."

Later still, after Sarah had finished brushing her hair, she turned out the bathroom light and found her way through the dark, almost-cold bedroom to the bed. She snuggled up to Alex, and he held her in his arms.

"Mmm, you're nice and warm," she said.

"Warmer than you think."

He kissed her forehead, then the tip of her nose, then her lips. She kissed him back and moaned softly as she felt his tongue seek out hers. Then his lips pulled away from hers and brushed over her chin to her throat, and his left hand found its way to the front of her nightgown and settled lightly on her breast. She clung to him and whispered his name in his ear.

They made love. Slowly, at first, and then with increased passion, and Sarah felt her body release control, give itself up to ecstasy.

Alex clung to her, his chest rising and falling in deep breaths. She stroked the back of his neck and thought how much she loved him, how much she needed him.

She drifted into sleep.

† † †

Much later she awoke with a start to loud whispers and shadows moving about the room.

Sarah raised herself on her elbows and listened to the winter wind moaning outside, forcing itself through the pine trees and pushing against the house, trying to find a way in. The old house groaned, and its windows chattered from the cold.

Beside her on the bed Alex snored softly. Sarah eased her head down on the pillow and closed her eyes.

She had a difficult time falling back to sleep.

The next day was Saturday, so Alex and Brian were both slow to get out of bed. Sarah, though, had a full day ahead of her at the shop, so she had already showered and dressed and finished her coffee and toast by the time Alex and Brian wandered into the kitchen.

"Are you leaving already?"

"I've got an eight o'clock appointment," Sarah said.

"Are you coming home for lunch?"

"I doubt it. It looks like you two guys will be on your own all day. Do you think you can handle it?"

Alex looked down at Brian. "What do you think? Can we have fun without your mom around?"

"I guess," Brian said tentatively. "We could watch cartoons."

"Satisfied?" Alex asked Sarah.

"Not really," she said, and kissed him good-bye.

Outside, the sky was overcast, and the breeze had a sharp edge. Sarah ducked her chin into her coat to keep her face out of the wind, lowered her already watering eyes, and walked around the house toward the garage, digging in her purse for the key to unlock the side door. She raised her eyes and stopped abruptly.

The side door to the garage, which should have been shut and locked, now stood wide open.

Sarah hesitated, then went forward, shaking her head as if to scold Alex. He must not have closed it all the way last night, she reasoned, and the wind blew it open.

She entered the garage and pulled the door shut behind her.

The big overhead heater was roaring merrily in the far corner of the garage, trying to keep pace with the cold air that had been pouring in through the door. Sarah walked around the front end of the Wagoneer. When she put her hand on the door latch, she noticed that the side window was open. In fact, it was rolled all the way down.

She frowned. Hadn't she closed it last night? When she'd parked the Wagoneer, Alex and Brian had been standing by the side door, she remembered, so she'd felt slightly more rushed than usual because she didn't want to keep them waiting.

So maybe I forgot to close things up, too, she thought. She smiled to herself. I guess we're both getting absentminded in our old age.

Sarah pulled open the car door, then stopped.

She stared down at something on the seat—three things, actually. At first she thought they must belong to Brian. Toys, perhaps. They were the size of Ping-Pong balls, but misshapen and fuzzy and gray. She reached down to pick up the nearest one. Then her fingers jerked back when she saw something attached to the fuzzy ball.

A tiny pink foot.

Sarah grimaced and leaned in for a closer look, keeping her hand high on the back of the seat. All three "balls" were the bodies of mice. No heads, just the bodies.

"Yuck," she said, shuddering with disgust.

She stepped back out of the car, then walked around the front of Alex's Celica to his workbench, which was flanked by an old power mower and a new snow blower. The workbench held only a toolbox and a row of coffee cans that were filled with nails, screws, nuts, and bolts. The wall beside it was hung with saws, rakes, shovels, a thick coil of yellow electrical cord, the "weed eater," and the electric hedge clippers.

The sight of the clippers made Sarah smile in spite of herself. She remembered the one and only time that Alex had used the old-style hedge clippers, used them for less than an hour before he'd gone right out and bought the electric clippers. As far as she knew, he'd never used the old clippers again. They'd hung above the workbench, their wooden handles forming an inverted "Y" below their long, sharp blades. She noticed now that the old clippers were no longer on the wall. She wondered if Alex had stored them away, out of sight.

Sarah squatted down and looked under the bench. There were several paint-spattered tarps folded up next to a dozen or so paint cans, most of which had been opened and resealed. Next to the cans was a cardboard box containing paintbrushes, rags, and stirring sticks. She shook out a rag and took it back to the Wagoneer.

"Darn you, Patches," she said.

Sarah used a flat paint stirrer to push the mouse carcasses onto the rag. She gingerly folded up the morbid contents, then stepped outside. The cold wind whipped open the flap of her coat. She carried her bundle to the side of the house and dropped it in the large plastic trash barrel near the side steps. She'd suspected that the old house had mice, although she hadn't seen any before this morning. And she could picture Patches busily carrying his three kills out to the open garage last evening while the three of them were preoccupied on the front porch with the Christmas tree.

Three blind mice, she thought, smiling grimly.

As she walked back into the garage, she checked her watch and realized that this little episode had made her late for her first appointment.

Even so, before she drove away, she searched the inside of the Wagoneer from front to back. But her search was fruitless; she did not find the heads.

Lord Doom slashed down with the Sword of Power and struck the Queen of the Hill People across her battle helmet, knocking her to the ground. She lay there, dazed, unmoving. Lord Doom put his steel-clad foot on her back and raised the Sword in a gesture of victory.

The Hill People dropped their weapons, hung their heads, and wept. Without their Queen they were defenseless against the forces of Lord Doom. Now they would have to submit to him. The Hill Planet would become a planet of slaves.

At least for a while, Brian knew.

Before the half hour was up, the Heroes of the Universe would fly in on their starship and save the Hill People and rout the forces of Doom, just as they did every week. And just as he did every week, Lord Doom would manage to escape, thanks to his Sword of Power.

Brian knew that the Sword was more than just a weapon to knock people down with. Whoever wielded it could control people's minds. It could make them see things that weren't there, make them afraid. Sometimes even the Heroes were fooled by the images Lord Doom conjured up with the Sword of Power.

A commercial for breakfast cereal came on just as Alex walked into the family room.

"Are you ready to go, Brian?"

"Where're we going?"

"Shopping, remember? We need to start looking for your mother's Christmas presents."

"We do?"

"Yes."

"Oh . . . Can I watch the end of Heroes of the Universe?"

"Absolutely," Alex said. "First things first."

He sat on the couch next to Brian and watched commercials. When they ended, the screen was filled with a figure draped in black, a figure with a hideous steel mask for a face.

"Who's that evil-looking character?"

"Lord Doom."

"Oh, right. Is he as mean as he looks?"

"He's pretty mean, but mostly it's because he has the Sword of Power. It'd be neat to have something like that, don't you think?"

"Something that made you mean?"

"No, Dad, something that made you real powerful."

"Oh, I suppose. Is that something you're going to ask Santa to bring you?"

"No. He couldn't."

"Why not?" Alex asked, interested.

"Because they don't make them yet. Eddy Teesdale said so."

"Oh, well, maybe we could make one."

Brian turned to face Alex, the TV show suddenly forgotten.

"Really?"

"Yes, I think so. Let's see, we could— Now I don't mean a *real* sword, you know."

"I know."

"Okay, we could cut it out of cardboard, maybe three or four thicknesses, and tape them together. I'll tell you what: I'll get you the cardboard, you draw the Sword of Power on it, and I'll cut it out for you."

"I can cut it out."

"You mean with your little scissors? I don't know, it might be too hard for you."

Brian hadn't been thinking of his blunt-nosed scissors. He'd been thinking of the box cutter, with its rusty, sharp razor blade. He'd snuck it out of the basement last night, while Alex and Sarah were carrying out the boxes of ornaments. Then he'd hidden it in a corner of his toy chest.

"I can cut it, Dad."

"Your scissors might not be sharp enough."

"I think I can do it," Brian said. "I'm sure I can."

10

ON SATURDAY NIGHT ALEX took Sarah and Brian to dinner at a seafood restaurant in Manitou Springs, west of town.

Alex ordered Hawaiian spearfish, and Sarah decided on trout. Brian's salmon steak had come from the children's menu—guaranteed boneless—but Sarah checked for bones, anyway, before she allowed him to eat.

While they ate, they talked about their party.

A month ago they'd both felt that they were settled in enough to show off their new old house, and after some discussion, they'd decided to have a New Year's Eve party.

"That's only three weeks from next Thursday," Sarah said, reaching for her glass of Chablis, "and we haven't even sent out the invitations."

"Can't we just call people on the phone?"

"Alex."

"Okay, okay, just kidding. So when are we doing the mailing?"

"I'd say right away."

"Tonight?"

"You can't tonight, Dad."

They both looked down at Brian.

"You promised you'd help me make a sword, remember?"

"A sword?" Sarah looked at Alex and raised her eyebrows.

"A Sword of Power, Mom."

"Oh?" Her eyebrows remained arched.

"Like Lord Doom's."

"Exactly like it," Alex said. "Except made out of cardboard."

"Oh." Sarah's face relaxed in a smile.

"But only because we're fresh out of nova-hardened, laser-polished titanium. Right, Brian?"

"Huh?"

Sarah laughed. "Okay, so we'll do the invitations tomorrow. And while we're at it, we can do our Christmas cards." Her eyes brightened. "Another first for us," she said. "We can combine our Christmas-card lists."

"Mine isn't very long," Alex said. "Just a few friends back in Albany. And Joseph Pomeroy . . ."

Alex frowned briefly and looked away. Sarah knew what he was thinking, and she realized that neither of them had mentioned Christine Helstrum since last night. They'd tried to carry on as if she didn't exist.

"Maybe they've caught her by now," Sarah said.

"What?" Alex looked at her, then smiled faintly. "Oh. Right. We can hope."

"Caught who?" Brian asked.

"No one," Sarah said. "Now how about some ice cream for dessert?"

After they got home from the restaurant, Alex brought up an empty cardboard box from the basement.

"Is that my Christmas-ornament box?" Sarah asked.

"Only temporarily," Alex said. "Soon it will be a Sword of Power."

"You're going to cut up my ornament box?" Sarah asked with mock horror.

"Sorry, babe. The good guys need weapons, too, you know. Besides, I forgot to pick up a box when Brian and I were out today."

"But shouldn't you make it out of wood or something?"

"This is quicker, cleaner, and easier. Besides, for wood I'd need a jigsaw, and even if I had one, I wouldn't know how to operate it."

"Oh. But my *ornament* box?"

"I promise I'll replace it before we take down the ornaments, okay?"

"Well . . ."

"We need this cardboard to defeat Lord Doom. Right, Brian?"

"Yeah!"

"Well . . ."

Alex kissed her on the forehead. "I knew you'd understand." Then he said to Brian, "Where shall we do this, in the kitchen or in your room or—"

"*Not* in the kitchen," Sarah put in.

"I guess we go upstairs, then," Alex said, and Brian followed him up to his room.

Brian's room was cluttered but comfortable, with the bed and dresser to the left, a small desk and bookcase under the windows, and a large wooden toy chest in the corner near the closet. The walls were decorated with posters, *Star Wars* being the predominant theme.

Brian knelt beside his father on the floor at the foot of the bed. Alex used a large pair of scissors to cut the flaps from the box, then slit open the box itself until there was a small stack of cardboard sheets. The sheets were in two sizes: one nearly square, the other much longer than wide. Alex separated out the six longer pieces.

"This should be enough," he said. "Do you want me to draw the sword for you?"

"I can do it."

"Okay. When you get it the way you want it, give a holler and I'll cut it out for you, okay?"

"I can do that, too."

"You'd better let me do it, Brian. I'll—"

They both looked up at Sarah standing in the doorway. Brian thought that she looked kind of scared.

"Frank O'Hara's on the phone," she said.

Without a word Alex followed her out of the room.

Feeling rejected, Brian knelt there for a moment. Then he shrugged his shoulders, went to the corner of the room, and opened up his toy chest.

The chest represented an archaeological dig into Brian's life. The bottom strata consisted of forgotten infant's playthings covered by a layer of stuffed animals and brightly colored plastic push toys over which was heaped a confused mixture of boxed games, plastic monsters, sporting equipment, and an occasional toy gun. Brian knew that his mother didn't approve of guns, real *or* toy, and he remembered that she'd been reluctant to let him have these few, even after he'd pleaded, "Gosh, Mom, all the other kids have them."

Brian rummaged in his toy chest. Then he found what he was looking for: a small shoe box wrapped with a thick rubber band to hold the lid in place. He sat cross-legged on the floor and opened the box. It was filled with well-worn crayons, pencils, and nontoxic multicolored felt-tip pens.

Brian picked out a black pen, then knelt beside a long piece of cardboard and drew the outline of a sword. When he was finished, he sat back on his heels and frowned.

His drawing did not look anything like his mental image of Lord Doom's Sword of Power. For one thing, it was too short—

he'd used only half the length of the piece of cardboard. And the handle was all wrong.

Brian set aside the drawing and tried again, using a fresh piece of cardboard.

The second drawing left him only slightly more satisfied. The sword was certainly long enough, but it still didn't look right to him.

"The blade's *different*," he said out loud.

He tried again. And again. After six drawings he still didn't have it right.

He looked back through all his drawings, thinking that maybe he'd missed something, that maybe *one* of them looked okay. But none of them did. He pushed them away in disgust, and one of the cardboard rectangles flipped over, revealing a clean brown surface.

Brian smiled.

Six more tries, he thought.

But when he turned over the other five sheets of cardboard, his smile faded. Only one sheet was any good. Two were filled with large red letters and printed pictures of soup cans, and two more were ruined by crusty patches of old glue.

Brian pulled the two "good" pieces toward him and picked up his black pen. He carefully drew the outline of a sword. But even before he'd finished, he knew it wasn't right. He pulled the last sheet of cardboard toward him.

One more try, he thought grimly.

He held the pen above the clean surface, closed his eyes, and tried to picture Lord Doom with his Sword of Power raised high. He concentrated on the sword, on the way the edges of the blade tapered to a point. *That's* what he hadn't been able to get right—that long, smooth curve of the blade.

Suddenly, Brian opened his eyes. His smile returned. He'd seen that curve before, right here in his own house.

"I can *trace* it," he said aloud.

He went out into the hallway, passing his father's den, where Alex was still talking on the phone. Brian went downstairs to the kitchen. He stopped short in the doorway. His mother was standing by the telephone, the receiver to her ear, a worried look on her face. Brian's eyes shifted toward a certain drawer under the kitchen counter, then moved back to his mother.

I'll have to come back later, he thought, when no one's around.

Sarah followed Alex from Brian's room. He stepped into his den and picked up the phone at his desk, and Sarah went downstairs to the kitchen. When she lifted the receiver, Frank O'Hara was speaking.

". . . wife said you both wanted to be on the line."

"I'm here," Sarah said.

"Oh, okay. I'm not sure how much of this you two would like to hear. A lot of—"

"Have they caught Christine or haven't they?" Alex asked, his voice abrupt.

"No, I'm afraid not."

Sarah felt her chest tighten.

"That is, not yet. But I'm sure it won't be long before they do."

"That's what you told me yesterday," Sarah said, trying to keep her voice calm.

"I know, but—"

"So what exactly are the police doing?" Alex asked angrily.

Sarah heard O'Hara sigh.

"Look, Mr. Whitaker, *I'm* not in charge of things, okay? I'm not even a cop anymore. The only reason I looked into this and called you was as a favor to your wife. She sounded genuinely concerned on the phone yesterday."

No one spoke for a moment.

"Okay," Alex said, somewhat mollified. "I'm sorry. I didn't mean to blame you for anything. I just want to know what's being done."

"First of all," O'Hara said matter-of-factly, "there's a statewide search for her. And on the off chance that she's made it out of the area, her description has been sent to every state police agency in the country, including Colorado's. The minute she shows her face, they'll get her. But I'll tell you something else: I doubt that she's even alive."

"What?"

"And I'm not the only one, either," O'Hara said. "You see, on the night that she escaped, it was—"

"That's something no one's explained to me yet," Alex said bitterly. "Just how could they let her get out?"

"Apparently she picked a lock that allowed her access to a maintenance tunnel, crawled through it for a few hundred yards to a building outside the main compound, then climbed a ten-foot-high fence and walked into the woods."

Sarah was gripping the phone tightly enough to make her fingers ache.

"As I was saying," O'Hara continued, "on the night she escaped, it was barely twenty degrees outside and snowing heavily. In fact, it snowed for several days after that. Now you have to realize that she escaped wearing nothing more than a hospital gown and slippers. She might have brought a blanket with her, but that was her only protection against the cold. Also, the Wycroff state hospital is surrounded by miles of heavy woods. A *sane* person could get lost out there."

"She might be insane," Alex said, "but she's not stupid."

"No," O'Hara said, "she's not. And I grant you there's a chance she survived the woods. However, I strongly doubt it. But even if she did, I wouldn't worry about it if I were you."

"Not *worry*? That's easy for you to say."

"Yes, Mr. Whitaker, it is easy for me to say. I was a cop for thirty years and sent quite a few people to prison, and a lot of them threatened to get me when they got out. Well, here I am without a scratch on me. You know how many of them even *tried* to get even with me? Not one. That's because your average criminal has a short attention span and—"

"Christine Helstrum is not an average criminal," Alex said grimly.

Sarah heard O'Hara sigh again.

"The best thing is for you two not to let yourselves get upset. Just carry on with your lives. It's been nine days since Christine escaped, and there's been no sign of her. The odds are she's dead."

"The odds," Alex said sarcastically.

"It's likely," O'Hara said. "Eventually, maybe not until spring, but eventually, someone will find her body out there in the woods. I'm not just saying that to put your minds at ease. I'm saying it because I think it's true."

No one spoke.

"If I hear of anything more," O'Hara said finally, "I'll give you a call."

"Thank you for your help, Mr. O'Hara," Sarah said. "We appreciate it."

"It's no problem. Just try not to worry."

Sarah set the receiver in its cradle and stared at it. She wanted to believe O'Hara. She wanted to believe that Christine was dead. But she kept thinking about how she'd escaped from the hospital. She'd used cunning and endurance and strength. Sarah wondered if a woman like that would allow herself to die in a snowstorm.

† † †

Brian was tucked into bed that night with no further mention of making his Sword of Power. He wondered if his dad had changed his mind about helping him. Or if the phone call had made him forget.

It doesn't matter, Brian thought, smiling to himself, his eyes closed in the dark. Now I know how to make it myself.

Later that night Brian dreamed that he and Eddy Teesdale were in the school playground, climbing an impossibly high jungle gym, trying to get away from a scary-looking woman with a huge knife. She held it between her teeth, as if she were a pirate, and climbed up after them. Soon Brian and Eddy reached the top of the jungle gym. There was nowhere to go. The ground was far below them, too far to jump. They could do nothing but sit and wait and watch the woman climb toward them. . . .

Brian sat up in bed, his heart pounding.

The room was dark except for the Mickey Mouse night-light that glowed faintly above the light switch by the door. The dream was quickly fading—only a few traces remained: the jungle gym, the woman, the knife.

The knife, he thought.

He climbed out of bed.

The room felt cold, so he put on his blue terry-cloth bathrobe over his pajamas and tugged his slippers onto his bare feet. Then he tiptoed down the hall. When he reached the doorway of his parents' bedroom, he peeked around the corner. They were silent and still beneath the covers. Brian walked softly past the door and down the stairs.

It was dark. The once-familiar articles of furniture were now black, vague, misshapen things. The doorways were shadowy openings, like the entrances to forbidden caves.

Brian found his way to the kitchen and switched on the light, then squinted from the brightness. He took a few steps across the tile floor, then turned and looked behind him. The short hall beyond the kitchen doorway was dark—seemingly darker than when he'd walked through it a few moments ago. He felt exposed under the overbright kitchen light, as if someone were out there in the darkness, watching him.

He backed away from the doorway and bumped into the kitchen drawers by the sink.

The top drawer held silverware. The bottom one was filled with sandwich bags, plastic wrap, aluminum foil, empty paper sacks, and pairs of light bulbs in flimsy cardboard cartons.

Brian tugged open the middle drawer. It was heavy with kitchen gadgets and utensils. And knives.

He moved aside a cheese grater and a bread knife before he saw what he was looking for. It was a heavy-bladed butcher knife with a black wooden handle. Brian knew that he shouldn't be doing this, and he felt a slight thrill of excitement as he reached in and grasped the handle. He'd seen his mother use the knife once to chop up something for a stew, but he'd never actually held the knife before. It was heavier than it looked. He held it in both hands and raised it up, his arms straight out before him, the way he'd seen Lord Doom stand.

His eye ran up the sharp edge of the wide blade to its point. The blade was nearly as long as his arms, and the shape was perfect, just like the Sword of Power. Of course, *this* sword was curved only on one side, whereas *that* sword was curved on both sides. But he could take care of that on his drawing.

He shut the drawer by leaning into it with his hip, then crossed the kitchen and turned out the light. He held the knife before him as he found his way to the stairs, daring anyone who might be hiding in the shadows to try to get him.

He tiptoed up the stairs and down the hall toward his room. Even though he was certain his parents were still asleep, when he neared their room, he held the knife in his left hand down at his side, its point near the carpet, its blade shielded from view.

But as he passed before his parents' room, he heard his mother call his name.

Sarah awoke from a light sleep.

She'd heard a noise downstairs. It had been a distinct, metallic-sounding noise—a muffled crash. Patches? Sarah wondered. She sat up in bed, and Alex stirred beside her.

Then she heard a creak on the stairs. Then another. Her hand was on Alex's back, ready to shake him out of his sleep. A form slid past their doorway.

"Brian?" she said.

"What, Mom?"

"Are you okay, hon?"

"Yes, Mom," Brian said, and disappeared.

Sarah slipped quietly out of bed. She padded in her bare feet down the cool hallway to Brian's room, hugging herself through her thin nightgown. When she got to his room, Brian was already in bed, the blanket pulled up to his chin. Sarah sat on the edge of the bed and reached down to stroke his hair.

"Why were you up?"

"I was, um, getting a drink of water."

"Did you go downstairs?"

"Yes."

"How come? Why didn't you just go into the bathroom?"

"Um, I don't know."

"Well, next time, turn on the light, okay? It's not safe to go down the stairs in the dark. Okay?"

"Okay, Mom."

She kissed him on the forehead.

"Good night, pumpkin."

"Night."

Sarah walked back to the master bedroom feeling uneasy. She

had to admit that she'd been afraid, if ever so briefly, when she'd heard the creak on the stairs. She'd gone to bed with Christine Helstrum on her mind, and when she'd seen someone in the doorway, for a brief moment she'd thought . . .

Sarah climbed back into bed, angry at herself for succumbing to her imagination.

But when she closed her eyes, she remembered seeing Brian in the doorway. Before she'd realized that it was Brian, she thought she'd seen something at his side—the dull glint from the blade of a knife.

11

WHEN SARAH AWOKE SUNDAY morning, it was nearly nine. Alex was already gone from bed.

She recalled how upset he'd been after the phone call. She'd tried to make him—and herself—focus on the favorable things that Frank O'Hara had said. First, that Christine probably no longer remembered her threats to Alex. And second, that she might not even be alive.

But Alex had refused to listen to either suggestion.

"She's alive," he'd said to her, "and she'll never forget her promise to me."

They'd gone to bed without speaking further of the matter, a quiet tension between them.

Now Sarah got up, washed and dressed, then looked into Brian's room. His bed was empty. She straightened the sheet, blanket, and quilt and fluffed the pillows, then went downstairs.

A moment later, Alex came inside carrying the Sunday newspaper. Even though he was wearing a bulky cable-knit sweater, he shook his shoulders from the cold. He quickly closed the front door to shut out the frosty air.

"Hi," he said, smiling uneasily.

"Good morning."

Sarah crossed the foyer, and when she put her arms around him, she could feel the cold air clinging to his sweater. "How long have you been up?" she asked.

"Not long. I made coffee and mixed up some pancake batter and—"

"No kidding," she said.

"And I would have had the bacon strips separated and the grapefruits sliced, but Brian came down and wanted to know where the Sunday comics were."

Sarah smiled, thankful that for the moment at least things were back to normal.

While Alex finished preparing breakfast, Sarah read the comics with Brian. She encouraged him to read where he was able, and she carefully pronounced the words that were new to him. That was the easy part. The hard part sometimes came afterward.

"I don't get it, Mom."

"Well, maybe that one wasn't too funny."

"Then why is it in the comics?"

"Because it's *supposed* to be funny. Some people would think it was funny."

"Why?"

Sarah sighed and looked toward Alex for help. But he was idly poking at his pancakes, his mind elsewhere.

"Okay," Sarah said, "you see, Cathy thought that she was going to have a romantic dinner in a restaurant, and instead she ended up being stuck at home with all this ironing to do."

"Yeah?"

"That's the joke."

"It is?"

"Yes, well, see the joke's on *her*, because she thought she was going to have fun and instead she had to work."

"Why is it funny?"

"Okay, well, maybe it's not *too* funny. In fact, it wouldn't be funny at all if it happened to you, but since it happened to *her* and since she's here in the comics, well, we can laugh."

"We can?"

Sarah sighed again.

"You're right, Brian, it's not funny at all."

After breakfast Sarah asked Alex what he thought they should do today. He shook his head and said he didn't really feel like doing anything. But Sarah wouldn't let it go at that, and she began tossing around suggestions.

They almost always did something together on Sundays. If the weather was nice, they'd have a picnic in the park or hike in the mountains or visit the Cheyenne Mountain Zoo or go for a drive or just stay home and toss a Frisbee around the backyard and then cook hamburgers on the grill. If the weather was bad, they'd go to a movie or visit a museum or play one of Brian's board games.

They rarely went to church. It wasn't that Sarah and Alex didn't believe in a Supreme Being. They just didn't believe in organized religions. Nor did they believe in forcing one on their son. Of course, they did their best to teach Brian the difference between good and bad, right and wrong. But selecting a religion —or *no* religion—was up to him, they felt. So on the few occasions when they did go to church, they gave equal time to a number of religious denominations. One Sunday they might go to a Catholic high mass (Brian liked the "costumes and the smelly smoke"), and a month or two later they'd go to a Baptist revival meeting (Brian liked the excitement and the singing). Once, they "switched" Sunday to Saturday and visited a synagogue. Brian liked the chants.

But today no one seemed interested in anything Sarah suggested.

"Well," she said, "I know one thing we *need* to do today: buy party invitations and Christmas cards and get them addressed and ready to mail."

Brian groaned.

"You know what I'd like to do?" Alex said, a faint smile on his face. "That is, if everyone agrees."

"What, Dad?"

"Go ice-skating at the Broadmoor."

"All right!"

Sarah grinned. "But what about my Christmas cards?"

"There's a shop at the Broadmoor."

Before Sarah could say that there were less expensive places to buy cards, Brian jumped up from the table.

"I'll go find my skates," he said, and ran upstairs.

They drove west on Lake Avenue, which pointed directly at the main structure of the Broadmoor Hotel. Sarah had always thought that the sprawling seventy-year-old building looked like an enormous, elaborate cake—rose-colored and multilayered and topped with red tile frosting.

Alex steered the Toyota Celica around the horseshoe-shaped lot in front of the building complex. He found a space near the entrance to the drugstore marked 30-Minute Parking.

There were about a dozen customers inside, enough to make the small store seem crowded. Sarah guessed that she and Alex and Brian were the only locals, for everyone else was either picking out postcards or marveling at the unique selection of chocolate candies or merely browsing along the aisles of lotions and potions and grooming accessories, as if they'd never been in a drugstore before.

Sarah steered Alex toward the greeting cards, while Brian wandered off to more interesting areas of the store, those stocked with toys and candy.

The selection of party invitations wasn't as large as Sarah had hoped. However, she did find one design that she felt was satisfactory. As far as Alex was concerned, they were *all* satisfactory.

"Only twelve?" she said, looking more closely at the box. "At this price there should be twenty per box."

" 'When you care enough to send the very best' . . ."

"Very funny. So we'll have to get, let's see, four boxes."

"What? You're planning on having fifty couples in our house? A hundred people?"

"They won't all be couples."

"Do we even *know* that many people?"

"Sure, Alex, when you count the people from my shop and—"

"All your customers?"

"Not *all*, but there are a lot of them I want to invite. You don't mind, do you?"

He shook his head, smiling, and put his arm around her waist. "Of course not."

After Sarah had picked out several boxes of Christmas cards, they paid the cashier, then looked for Brian.

He was nowhere to be found.

They searched up and down every aisle and in the nook housing the candy display and in the rear by the lunch counter. He wasn't in the store.

Sarah fought back a feeling of alarm.

"Maybe he went out to the car," she said, and started for the door.

Alex put his hand on her arm.

"I don't think so," he said. "Come on."

She followed Alex through the other entrance to the drugstore—the one that led directly into the hotel.

Sarah could imagine Brian setting off to explore new territory and turning down one hallway after another and becoming hopelessly lost.

Well, not *hopelessly*, she knew. Eventually, someone would take the scared little boy to the front desk, where he would be well cared for until his mother arrived. Still, Sarah felt a sense of urgency about finding him.

She remembered an incident two years ago when she'd become separated from Brian at a department store. She'd searched frantically for him for over an hour, actually running through the aisles in the store, imagining that all sorts of terrible things had happened to him, until she'd been paged to a customer-service desk, where Brian was waiting for her, his eyes red from recent tears. He'd wandered into the toy section, and some older boys had teased him and pushed him around until he'd cried for his mother. Then, of course, they'd laughed at him, which had hurt even more.

Sarah and Alex entered a short, wide carpeted hallway with a wall filled with old framed photographs on the left and an information desk on the right. Beside the desk, nearly hidden in the corner, was a glass case with a mannequin of an American Indian wearing a red plaid shirt, blue jeans, and a cowboy hat and seated in a straight-backed wooden chair. Sarah had always thought the display seemed out of place, incongruous with the rest of the hotel. The dummy looked like a carefully preserved mummy.

And there was Brian, standing with his nose and hands pressed to the glass.

"Brian." Sarah's tone was part relief, part scolding.

"Hey, Mom, Dad, look at this. Is he real?"

"Brian, I wish you wouldn't wander away like this," Sarah said, feeling herself calm down.

"Huh?"

"We thought you were lost."

"I wasn't lost," Brian said. "I was right here."

"Right," Alex said. "Let's go skating."

They went outside to the car. The sunlight seemed especially bright now, and although Sarah knew the temperature must still be in the thirties, the sun felt warm on her face.

"Why don't we walk to the arena," she said.

Alex unlocked the passenger door and put the sackful of cards in the backseat.

"We can't leave the car here," he said, pointing at the thirty-minute parking sign.

"Oh."

"But why don't you and Brian walk, if you want to, and I'll meet you inside."

Sarah looked at Brian.

"How about it? Do you feel like walking around the lake?"

He shrugged his shoulders. "I guess."

"We can see the geese."

His face brightened. "Okay!"

Alex climbed into the car, and Sarah and Brian went back into the drugstore, then out through the connecting hallway and past the glass-encased Indian to the hotel lobby. A hand-carved marble staircase spiraled up to their left. It was one of Sarah's favorite features in the hotel. However, she knew that Brian preferred high tech, so they continued on through the lobby and past the front desk to the escalators. Brian looked as happy as if he were on a ride at Disneyland.

When they got off the escalator at the top, they were once again on ground level, since this part of the hotel was built on a hillside. They walked through a large, open room where a scattering of hotel guests lounged on tasteful, comfortable furniture, then pushed through heavy glass doors to the main patio.

From mid-June until late September the large patio, which bordered on a small, placid lake, would be filled with people taking in the sun on chaise longues. But now the long chairs were folded up and stored away. The patio was empty, and the lake was covered with ice.

Sarah and Brian turned left onto the path. The cement walk had been shoveled clear, and snow was piled in windrows against the barren trees on each side. There were dozens of plump geese waddling around the edge of the frozen pond, poking their beaks through the snow as if they expected to find something good to eat. They looked up expectantly at Sarah and Brian. Sarah wished she'd brought bread crumbs for them.

"Don't their feet get cold?" Brian asked.

"Maybe. But they don't seem to mind."

There were a few other people strolling around the frozen pond, enjoying the bright sun and the brisk winter air. Sarah guessed that they were town residents rather than hotel guests—their winter clothing was more sensible than fashionable.

They reached the narrow end of the lake, and the path curved sharply around it to the right. As Sarah looked to her right over the flat white lake, she glimpsed a woman on the path behind them.

The woman had short brown hair and wore a long dark coat.

She seemed to be staring at Sarah and Brian. But when she saw that Sarah had noticed her, she turned quickly away, suddenly interested in some nearby geese that were poking their beaks through the snow.

Sarah took Brian's hand and walked quickly around the end of the lake, not stopping until they'd reached the World Arena. She looked back, but the woman was not in sight—only the dark leafless trees and the white lake and a scattering of people feeding the geese from the path.

Sarah pushed through the glass doors into the tiny lobby where Alex was waiting, a small pile of skates at his feet.

"Is something wrong?" he asked, looking at her face.

Sarah shook her head. "No," she said, but she couldn't help glancing back through the glass doors.

"What?"

"There was a woman," she said, "on the path. I think she was watching us."

"What did she look like?" Alex asked quickly.

"I'm . . . not sure. I just caught a glimpse of her face, and then she turned away. She was wearing a dark coat."

Alex's mouth came partly open; then he set his jaw and stepped to the door.

"Where?"

"She's gone now," Sarah said, putting her hand on his arm.

"I'm sure it was nothing, just someone feeding the geese. Come on, let's skate."

Alex stared out the door for a full minute before he turned away.

Since Alex had already paid, they went directly to the stadium seats, removed their coats and shoes, and put on their skates. There were only about a dozen others skaters on the ice, so Sarah and Brian and Alex had plenty of room to maneuver without worrying about getting in anybody's way.

Alex was a competent, if somewhat ungraceful, skater. He'd taken up the sport in his early teens, then dropped it after college, only to rediscover it shortly before he and Sarah had met. In fact, that was how they had met—skating at the Plaza Ice Chalet. Brian had taken a fall on the ice, and before Sarah could get to him, Alex was helping the boy back onto his skates. They had finished the day skating together.

Brian had been skating for a year and a half, and he still considered it an achievement to completely circle the arena without falling down.

Sarah was by far the best of the three. She was a better-than-average skater, she knew. After all, she'd been skating since she was Brian's age. But she always felt humbled when she skated here, because this was where Dorothy Hamill and Scott Hamilton, among others, had trained on their way to the Winter Olympics. However, it wasn't technical achievement that Sarah sought when she put on skates. What she loved was the freedom of movement and the feeling of floating through air.

They stayed on the ice for nearly an hour. By then they were all beginning to feel a bit tired, so they made their way to the seats where they'd left their shoes and coats.

Brian had his skates off and his shoes on almost before Sarah and Alex had sat down. He grabbed his coat and walked to the railing surrounding the ice, joining the other people who watched the skaters. Sarah smiled, remembering how she had always been reluctant to leave the skating rink when she'd been Brian's age. However, she winced when she pulled off her skates. Her feet were tired, and she was glad that they were through skating for the day.

She slipped into her shoes while Alex tied together each pair of skates by their laces. Sarah picked up her purse and coat, then looked around her.

"Have we got everything?"

"I think so," Alex said. "Where's Brian?"

"He's right over—"

Sarah stopped when she realized that Brian was no longer standing at the railing.

"He was there a minute ago," she said, a note of worry in her voice.

They searched the grandstands and the walkway around the ice. Brian was not in the arena. Nor was he in the lobby, where several people stood in line to buy admission tickets. They separately checked inside the rest rooms. When they stepped back into the lobby and looked at each other, Sarah could see panic in Alex's eyes. He pushed through the outer glass doors, with Sarah close behind him.

And there was Brian on the path by the lake.

He was not alone.

Walking beside him was the same woman Sarah had seen earlier. Her left hand was on her purse, which hung by a strap from her shoulder. Her right hand rested lightly on the back of Brian's head. She was leading him away.

12

ALEX, THAT'S THE WOMAN WHO was fol—"

Before Sarah could finish, Alex dropped the skates and ran toward the woman and Brian. Sarah ran after him.

"Get away from my son!" Alex yelled.

The woman started to turn just as Alex came up behind her, grabbed the shoulder of her coat, and spun her around with such force that her purse went flying, along with a sack of bread crumbs. Brian looked on, stunned.

A moment later, Sarah ran up and got her first close look at the woman's face and saw that she was easily in her sixties. The myopic eyes behind her glasses were wide, and her mouth was open in surprise and fear.

Alex, too, looked surprised. But he hesitated for only a moment before demanding, "What do you think you're doing?"

"The boy—" the woman said, pointing a trembling finger toward the lake, "he wanted to feed the geese. . . ."

"Oh, my God," Sarah whispered under her breath.

"Martha!"

Sarah turned and saw an elderly man hurrying anxiously toward them, dropping a sack of bread crumbs along the way. He pushed past Alex and held the woman by both arms.

"Martha, are you all right? What happened?"

"This man," she said, "grabbed me and nearly knocked me down."

The old man turned an angry face toward Alex, whose own face, Sarah noted, was red with embarrassment and shame.

"Oh, God, I'm so sorry," Alex said. "Please forgive—"

Alex stepped toward the couple, and the man stuck out his arm, palm forward, to ward him off.

"Stay away from us," he said angrily.

"The little boy—" the woman said, looking down at Brian, "he asked me if he could feed the geese. I said of course. I didn't see the harm . . ."

"I'm terribly sorry," Alex said, a slight tremor in his voice. "I . . . thought you were someone else."

"Get away from us." The man's voice was a mixture of anger and disgust. "If you don't, I'm going to get the police." Then he turned toward his wife, and his tone softened. "Are you sure you're all right, Martha?"

"Yes . . . yes, I think so."

Alex started to apologize again, and Sarah put her hand on his arm.

"Come on, Alex," she said gently.

"I'm sorry." Alex looked toward the couple, then shifted his gaze to Sarah's eyes. "I thought she was . . ."

"I know. I did, too." Sarah said. "Come on, let's go."

Sarah and Alex and Brian walked toward the ice area, all of them slightly shaken, as if they were leaving the scene of an accident. Sarah glanced back once and saw the man pick up the woman's purse and brush off the snow.

Brian looked up at his father, tears of confusion in his eyes.

"Dad, why did you do that?"

"Your father just . . ." Sarah began.

"I made a mistake," Alex said softly.

† † †

As soon as they got home, Brian went upstairs to play in his room. Alex sat at the kitchen table while Sarah put a kettle on the stove. She set the table with mugs, napkins, spoons, a tin of tea bags, and a bowl of sugar.

Alex stared down at his hands and said, "I can't believe I lost my head like that."

"It was partly my fault," Sarah said.

"No."

"I told you that woman had been following us when really she was doing nothing. Just feeding the geese."

Alex shook his head.

"You could have said nothing," he said, "and it wouldn't have mattered. When I saw her from behind, her size, her hair, leading Brian away, I . . . I thought it was Christine. I've never felt such rage, Sarah. It blinded me. I was ready to—" He squeezed his eyes shut, then opened them and looked up at her. "Thank God I didn't hurt that poor woman."

Sarah stepped behind Alex's chair and gently rubbed his neck. It felt knotted with muscle.

"It was stupid of me to lose control," Alex said. "Frank O'Hara was right. The best thing for us to do is to carry on with our lives and forget about Christine Helstrum. Besides, she's probably dead."

The kettle whimpered, then screamed.

Sarah turned off the burner, brought the kettle to the table, and poured steaming water into their mugs.

"I agree," she said. "It won't do either of us any good to jump at ghosts. We've got more important things to think about." She set the kettle on the stove, then sat at the table and moved her tea bag around in the cup with a spoon. "For instance," she said, trying to put some cheer back into her voice,

"Christmas cards and party invitations. What do you say? Do you feel up to it?"

"Sure," he said, reaching for her hand, a faint smile on his lips. "But first I want to go up and speak to Brian for a minute. I owe him an apology, or at least an explanation."

"About Christine?" Sarah sounded concerned.

"No," Alex said. "I'll leave her out of it."

Brian took the butcher knife from his toy chest.

He thought back to last night when he'd carried it to his room and almost been caught by his mother. In fact, he'd barely managed to slide it beneath the bed and climb under the covers before she'd come in to ask why he'd been up. He'd said he'd been getting a drink of water. That was a fib, and he knew it, and he knew it was wrong and that he could be punished for it. But he also knew that taking the knife was more serious, more wrong. So after his mother had kissed him good night and gone back to her bedroom, he'd hidden the knife in his toy chest and covered it with several layers of playthings.

Besides, he thought, I'm not gonna *keep* it.

He held the thick wooden handle in both hands and raised his arms so that the light played off the blade.

I'm just gonna *borrow* it for a little while.

He laid the knife lengthwise on the long piece of cardboard. He was pleased to see that his drawing surface was just long enough to accommodate it. Then he pulled the cap from his black drawing pen, knelt down, and began to trace the handle of the knife.

Brian heard Alex's voice.

He froze, his left hand pressed flat on the knife handle, his right hand holding the pen. His mouth was open, and his eyes were riveted on the open bedroom door.

The voice faded.

Brian rose and walked out of his bedroom to the empty U-shaped hallway. He wondered if his father was upstairs. His eyes scanned the open doors: his parents' bedroom to his left, his father's den straight ahead at one corner of the U, the guest bedroom next to that, the bathroom next to that at the other corner of the U, and the large sitting room across the open stairwell from where he stood.

Then he heard his father's voice again. Brian stood at the railing and looked down the stairs. He realized that the voice had drifted up the stairwell. Then he heard his mother, and he knew for sure that they were both down there, probably in the kitchen.

Brian went back to his room and stood for a moment in the doorway. The cardboard and the long butcher knife were in plain view in the middle of the floor. He closed the door behind him. But he realized that with the door closed he wouldn't be able to hear if anyone came up the stairs and walked to his room.

He opened the door. Then he dragged the cardboard and the knife around to the far side of his bed, out of view from the doorway. Now if anyone came upstairs, he'd be ready to push the knife under the bed.

Once again he began to trace the handle of the knife with his drawing pen. The handle had a round knob that bulged forward from the bottom, and then it was smooth and straight up to the bottom edge of the blade. The bottom of the blade jutted out several inches from the handle and then began its long, gentle curve up to the point.

As Brian began to trace the cutting edge of the blade, his pen seemed to stick to the cardboard. He examined the cardboard and then the pen. There was a notch cut into the side of the plastic pen. He realized now why the pen hadn't moved smoothly—the knife blade was cutting into it. And for the first time since he'd taken the knife, he realized how sharp and dangerous it was.

He carefully finished tracing the cutting edge of the blade.

Then he flipped the knife over, positioned it just right, and began retracing the cutting edge so that his cardboard sword would be double-edged.

Suddenly he saw movement out of the corner of his eye, and his head jerked up.

But it was only Patches. The big orange-and-white cat meowed and sniffed at the cardboard and the point of the knife blade.

"Watch out or you might cut your nose," Brian said.

Patches walked stiff-legged around the cardboard, eyeing it suspiciously, then rubbed up against Brian with his tail in the air. Brian tried to ignore the cat and finish his tracing.

"What are you doing, Brian?"

Brian looked over his bed. His father stood in the bedroom doorway.

"Uh, nothing," Brian said, and pushed the knife under the bed. "Just playing."

"Can I talk to you for a minute?"

Brian was certain that his father had seen the knife and was going to get mad at him. But it was something else entirely. He wanted to talk some more about the woman by the lake today. Brian didn't quite understand what it was all about, so he just nodded a few times and said, "Yeah."

Then his father was finished and got up to leave the room. Brian saw his eyes fall on the stack of cardboard pieces in the corner.

"How's your Sword of Power coming?" Alex asked.

"Okay, I guess."

Alex walked over and picked up the cardboard sheets and began shuffling through them.

"Not bad," he said. Then he saw the piece lying beside Brian's bed. "Is that your latest one?"

"Yes."

Alex stepped to the bed and bent down to retrieve the cardboard. Brian didn't move or even breathe. If his father saw the knife under the bed, it was all over. He wasn't sure what his father would do to him. He seemed to remember being spanked very hard several times, but he thought that was a long time ago by Ted. He tried to remember what Alex did when he got angry, but he couldn't remember ever seeing him angry. Except today, when he'd grabbed that woman.

"Hey, this is really good," Alex said, holding up the cardboard with the tracing of the double-edged sword.

"Thanks, Dad," Brian said. He was watching Patches pawing at something under the bed.

"How did you manage to get the lines curved so nice?"

"I, um, sort of traced it."

"Well, you did a good job. Would you like me to cut it out for you now?"

"I can do it," Brian said, thinking of the box cutter that he had hidden away but mostly just wishing that his father wasn't here right now. Then he remembered that he wasn't supposed to have the box cutter any more than he was supposed to have the knife.

"Maybe you should let me."

"Okay," Brian said quickly.

He helped his father pick up all the pieces of cardboard, and he was greatly relieved to follow him out of the bedroom.

Alex tossed and turned in his sleep that night, keeping Sarah awake.

She knew what was troubling him: the scene today at the Broadmoor. It troubled her, too. Not just that he'd nearly attacked an old woman, which was disturbing enough, but that his actions had been so totally out of character for him. He was warm and emotional, of course, but also solid and logical. Thoughtful. She could depend on that quality in him. In fact, she knew, in the short time that they'd been married, she'd come to depend on almost everything about him. Not financially dependent, of course, but emotionally, psychologically.

That's it, she thought with a wry smile. I'm psychologically addicted to him.

This was something new for her, since she'd never felt that close to Ted Saunders, even when their marriage was going smoothly. And during her three years of being a single parent—after her divorce from Ted and before she'd married Alex—she'd become totally self-reliant, quite able to take care of herself and her son. Her friends all praised her for being able to "make it on her own," to carry on without having to rely on some man, to get by without *needing* someone.

She'd begun to believe it herself—that she could get by with what she had and that she didn't need anything else in her life.

Not the child-support payments, which came sporadically from Ted. Not sex, which she'd thought she'd long for, but didn't, after her separation from Ted. And not more love—Brian gave her all she'd ever need.

Then she'd met Alex. And her life, which she'd thought had been just fine, had somehow become easier, better.

And now she needed him. She counted on him. Not just for the "big" things, like making the house payments or taking care of her and Brian when they'd both come down with the flu or simply loving her. She counted on him for the "little" things as well: starting the lawn mower and listening to her complain about a rude store clerk and holding Brian's hand when the three of them went for a walk. The more she was with him, she realized, the more she'd grown to need him. And she knew in her heart that he needed her just as much.

Maybe that's not such a good thing, she thought, staring up at the dark ceiling. Maybe it weakens you to give up so much of your self-reliance.

She turned her head and looked at Alex stirring in his sleep beside her. She smiled in the darkness and reached out and touched his back.

But we're stronger together, she thought, stronger than either of us was apart.

Besides, she knew, Alex would always be there for her. It wasn't that she *needed* him to lean on. But it was comforting to know that he was there if she did need him. He was solid and strong and logical. She'd never doubted that for a minute.

Until today.

When he'd gone after that woman, it had been like watching a stranger, a reckless and violent man. Of course, he'd thought that Brian had been in danger, that the woman was Christine Helstrum.

But she wasn't Christine. She was just an old woman who'd been feeding the geese, and Alex had nearly thrown her to the ground. It had been a terrible thing for Sarah to witness. More than witness—to be a part of. Because she believed that she would have done the same thing had not Alex been there.

What would they have done, she wondered, if the woman *had* been Christine?

As disturbing as that was to her, she had a thought that frightened her even more:

What would Christine have done?

13

SHE HUDDLED IN THE DARK, eating.

She felt pleased with herself. And why shouldn't she? After all, she had everything she needed: a safe hiding place, all the food she could steal, and an easy way to get into Alex's house.

I could kill them right now, she thought, licking crumbs from her fingers. I could get into the house right now and kill them in their beds.

That thought doubly pleased her. But it also troubled her, because she knew that once they were dead, the game would end.

Like with the mice, she thought.

She remembered setting out crumbs for them and then waiting, holding perfectly still for hours, waiting for them to come out of hiding, to test the air with their tiny pink noses, and finally to creep closer, close enough for her to snatch. First one. And then another. Three in all. But after she'd caught three, the little game had been over.

Although it had given her the idea for the *real* game.

She smiled now, remembering snipping off their heads with the hedge clippers and putting them on the seat of the car. She wondered if the three of *them* had gotten the joke.

Three blind mice.

See how they run, she thought.

She stretched out her legs on the floor and leaned back against the wall.

"They all ran after the farmer's wife," she sang softly in the dark.

"Who cut off their heads with a carving knife."

She put her hand over her mouth to stifle a laugh.

But he mustn't die too soon, she thought. He must suffer first. The way I suffered. Suffered every day I was locked up. Every day for two years thinking about my son. Two years of trying to get out. Two years of being probed and drugged by idiots in white coats. Two years? Or was it four? No matter. *Now* is what matters.

And now, she knew, she was in control of things. She could do whatever she wanted.

She folded her arms and hugged herself against the chill air. That was the only thing that she didn't like about her hiding place—it wasn't very warm.

A sweater would be nice, she thought.

She closed her eyes in the dark and tried to imagine how good she'd feel with a nice warm sweater on beneath her coat. She concentrated on the sweater. It was a pullover, and it was pink. She realized it was just like a sweater she'd once owned, back in a happier time, back when Timothy was still with her.

Timothy. Poor little Timothy. If only he were alive.

But how he'd cried. Always hungry. Always sick. Always something. Until she didn't think she could stand it any longer. She just wanted him to shut up, the cries going through her brain like knives until she yelled at him to shut up, and when he cried even louder, she hit him. And again.

She remembered the police coming and taking her away from Timothy without even giving her a chance to soothe him and say she was sorry.

And then later, after she'd been released, she found out that *he'd* taken Timothy.

He'll be sorry, she thought. He'll pay. Him and his wife and . . .

Her eyes opened wide, and she stared into the blackness.

She's never seen me, she thought. I could walk right up to her and she wouldn't even know it was me.

Now she grinned, shivering with cold and, perhaps, delight.

He'll pay, she thought.

14

EVEN THOUGH SARAH HAD Mondays off, she rose with Alex and Brian, made their breakfasts, and got them off to their respective schools.

Neither she nor Alex mentioned yesterday's incident at the Broadmoor. And really, what was there to be said? It was over and done with. Alex had made a mistake—a frightful mistake, to be sure, but still just a mistake. He'd apologized, and there was nothing more to be said. He had said more, though. He'd promised to put Christine out of his mind and carry on, business as usual. Sarah wondered if things could ever be "as usual."

"They can if you try," she said out loud.

Patches meowed and rubbed against her leg. Sarah scratched him behind the ears. Then she poured herself another cup of coffee, sat down at the kitchen table with a pen and a notepad, and began making a list of gifts. It was only two and a half weeks until Christmas, she knew, and now was as good a time as any to get started. She already had a good idea of what she wanted to get for both Alex and Brian, but the act of writing helped her focus her attention.

Things as usual, she thought. Christmas shopping.

Her first stop was across town—the Citadel Shopping Center.

The lot was already more than half-filled with cars despite the fact that it was only nine-thirty in the morning. Sarah parked as close as she could to the entrance of May D&F, locked the car, and pulled her coat closed against the fresh breeze. The outside of the store was draped in bright holiday decorations, contrasting nicely with the overcast sky, which promised snow. The scene lifted Sarah's spirits and put her in the proper holiday mood to jostle her way through the happily harried shoppers.

The first thing she bought was a robe for Alex. She held it at arm's length and pictured him in it. "Cuddly" was the word that popped into her mind. She smiled and handed her VISA card to the salesclerk.

Sarah spent nearly two hours in the store buying Brian two pairs of corduroy pants (one forest green, one burgundy); a sweater (off-white with multicolored deer across the chest); a pair of blue jeans; two rugby shirts (one with blue and white stripes, one with green and yellow); and a new parka (not that there was anything wrong with his old one other than that his wrists were starting to show at the ends of the sleeves). While she was picking out some socks and underwear for him, she got the idea to take a chance with Alex.

She walked over to the men's underwear section and eyed the briefs. She knew that the microbriefs would be going too far, although she'd like to see Alex in something like that at least *once.* She knew she was even taking a chance on the bikini briefs, since Alex seemed to be fairly conservative, if not regimental, about wearing jockey shorts.

But, she thought, if nothing else, it would be good for a laugh. Maybe even a blush from Alex.

She bought a package of three in deep, rich sexy colors.

Sarah had carried her armload of booty out to the car before she realized she'd forgotten something on her list. She locked the car and walked back to the Fashion Bar. She'd already had in mind the color of sweater that she wanted to buy for Alex, but once she saw the assortment, it took her a good twenty minutes to make her selection: a V-necked ivory cashmere. She couldn't decide whether a turtleneck or a dress shirt would look better underneath, so she bought both.

She was splurging, she knew, something she usually didn't do. But, number one, this had been a very good year at the shop, so she had more money to spend (that is, charge now, pay later). And, number two, she wanted this Christmas to be something special. It already was special, she knew, their first together in their new house. She also knew that there was more to Christmas than simply material things.

But a few extra presents under the tree couldn't hurt, she thought happily.

Before she left the shopping center, Sarah bought a game for Brian—actually, for all three of them. The one she picked looked challenging but not too complicated. The side of the box said "For Ages 8 and Up," but she figured that Brian, at 6½, could probably handle it.

In fact, she thought smiling, if his checker playing is any indication, he'll probably beat us both.

Sarah drove north on Academy Boulevard. Several miles later, when most of Colorado Springs lay behind her, she turned into the lot of Hobby Town. She'd never been to this store before. However, she and Alex had both seen the ads that Brian had clipped from several weeks' worth of Sunday papers—the ads for the radio-controlled car. They'd discussed more than once whether he was too young for such an expensive "item" (they both hesitated even to call it a "toy"), and they'd questioned him several times (cleverly, they hoped) to test his resolve about the car. In the end, they'd decided to buy it. Alex had tipped the scales in favor of purchase:

"It's something that will last for years," he'd said. "Besides, if Brian doesn't play with it, I will."

The car, a Volkswagen dune buggy with fat tires and a raised rear end, was much larger than Sarah had imagined. At first she thought that the salesman, who was a gum-popping young man with thick glasses and a nerd-pack stuffed with pens, was trying to take advantage of her ignorance. But after he painstakingly pointed out that each feature mentioned in the ad exactly matched each feature of the car itself, she tentatively handed over her charge card.

It was well after noon by the time Sarah drove south toward town. There were still a few items left on her list, but she was too hungry to go on without lunch. She paid for the salad bar at a fast-food restaurant. After carrying her Styrofoam plate along the row of pathetic-looking vegetables, she wished she had ordered a greasy burger and fries.

There were only two more items on her gift list, both for Alex: a book and a tennis racket.

The book was something she'd been considering buying for several months, ever since Alex had pointed it out to her at the bookstore downtown. It was a rare, old book on world history—a first edition and in very good condition. The price was five hundred dollars.

Sarah found a parking place on North Tejon one block from the store.

The book was still resting under its protective glass cover. It lay open, displaying a map, a richly colored plate of fourteenth-century Europe. The facing page contained rows of crisp black text.

Sarah remembered how Alex had gazed for long minutes at the book, how he'd questioned the saleslady about it. She knew that he wanted it, not to *use* but simply to have, to cherish. She also knew that he considered five hundred dollars too much to spend.

Which was why she'd been debating whether or not to buy the book. She was also troubled that Alex might be embarrassed if she "outdid" him at Christmas. Although he'd never said as much, she knew that he was at least mildly bothered that she earned more at her shop than he did from teaching. She didn't want to exacerbate those feelings. On the other hand, she wanted him to have the book.

She hesitated, then motioned to the saleslady.

Sarah left the store with the book, which was carefully packed in a thick cardboard box, tucked under her arm. She turned right, away from her car, and walked a block and a half to the sporting-goods store.

Sarah had played tennis since she'd been in high school. She wasn't very good, but she enjoyed the sport. Last year she'd tried to get Alex interested in it. He'd loved it from the start, and although he'd never really played before, Sarah was amazed at how well he did, even though he'd been forced to use one of her old rackets. He'd considered buying one for himself. However, he'd kept putting it off until fall had given way to winter and tennis to ice-skating.

Sarah asked a clerk for directions, then made her way toward the rear of the store where the tennis equipment was displayed. As she passed by the hunting and fishing section, something caught her attention.

A salesman was showing a revolver to a middle-aged couple, obviously husband and wife.

"It's for her," Sarah heard the husband say.

The salesman handed the gun to the woman. He was one of two clerks standing behind a glass case that served as a counter. The wall behind them was lined with rifles and shotguns, and the glass case was filled with handguns.

The woman turned the gun this way and that in her hands as if she were quite familiar with it. She sighted down the barrel at the floor behind the salesman.

"It has good stopping power," the salesman said.

"That's what we're looking for," the husband said. "My job takes me out of town more often than it used to."

"I'm sure I'll never have to use it," his wife said. "But it will make me feel safer at home."

"Have you ever fired a gun before?" the salesman asked her.

"Oh, yes," she said.

"May I help you, ma'am?"

Sarah came out of her reverie. The other salesman was looking directly at her.

"Oh, no. No, thank you."

Sarah walked quickly to the rear of the store, feeling guilty at having been caught eavesdropping. She tried to summon up her earlier feelings of joy, her Christmas spirit, by immersing herself in selecting a tennis racket for Alex. But she stood before a display of scores of rackets, unable to concentrate, and she ended up picking the one nearest at hand and handing it to the salesclerk.

She was thinking about the incident yesterday at the Broadmoor. What could she have done if the woman with Brian had been Christine? She wasn't especially strong, and she certainly wasn't skilled at self-defense. What could she do to protect herself and her son against a madwoman? Hit her with this tennis racket?

Or should she have something at her disposal that was better suited for the purpose?

"I'm sure I'll never have to use it," she'd heard the woman say a few minutes ago, "but it will make me feel safer at home."

Sarah found herself walking back to the hunting section.

"May I help you, ma'am?"

It was the same salesman who'd spoken to her before. He was a heavyset man with a small mustache. He wore a long-sleeved white shirt that was beginning to fray at the cuffs. His tie was tacked firmly in place.

"I . . . yes," Sarah said.

The man waited, a half smile twitching beneath his mustache.

"Yes?" he asked.

"Oh, well, I was thinking of protection. For my family. At home."

"I see," the man said. "So you'll want something that both you and your husband can handle. Are you familiar with handguns?"

"No . . ."

"Then we'd better stick with a revolver."

The man slid open the rear of the case, then squatted down behind it. Sarah felt foolish standing alone at the counter. She looked around, half-expecting to see someone she knew. What if they came over and asked what she was doing?

She was ready to walk straight out of the store when the man rose from behind the counter. He was holding a gun.

"This is a Colt," he said. "It fires a .38 special, which is all you'll ever need, believe me. Most people think they need a Magnum, probably because of all the Clint Eastwood movies. You know what I mean?" When Sarah didn't answer, the man cleared his throat and held out the gun, butt first. "Here," he said, "get the feel of it."

Sarah hesitated, then set her packages on the counter and took the pistol from him. It was the first time she'd ever held a gun, and she was surprised by how heavy it was. She was also surprised at how it seemed to fit perfectly in her hand. She turned her hand, palm up, and stared at the weapon.

"It has a two-inch barrel," the salesman said, "which is no good for target practice, but for around the house, it's sufficient. You know, most shootings occur at less than twenty feet, which is probably longer than any room in your house."

Sarah was about to say that their living room was longer than twenty feet, then realized how ridiculous that would sound. She tried to picture herself standing in that room, perhaps by the Christmas tree, showing Alex and Brian the gun, explaining to them that although she hated it and considered owning it immoral and that she believed in a civilized society and law and order and the protection of the police, she'd bought the gun for their own good and would not hesitate to use it, to shoot bullets into someone, to kill another human being.

Sarah shook her head no. She laid the small, blue ugly thing on the countertop.

"No," she said softly.

She picked up her packages from the counter and walked through the crowded store toward the entrance. All the way she felt the man's confused stare on her back. But by the time she'd reached the parking lot and climbed into the Jeep, she'd pushed the incident from her mind.

Sarah made two stops on her way home. One was to buy a bottle of White Linen cologne for Kay Nealy. Sarah didn't particularly care for that scent, but it was Kay's favorite. The other stop was for wrapping paper, ribbons, name tags, and tape.

When she got home, she made several trips from the garage to the living room, setting everything on the floor in front of the tree. Alex and Brian weren't due home for almost two hours. She figured she could get all the presents wrapped and placed under the tree before then—a nice surprise for Brian, since a decorated tree wasn't truly a Christmas tree until there were presents lying beneath it.

Sarah made tea, then brought a steaming cup and a pair of scissors into the living room. She'd begun to recapture the holiday mood she'd been in earlier today. To help things along, she plugged in the Christmas-tree lights and switched on the small stereo set. She searched the dial for Christmas music. Finding none, she settled for a station that billed itself as "easy listening."

She sat cross-legged on the floor before the tree, surrounded by packages and brightly colored paper, and began working. Patches strolled in, toyed for a while with some ribbons, then curled up in a chair at her side.

An hour later she was nearly finished with her wrapping. In fact, she was on the last gift, Alex's book, when she heard the kettle whistling from the kitchen.

She shook her head, smiling at her absentmindedness, and got to her feet. Then she stopped and held perfectly still. She stood in the midst of colorful presents, empty shopping bags, and scattered scraps of paper. Patches raised his head and meowed. The kettle screamed shrilly from the kitchen like a small wounded animal.

I turned off the stove, Sarah thought. I remember. I turned it off before I poured water into my cup.

The kettle continued its one-note, off-key song of pain.

Maybe Alex and Brian came in without my noticing, she thought. One of them turned on the burner under the kettle.

She moved slowly to the doorway and peered out into the foyer and the hall leading to the kitchen.

"Alex?" she called.

No answer.

The kettle continued its shrill cry.

Sarah moved toward the kitchen.

"Alex?"

The kitchen was empty. The kettle sat on the stove on the left rear burner, the one she always used to heat water. The coil beneath it was orange red from heat, and she could see that the dial had been turned to "high." The kettle continued to scream as steam shot from the spout and condensed on the wall by the stove, leaving a patch of tiny drops.

Sarah felt a bead of perspiration run down her side.

She took one step into the kitchen, then nearly jumped out of her shoes when Patches brushed past her leg. She slowly walked into the kitchen, glancing warily over her shoulder and wincing from the howl of the steam. She lifted the kettle, set it aside, and turned off the burner.

I'm positive I moved this before, she thought, *and* turned off the burner. But maybe not. Because if I did . . .

She turned, her back to the stove, and scanned the room. Nothing seemed to be out of place. Even her purse sat open on the kitchen table, exactly where she'd left it.

Then she felt cold air on her right hand.

Sarah turned to her right, frowning, and stepped toward the laundry room. She was halfway through the doorway when she froze. The outside door was to her left. She distinctly remembered locking it before she'd left the house this morning. There was no question in her mind—she'd locked that door.

Now it stood wide open.

For a moment, she didn't move, frozen by fear and indecision—run out the back door? or the front door? or call the police?

She knew she had to do something, and now, because there was someone in the house.

15

SARAH HESITATED A MOMENT longer, then hurried across the kitchen and phoned the police.

They found her standing half in and half out of the front door, with her hand on the knob and her cat tucked under her arm. She looked ready either to run from the porch or else jump back inside and slam the door shut.

"Are you the lady who called the police?" one of the cops asked.

He was over six feet tall, Sarah guessed, with dark eyes and black sideburns jutting from beneath his cap. His partner, a woman, was shorter than he but taller than Sarah. Her hair was blond and pulled back in a small bun. She was dressed like the man: black shoes with rubber soles; dark trousers; and a waist-length zippered jacket open to reveal a wide belt from which hung a night stick, a two-way radio, and a holstered revolver.

"Yes, there's been someone in the house." Sarah spoke rapidly in a low voice. "Maybe they're still in there, I don't know. The back door was open, so they could have slipped out."

"Did you see anyone?" the woman asked.

Her name tag said "Pearl," and Sarah wondered if that was her first name until she saw that the man's tag read "Maestas."

"No, but someone turned on the kettle."

The cops glanced at each other.

"In the kitchen," Sarah said. "Someone was in the kitchen."

"Is there anyone else in the house?" Maestas asked. "Any other member of your family?"

"No."

He nodded, then said to Pearl, "Go around and check the rear of the house and the back door. I'll meet you inside."

Officer Pearl stepped off the porch just as Alex drove into the driveway. He braked the car abruptly, then jumped out, leaving Brian sitting inside.

"My husband," Sarah said to Maestas, who nodded, then went into the house.

"Sarah, what's going on? Are you all right?"

"Oh, Alex, thank goodness you're home. Someone's been in the house. They came in the back door."

"While you were here?"

She nodded yes.

"Did you see who it was?"

"No."

"Could it have been . . . ?"

"I don't know, Alex. It could've been anyone."

Sarah described how she'd checked the doors before she left the house that morning to go shopping. Then she explained how she'd been in the living room wrapping presents and heard the teakettle whistling, then discovered that the back door was open.

Alex was frowning.

"The kettle?"

"Yes. Whoever came in must have turned on the stove."

Alex gave her a quizzical look.

"But why?"

"How should I know?" Sarah's voice was tight.

"Okay," Alex said gently. He looked over her shoulder. "Brian's sitting in the car. Maybe I should get him."

"I'll go."

Sarah found Brian waiting not so patiently in the Celica.

"How come there's a police car?" he asked, his eyes wide with wonder.

"Because . . . someone left the back door open, and they just want to see that everything's okay."

"Oh . . . Can we look inside their car?"

"I think we should go up to the porch," she said.

The porch was empty. Alex and the two policemen were waiting in the foyer.

"They've searched the whole house," Alex said. "The upstairs, too. There's no one in here."

Sarah felt Brian pressing against her side. She realized that he'd probably never been this close to uniformed policemen, and their presence frightened him. She put her hand on his head.

"Did you check the basement?" she asked.

"The outside door is locked," Pearl said.

"What about the inside door?"

They all followed Sarah down the short hallway and through the kitchen to the laundry room. The basement door was closed, and the bolt was set firmly in place.

"Locked tight," Maestas said.

"Shouldn't you check the basement, anyway?"

Maestas looked at Sarah. "No one could go through this door and then lock it from *this* side." Then he shrugged. "But we'll search down there if you like."

"I . . . guess it's not necessary."

"I'll do it," Pearl said. She stepped past them and slid open the bolt. "It's no problem."

"Whatever," Maestas said under his breath.

After Pearl had gone down the stairs, Maestas asked if anything had been stolen. Sarah and Alex looked at each other for an answer. Then they made a quick search of the rooms on the first floor—the television set, the stereo, Sarah's good silver in the polished box in the sideboard in the dining room. Nothing was missing. Back in the kitchen Maestas pointed to Sarah's purse on the table.

"How long has that been there?"

"Since I first got home."

Sarah looked through her purse and found her checkbook and her wallet inside. She went through the wallet, counting off her credit cards and thirty-seven dollars in cash.

"It's all here."

"If someone came in the house, then I guess you scared them off," Maestas said.

Sarah looked at him.

"What do you mean, 'if'?"

Before Maestas could answer, Pearl came into the kitchen.

"Anything?" Maestas asked her.

She shook her head no. Maestas looked smug, Sarah thought. When she spoke, it was directly to him.

"What did you mean a minute ago when you said, '*If* someone came in the house'?"

"See, when you get a back-door thief, the first thing they'd take would be a purse lying in the open like that." He shrugged. "No one took the purse."

"What about the kettle?" Sarah demanded.

"Yes, well . . ." Maestas cleared his throat. "Is it possible that you left the burner on and—

"No."

"—and then forgot about it?"

"No," she repeated. "Absolutely not. Besides, the back door was wide open."

"Are you certain it was closed when you left the house this morning?"

"Yes, we're certain," Alex said firmly, coming to Sarah's defense. "If my wife says it was closed, then it was closed."

"We didn't mean to imply otherwise," Pearl said. She cast a hard glance at Maestas. "I'll get a report form from the car."

Later, after Sarah had helped them fill out the official form, Alex walked them to the door.

As Sarah passed by the living room, she saw Brian on his hands and knees in the midst of the wrapped packages.

He looked up at her, his eyes wide with delight.

"Look at all the presents!"

Sarah sighed and shook her head. She'd meant to hide all but a few of the gifts she'd bought for Brian. Those few would be placed under the tree and tagged "From Mom and Dad," but the majority of them would be tagged "From Santa" and wouldn't be set out until after Brian had gone to bed on Christmas Eve.

She picked up the scissors and tape and scraps of wrapping paper.

"Why don't you place all the presents under the tree," she said, "so they'll look real nice."

"Okay, Mom."

Sarah put away her wrapping paraphernalia, then went to the kitchen to start dinner. Before she removed anything from the cupboards, though, she checked to see that the outside door and the basement door were both shut and locked. She knew that the police—at least Officer Maestas—doubted her story. Perhaps, she thought, she'd be dubious, too, if it had happened to someone else. After all, now that it was over, it did seem a bit silly. And it was *possible* that she'd left the back door open and forgot to turn off the burner. . . .

She shook her head.

No, she thought, absolutely not.

Alex came in the kitchen.

"They're going to drive around the neighborhood," he said, "and look for any 'suspicious persons,' not that it'll do much good. Are you all right?"

"Fine."

"You sure?"

Sarah nodded and smiled. "Except I don't think they quite believed me."

"*I* believe you, Sarah." He went to her and put his arms around her waist. "If you say that's what happened, then that's what happened."

"You don't think I'm just being forgetful and maybe imagining things like . . ."

He gave her a half smile. "You mean, like I did yesterday at the Broadmoor? No, I don't think that. I think someone opened the back door, maybe a kid, maybe it wasn't quite shut all the way and locked—who knows? And when they heard you, they ran. That's what probably happened. But one thing's certain—it wasn't Christine."

"How can we be sure?"

"Because it's nonsense," he said. "Why would she come in and just turn on the teakettle?"

Sarah shook her head. "I don't know. Unless . . ."

"What?"

"Unless she's toying with us."

Sarah was remembering something from a few days ago—finding three headless mice on the front seat of the Wagoneer.

That night, Alex lay on his side, snuggled tightly against Sarah's back, fitting her as closely as a pair of spoons. He stroked her hip and kissed her neck.

"I love you," he whispered in her ear.

"I love you, too."

She reached back and touched him, and for a while they caressed. Then thoughts of Christine began to intrude into Sarah's mind. She tried to ignore them, turning to face Alex, pressing her body against his, stroking him, concentrating. But her mind conjured up the image of Christine standing downstairs in the kitchen. Sarah buried her face in Alex's chest. She wondered if something similar was occurring to him, because his hand had become still, resting on the small of her back.

After a moment she said softly, "I'm sorry."

"I am, too."

They did not make love.

The next day, while Sarah cut the hair of her first customer, Paul Unger, she told Kay Nealy about hearing the kettle and finding the back door open.

"God," Kay said, "that's nothing. Once, we went on vacation for two weeks and left the *front* door open the whole time *and* the sprinkler on in the backyard. Do you think any of the neighbors would come over and shut it off? Hell, no. When we finally got home, it looked like a rice paddy back there. *Plus*, all the stray cats in the neighborhood had turned our living room into a feline bordello."

"A cathouse?" Kay's customer said, and they both laughed.

"I called the police," Sarah said.

"Really?" Kay turned to face Sarah, her scissors and comb poised above her customer's hair, the smile fading from her lips. "Why?"

"Because I thought someone was in there. I'm certain that I didn't leave the stove on or—"

She stopped when she saw that Kay was looking toward the front door. A woman had just entered the shop.

The woman was somewhere between thirty and forty, Sarah guessed. It was difficult to tell, because she wore heavy makeup. She had a broad nose and thick, dark eyebrows, and her lips were painted a deep cranberry. Her rumpled brown coat was a size or two too small for her thick frame, and her shoes looked as if they pinched her feet. She wore a plaid wool scarf around her neck. A black purse was clutched under her left arm.

"It's crowded," the woman said, eyeing them all. She fidgeted, as if she were ready to bolt from the shop.

"May I help you?" Sarah asked.

"It looks like she needs all the help she can get," Kay's customer said under her breath.

Sarah shot her a glance, then looked back at the woman.

"I'd like to get my hair done," the woman said softly. "By Sarah Whitaker."

"I'm Sarah," Sarah said.

The woman smiled quickly, then nodded, staring at Sarah, saying nothing, waiting.

"What did you want to have done?" Sarah asked.

"Oh," the woman said, surprised. "I don't know. I guess a haircut."

"Okay. Excuse me for a minute, Paul."

Sarah walked to the desk and looked through a few pages of the appointment book. The woman seemed to be wary of the other people in the shop. She edged toward the desk and Sarah.

Sarah said, "It looks like I—"

"And color it, too."

"Excuse me?"

"I want my hair colored, too."

"Oh . . . Okay, fine. It looks like I can get you in this Thursday, day after tomorrow, at eleven."

"Not tonight?"

"I'm afraid not. I'm booked solid until then."

"Oh."

"Shall I put you in?"

The woman glanced at Kay and the two customers, then at Sarah.

"Can you get me in at night?"

"Well, let's see." Sarah began turning pages of the appointment book. "Not until Friday of next week."

"No, I don't want to wait that long. Thursday's okay."

Sarah picked up a pencil. "What's your name?"

"Mrs. Green."

Sarah nearly said, "We're on a first-name basis here," but thought better of it. She wrote down the name. "What's your phone number. If there's a cancellation tomorrow, I could have you come in then."

"I don't have a phone," Mrs. Green said. "I just moved to town."

"No problem," Sarah said. There might be a problem with your hair, though, she thought, looking at it closely for the first time. It was a limp and lusterless brown, cut squarely a few inches above her shoulders. Sarah filled out an appointment slip and handed it to Mrs. Green. "We'll see you on Thursday," she said. "Oh, by the way, who recommended me to you?"

A smile quickly touched the woman's face, and then it was gone. "Mrs. Ettle," she said. "Kay Ettle."

"Ettle?" Sarah wrinkled her brow. "I don't recall the name."

"You might," the woman said, then turned without another word and hurried out of the shop.

The moment the door closed behind her, Kay's customer let out a laugh.

"That looks like an all-day job," she said, making Kay grin and shake her head. Even Paul Unger smiled. Sarah didn't think it was funny, though. There had been something disturbing about Mrs. Green, and it wasn't only her unkempt appearance. Sarah wished now that she'd told her she was booked solid for the next *month*.

Sarah picked up her scissors and comb from the shelf in front of Paul.

"Sorry about the delay," Sarah said.

She stood behind him, looking down at the back of his head. Suddenly she realized what had disturbed her about Mrs. Green, disturbed her as much as her odd behavior. Seen from behind, Mrs. Green had looked very much like the elderly woman at the Broadmoor, the one Alex had mistaken for Christine Helstrum.

The thought gave her a chill. Had Christine just been in her shop?

No, she thought, that's ridiculous. Christine wouldn't simply walk in here.

But the possibility stayed in her mind throughout Paul's haircut and after he left.

I don't really know what she looks like, Sarah thought.

She picked up the phone and punched out a familiar number. She noticed that her hand was shaking slightly.

"Thomas Jefferson High School," a woman's voice said.

Sarah started to speak, then hung up.

She was thinking how ridiculous it would sound to Alex if she had him paged to the phone and then asked him, "What does Christine look like? I think she just came in and made an appointment for a color and cut."

Maybe there's another way, she thought, a way that will set my mind at ease without bothering Alex. And won't make him think that I'm jumping at shadows.

And so, when her one o'clock appointment canceled out, Sarah didn't hesitate to put on her coat and tell Kay she'd be back at two-thirty.

She drove to the Penrose Public Library.

16

THE LIBRARY WAS ON CASCADE Avenue, a few blocks north of Colorado Avenue.

Sarah tried to remember when she'd last been here. Too many months ago, she thought with dismay. Before she'd met Alex, she'd come to the library nearly every other week to pick up two or three books. She loved to escape into the world of fiction, particularly historical fiction, which she felt could teach her something while entertaining her. And for the three years between her divorce from Ted and her marriage to Alex, reading was her primary entertainment. However, after meeting Alex, her life had changed dramatically. And although she still read, she now lacked one of her earlier motivations: escape. Her day-to-day life seemed so good now that she had no desire to escape from it.

Sarah passed by the fiction department and walked to the rear of the library. Stored here were thousands of back issues of newspapers and magazines, all carefully preserved on spools of microfilm.

Sarah didn't know exactly which newspapers were kept here or even whether any of them were out of state. However, she reasoned—hoped, actually—that if there were any out-of-state papers, the *New York Times* would be one of them. Furthermore, she hoped the *Times* would've carried the story of the murderer, Christine Helstrum. And, perhaps, a photograph.

An assistant librarian, a young man with a neatly trimmed beard, assured her that they did have the *Times*. He led her to a long row of metal cabinets, then asked her which month she wanted.

Sarah did not know precisely when Christine had been arrested. Alex had told her that his first wife and their son had been killed four and a half years ago. Frank O'Hara had said that Christine had been under treatment at Wycroff for four years. Sarah decided to begin with December and work backward.

The young man threaded the spool through the viewing machine and showed Sarah how to operate it. She began to scan four-year-old news stories.

She'd gone only as far as December third when she found a small item:

HELSTRUM FOUND INSANE

Albany, NY—Christine Helstrum was found innocent by reason of insanity yesterday of the murders last August of Laura Whitaker and her two-year-old adopted son, Timothy. The jury deliberated only five hours before returning their verdict. The judge's ruling on Helstrum is expected next week.

Sarah scanned ahead until she found the item about Christine's "sentencing." She read what she already knew: Christine had been committed to the Wycroff State Mental Hospital. There was no photograph.

Sarah rewound the spool, then asked the assistant librarian for the spool containing August of that year.

She scanned microfilm for the next half hour before she found the first article about Christine Helstrum. There was an accompanying photograph. It showed Christine being led from a courtroom, where she'd been formally charged with murder. However, her face was mostly obscured—she'd raised her handcuffed hands just as the photographer had snapped the picture.

Sarah had intended to search for a photograph and nothing more, but she found herself reading the article.

In fact, in the weeks and months (and spools of microfilm) that followed the murder, there appeared a number of related articles. Several aspects of the murder had piqued the interest of both the newspaper and the public. For one thing, it was revealed that Christine Helstrum had been an abused child and that she had in turn abused her son and eventually killed him—that is, the *Times* was careful to say, *allegedly* killed him. For another, Christine had had little trouble gaining access to the files of the adoption agency, which enabled her to find her son and his adoptive parents. And for another, the murder of Laura Whitaker had been unusually brutal. Her autopsy revealed that she had been stabbed thirty-nine times in her face, neck, arms, chest, and abdomen and that she had received numerous "defensive wounds," as the coroner described them—deep slashes across her forearms and the palms of her hands, received while trying to fend off her knife-wielding attacker.

Sarah stopped reading. There was a bitter taste in her mouth, and her stomach felt queasy; for a moment she thought she might become physically ill.

When Alex had described Laura's murder to her, it had all been so overwhelming that she hadn't really thought about the details. And later, she'd blocked all but the larger facts from her mind. But now, as she sat alone reading in the harsh and impersonal light of the viewing machine, she began to imagine what it must have been like for Laura.

Sarah had nothing in her own life to compare with Laura's experience. However, she remembered once as a child when she'd cut herself with a knife. She'd been playing in the backyard of her house near her mother's flower garden, and she'd found an old, rusty steak knife that her mother used for digging up weeds. The knife was not sharp, its blade dulled by constant contact with dirt and small stones. But it was sharp enough to open a cut on the side of Sarah's left thumb. She still carried the scar: a thin white horizontal line near the base of her thumbnail.

She couldn't remember exactly how she'd cut herself, but she remembered very well the aftereffects: the sharp pain that came not instantly but a measurable fraction of a second after the blade had opened her skin. She'd dropped the knife and cried out not only in pain but also at the horror of seeing the blood drip from her body and fall to the ground. She'd also seen a faint pink smear on the dirty, now evil-looking blade of the knife. Somehow that had been the most frightening thing of all—proof that there were things in the world that were evil and dangerous, things that could hide their true nature until they were close enough to harm you.

She'd run screaming to the back door of her house, her thumb on fire from pain and her arm beginning to throb clear up to the elbow.

Sarah looked at the tiny scar on her thumb, remembering how much it had hurt. She tried to compare that with the pain that Christine Helstrum had inflicted upon Laura Whitaker.

Deep slashes in her hands and forearms.

Sarah clamped her jaws, swallowed hard, and pushed back her chair with a screech. She stood and walked hurriedly to the drinking fountain.

And stab wounds, she thought, nearly forty of them.

She pressed her eyes closed and tried to push the images from her mind. Then she leaned over and drank from the fountain, letting the cool water wash the sour taste from her mouth. She returned to her seat and began scanning through weeks' worth of news without reading, without wanting to.

September and October passed before her in a black-and-white blur. Sarah occasionally stopped the rush of words, but only long enough to ensure that she didn't miss the one thing she sought. She inadvertently picked up news of the trial.

Christine's defense attorney had tried to portray her as a victim of her past, the only daughter of a mentally disturbed mother and an alcoholic father, both of whom abused her—mentally, physically, and sexually.

Sarah tried to imagine the anguish Alex must have felt during the trial. For several weeks attorneys and expert witnesses in psychiatry argued in open court about who truly was the victim, turning the trial into a media event. Alex was not even allowed the privilege of mourning in private. Not only did he have to testify and describe the awful scene he'd found at his home and relate the dying words of his wife, but each day he had to sit in the courtroom barely more than an arm's length away from the woman who had destroyed his family.

Bad turned to worse when Christine took the stand. Almost immediately she was screaming obscenities at the judge and the jury and at Alex Whitaker. She swore she'd get even with him for "murdering her son" if it was the last thing she ever did.

There was a photograph.

It showed Christine Helstrum being forcibly led from the courtroom by a pair of hulking marshals. Her eyes were wide with hatred, and her mouth was open in mid-curse.

As Sarah stared at that face, she felt a knot of fear tighten in her stomach. She stood up abruptly, nearly knocking over her chair. Then she hurried from the library, the spool of microfilm still in the viewing machine, the face of Christine Helstrum still glaring from the screen.

It was a familiar face, one she'd seen that very morning in her shop—the face of Mrs. Green.

Sarah stood in the reception area at Thomas Jefferson High School and waited for Alex. She was too upset to sit.

She'd also been too upset to drive, at least safely. In the few miles between the public library and here she'd run through two stop signs. The second time, she'd barely avoided a collision with a pickup truck. She'd left the car in a Faculty Only parking area, rushed into the school building and then into the first office she'd seen, and demanded that Alex be paged immediately. It was an emergency, she'd said.

The secretary, Miss Horst—a plain-looking young woman with dark-framed glasses and long bleached-blond hair—had eyed her suspiciously before she'd paged Alex to the reception area. She was still keeping a wary eye on Sarah when Alex came through the door.

"Sarah?"

"Alex," she said, hurrying to him, "thank God you're all right."

"What? What's wrong? They said it was an emergency."

"It's Christine. She's here."

"What?"

"She's here in Colorado Springs. I was afraid she may have tried to get to you before I could warn you. We've got to call the police."

"Sarah, what's—"

He stopped, glancing over her shoulder toward Miss Horst. Then he took Sarah by the arm and led her into the hallway. It was deserted except for two rows of gray metal locker doors, one on either side of the wide linoleum floor. Each row was broken at regular intervals by classroom doors, which threatened to erupt at any moment with noisy students.

"What's going on?" Alex asked. "What happened?"

Sarah took a deep breath. "I know this sounds crazy, but Christine came in my shop this morning."

Alex opened his mouth to speak, but Sarah rushed ahead.

"I didn't know it was her at first. She was just a strange woman who called herself Mrs. Green. But she was *very* strange—the way she acted, the things she said. And when she was leaving, I realized that from behind she looked like the woman you'd mistaken for Christine at the Broadmoor."

Alex searched her face.

"Did she do anything? What did she say?"

"It wasn't that, it was more a feeling I had about her. So I went to the library and looked through back issues of the *New York Times* until I found a photo of her. Alex, it was her in my shop."

Alex's expression had changed to fear.

"What exactly did she look like? The woman in your shop."

"She was taller than me, a few inches at least, maybe five feet seven or eight. And heavy looking, not fat exactly. Thick. I'd say a hundred and fifty. Her hair was brown and hung straight, almost to her shoulders."

"What about her face?"

"Alex, I know it was her. The photo was of her staring right at the camera as she was being led from the courtroom. It was the same woman."

Alex licked his lips, his face pale. Then he gave a start and grabbed Sarah's arm.

"Brian," he said. "What if she's found his school?"

"I never considered . . . all I thought about were her threats to you."

"We'd better call the school."

Sarah followed him back into the office. She fought a growing sense of panic as she pictured Brian, small and helpless, playing outside in the school yard, unaware that the woman approaching him was a threat to his life.

17

SARAH DROVE BRIAN HOME IN the Jeep, and Alex followed in the Toyota.

Before they'd gone to get Brian, Alex had phoned the school and said they were coming—a family emergency, he'd said—and that under no circumstances was Brian's teacher to allow him to leave with anyone before they got there. Alex had left the matter of his own afternoon classes in the hands of Miss Horst. Then he and Sarah had hurried out of the office. He'd driven as fast as the traffic and the lights would allow, with Sarah beside him, neither of them speaking. They'd gotten Brian out of class with the briefest of explanations; then the three of them had driven back to Jefferson High to get Sarah's car. Brian hadn't questioned any of this, seemingly knowing that adults often act in unknowable ways.

Now Sarah pulled into their driveway, letting Brian operate the remote garage-door opener. After the cars were parked and they'd all three gone inside, Sarah saw that Brian went upstairs to his room to play and Alex phoned the police.

Forty-five minutes later he was showing two uniformed policemen into the living room. They were not the same two who'd come before. One was overweight, red faced, and well into his fifties. His name tag read "Bauer." The other one, "Eastly," was a young black man.

Eastly nodded at Sarah, and Bauer sat on the couch. He opened a large black folder, clicked open a pen, and began writing at the top of a form.

"What's your name, please?" he said without looking up.

"Sarah—"

"Alex Whitaker," Alex said.

Alex stood in the middle of the room, his face pale and anxious looking. He was framed from behind by the large, brightly decorated Christmas tree.

Officer Bauer looked up at him, then turned to Sarah, who sat at the opposite end of the couch.

"I understand that you were the one threatened?"

"Yes. That is, I'm the one she approached."

"And your name?"

"Sarah Whitaker."

Bauer wrote it down. Alex fidgeted.

"And the name of the woman who threatened you?"

"Well, she said her name was—"

"Her name is Christine Helstrum," Alex said, then spread his hands. "Look, Officer, this woman is an escaped murderer. Four years ago in Albany, New York, she murdered my wife and . . . my first wife and our son. We just learned last week that she escaped from a mental hospital there. When they put her away, she swore revenge on me, and now she's here in Colorado Springs."

"Where did you see her?"

"I didn't see her. My wife did."

Bauer turned to Sarah, his pen poised.

"Would you describe her, please?"

Alex sighed in exasperation and began to pace the floor as Sarah described Christine and how she'd come into her shop this morning.

"Although she called herself 'Mrs. Green,' " she said.

Bauer wrote it down. "Are you certain that she's the same woman who threatened your husband?"

"Yes. I mean, I wasn't at the time. But afterward, I saw a photograph of her in the newspaper, and I *was* certain."

"Do you have the photograph?"

"No." Sarah described her visit to the library.

"And you're certain it's the same woman?"

"Yes." Sarah frowned, trying to recall the face of Mrs. Green in her shop and the face of Christine Helstrum on the view screen. "Fairly certain," she said.

Bauer nodded.

"I'm absolutely certain," Alex said.

Bauer glanced at him, then looked at Sarah.

"Exactly how did this woman threaten you?"

"Well . . . She didn't exactly threaten me. Not in so many words."

"What did she say?"

"She asked to make an appointment."

"An appointment?"

"To get her hair cut and colored."

Bauer wrote it down. "Did she say anything else?"

"Well . . . no."

"Look, Officer," Alex said, stopping his pacing in front of Bauer, "she didn't *have* to say anything. The fact that she's here is threat enough."

Bauer nodded understandingly. "Do you know why this woman"—he looked at his report—"Christine Helstrum, or Mrs. Green, would approach your wife in this manner?"

"No, I . . ." He spread his arms and shook his head. "Hell, no, she's insane. Who knows what she's going to do?"

Bauer nodded again, then turned to Sarah.

"When she left, did you see if she was with anyone?"

"No, I didn't see."

"Did you see her get into a car?"

"No."

"Was there a cab waiting for her?"

"I didn't see her after she left the shop, Officer. I'm sorry, I didn't even think to look."

Bauer smiled briefly. "It's not your fault. Did she leave you a phone number? An address?"

"No."

Bauer wrote some more. "Is there anything else you'd like to add?"

Sarah shook her head, then looked over at Alex, whose pacing had taken him near the doorway. Officer Eastly stood quietly behind him.

"Okay, then," Bauer said.

"So what are you going to do?" Alex asked, approaching the couch.

Bauer clicked shut his pen and slipped it in his shirt pocket. Then he carefully closed his folder and stood, grunting slightly from the effort.

"We'll turn this information over to the detective squad. I'm sure they'll want to come out here and talk to you."

"Is that all?" Alex seemed astonished.

"We'll keep an eye out during our patrol of this area for the woman you've described." He looked at Sarah. "The same goes for the area around your shop."

"And that's *all*?" Alex asked.

"That's all we can do for now," Bauer said. "The detectives will be in charge of this, and whatever more is done will be up to them."

"But this woman threatened my life." There was a note of pleading in Alex's voice.

"Four years ago," Bauer said. "Yes, I included that in my report. All I can tell you for now is that if you see this woman again call us immediately."

"Right," Alex said, and stalked from the room.

Sarah showed Officers Bauer and Eastly to the door, then went looking for Alex. She found him in the family room, standing at the window, staring out at the snowy backyard. Sarah thought it ironic that their roles had somehow become reversed. Earlier she'd been in a panic and had run to Alex not only to warn him but also to get his protection. After the police had been brought in, she felt more calm than before. However, it was obvious that Alex felt more upset. Now it was her turn to assure him that he was protected.

She touched him from behind, and he gave a start. Then he relaxed, and she put her arms around him, resting her head on his back.

"They're doing all they can," she said, meaning the police. "For now, anyway."

"It's not enough," he said quickly, firmly. "I've been thinking about . . ."

"About what?"

He hesitated. "About . . . buying a gun."

"No, Alex."

She let go of him and stood at his side, looking up at his profile. He stared straight ahead, frowning at the window, at the empty backyard.

"I won't have a gun in our house," Sarah said evenly.

Alex said nothing.

"It's too dangerous. With Brian in the house and—"

"Dangerous?" He turned his head to face her. "How dangerous do you think Christine Helstrum is?"

"The police are—"

"The police," Alex spat. Then he closed his eyes for a moment and sighed. Sarah thought that he looked exhausted. "I'm sorry," he said. "I know the police are doing what they can. But the thought that she may be here, that she may have found us, is almost too much to bear."

Sarah took a breath before she spoke.

"Maybe it wasn't her."

"What? But this morning . . ."

"I know," she said. "I was positive after seeing that old photo.

But just a while ago, when that policeman asked me if I was certain . . . I don't know. This woman, Mrs. Green, was very strange, and she made me think of Christine, and so I was in a weird frame of mind when I went to the library." She touched his arm. "I don't know now, Alex. The photo of Christine *looked* like Mrs. Green, I suppose, but . . . I don't know."

"I'm hungry."

They both turned to see Brian standing across the room.

"When are we going to eat, Mom?"

"Soon, hon." She glanced at Alex.

He gave her a faint smile. "How about now? I'm hungry, too."

Sarah got the rest of last week's beef stew from the freezer. She put it in a pot, then set it on the stove on low to thaw. While Alex started the salad, Sarah got out the bread and tomatoes for Brian's cheese sandwiches. But she couldn't find the American cheese. She thought there'd been an unopened pack of sixteen slices in the door of the refrigerator, but now there were only a few slices of Swiss in a Baggie and half a pound of cheddar wrapped in Saran Wrap. She shrugged and took out the cheddar.

After dinner, Brian went to the family room to watch TV, and Alex helped Sarah with the dishes. He lifted a wet glass from the drainer and began to dry it with a towel.

"What I said before . . ."

"What?"

"About the gun."

Sarah looked at him. He shook his head no.

"You're right," he said. "There's no place for a gun in our house."

"I know," Sarah said. "And I knew you felt that way."

Alex nodded. "Besides, we're completely safe in here."

When they were finished, Alex went in to join Brian. Sarah didn't feel like sitting, though. She needed to sort out her thoughts, and she needed to be *doing* something while she did it. She considered taking a walk, but it was too cold out.

She sighed.

There's always vacuuming, she thought.

Sarah decided to do the upstairs first, since Alex and Brian were watching a made-for-TV movie on the Disney channel. She knew that running the vacuum cleaner downstairs distorted the television picture—whether it was just simple interference or something to do with the wiring downstairs, she wasn't certain. She feared the latter, though, because of the age of the house.

They had two vacuum cleaners, one on each floor. This was a small luxury, which eliminated the chore of lugging one machine up and down the stairs, and which Sarah appreciated almost as much as if she'd had someone to do the vacuuming for her. She had to admit, though, that Alex sometimes helped her with this chore.

The upstairs vacuum cleaner was an old barrel-shaped model with a scuffed-up brown hose and a bagful of attachments. Sarah pulled it out of the closet in the sitting room.

She vacuumed the sitting room, then the hallway around the head of the stairs, the guest bedroom, Alex's den, and the master bedroom. Brian's room was last.

Sarah switched off the vacuum and picked up a pair of sneakers and a Nerf ball. She put the shoes in Brian's closet and the ball in his toy chest beside the cardboard-and-tape sword that Alex had made for him. Then she began vacuuming the carpet, starting at the door and moving toward the bed.

The carpet attachment struck something under Brian's bed.

"Another toy," Sarah said aloud, and shook her head.

She switched off the machine, got down on her hands and knees, and reached quickly under the bed with her right hand. She felt a tiny, sharp, biting pain and jerked her hand back in surprise. A drop of blood welled in the crevice between her index and middle fingers.

Sarah snatched a tissue from Brian's nightstand and pressed it between her fingers. The bleeding stopped almost at once, and she could barely see the tiny puncture wound. She dropped the blood-spotted tissue in the wastepaper basket, then looked apprehensively under the bed, thinking that perhaps she'd disturbed Patches and that the big cat was in one of his less pleasant moods and had bitten or clawed her.

But there was no cat beneath the bed. She saw something, though, and she used the vacuum attachment to drag it out.

Sarah stared in disbelief at the butcher knife.

She recognized it as one of hers. But it seemed so out of place here that it looked alien.

Why had Brian put it there? she wondered.

He'll have to explain why, she knew, and this bothered her. It wasn't his purpose for having the knife—whatever it might be—that bothered her. It was that he was keeping secrets and being sneaky.

She lifted the knife by the handle and carried it downstairs.

Alex and Brian were seated on the couch, their faces bathed in the glow of the TV set, their attention focused on the sounds and movements before them. They both glanced at Sarah and then did a double take when they saw she was holding a butcher knife.

"Brian, I found this under your bed."

Brian looked from her face to the knife and back again. His eyes were wide, and his face was flushed with embarrassment. Sarah realized that she could have been more subtle. She wondered if she should have spoken to Alex first and then approached Brian in a different manner. But it was too late to change tactics now, so she pushed ahead.

"Do you want to tell me how it got there?" she asked.

He opened his mouth to answer.

And all the lights went out.

18

THE DARKNESS WAS NEARLY ABsolute, and for a moment no one spoke. The only sound was the faint ticking of the heating pipes.

"Damn," Alex said.

Sarah saw him stand, silhouetted by the dim light from the window across the room.

"I'm scared."

"It's okay, son."

Sarah could barely make out Alex reaching down and taking Brian's hand. They moved toward her, a pair of flat black shapes.

"What caused that?"

"I don't know," Alex said. "Maybe a temporary power outage. It could be the whole neighborhood."

"But I see lights," Sarah said. Scattered points of lights could be seen through the trees that flanked their backyard.

"Then it's just us."

"I'm scared," Brian repeated.

"It's okay, honey." Sarah reached for him, aware of the butcher knife in her other hand. She considered setting it down, but it was too dark to see the end table. Besides, she'd felt at least a twinge of fear when the room had plunged into darkness. It wasn't that she wanted to carry the knife for protection; she just didn't want to leave it where someone else might pick it up. "Don't be afraid, Brian. It's just the lights."

"It's not the lights I'm worried about," Alex said. "It's the furnace."

Now Sarah realized why the water pipes were making ticking sounds: They were cooling.

"Where's our flashlight?"

"In the kitchen," Sarah said. "I think."

They moved in a tight group from the dark family room to the deeper recesses of the hallway. As they passed the dining room, Sarah sucked in her breath. She'd seen something move out of the black shadows on the floor of the foyer ahead of them.

"Don't step on Patches," Alex said.

The cat meowed, and Sarah relaxed. They crossed the foyer, then walked down the short hallway to the kitchen, moving slowly, as if they were all afraid they might trip over something. Alex fumbled through several drawers before he found the flashlight.

He thumbed the switch. Nothing happened. Then he banged the butt end of the flashlight in his palm and tried it again. This time it worked, casting a pale yellow-white circle on the wall.

"I'll check the breaker box," he said.

Sarah and Brian followed him through the kitchen to the laundry room, neither of them wishing to be left behind in the dark. Alex shone the light on the door to the basement. Then he slid back the bolt, turned the knob, and opened the door.

Alex's light danced across the floor of the landing and up the wall to the large gray metal box. The box was new, a replacement of the old fuse box, which Alex had insisted upon right after they'd moved into the house. It was something, Sarah knew, that she probably wouldn't have considered until after an incident like this one, when they'd be searching for new fuses.

Alex stepped onto the landing, opened the box, and shone his light on two vertical rows of small black levers. He strained to read the tiny paper tags, one beside each lever.

"The main switch kicked off," he said. "There must have been a power surge."

He flipped the little lever. Immediately, the bare bulb above his head went on, as did the kitchen light behind them, making them all squint against the brightness. Down below, the furnace roared to life.

"I wonder how long *this* has been on." Alex reached over and flicked the wall switch, turning off the overhead light.

He stepped toward Sarah, then stopped, one foot in the doorway, the other on the landing. He pointed his flashlight down the basement stairs.

"What's wrong?" Sarah asked.

"I thought I heard something."

He stood unmoving, his head cocked to one side, as if he were straining to hear through the muffled roar of the furnace. Then he shook his head and clicked off the flashlight.

"I guess it was just the furnace," he said.

He closed the door, then slid the bolt into place.

Much later that night Sarah was awakened by Brian. He was standing beside her bed and gently poking her shoulder.

"I'm scared, Mom."

"Wha—? Oh, don't be afraid, honey," she said, her voice thick from sleep. "The lights work okay now."

"But I heard noises. Downstairs."

"Noises?" she said sleepily. She pulled back the covers, careful not to wake Alex, and swung her feet to the floor. "You were just dreaming, pumpkin."

She stood, put her hand on Brian's shoulder, then walked him back to his room and tucked him in bed.

"Go to sleep now, everything's all right."

She kissed him on the forehead.

"But—"

"Shh, baby, go to sleep."

The next morning, right after his mother gently shook him awake, Brian climbed out of bed and took his Sword of Power from the toy chest.

"I don't think you have time to play with that now."

"I'm not. I'm taking it to school."

"Oh?"

"It's for show-and-tell."

Brian held the cardboard-and-tape sword in his right hand and let his eyes move along the smooth curve of the thick blade. His father had done a good job cutting it out.

"Are you sure that's what you want to take?" Sarah said.

Brian surmised that she didn't like his sword, and he guessed the reason was that in making it he'd "borrowed" her butcher knife without asking. He didn't have to guess that both she and his dad had been upset last night; he knew that for a fact. They'd made it very clear to him that knives were not toys and that not only shouldn't he be playing with them, but he shouldn't be hiding things like that in his room. At that point he'd almost admitted to having the box cutter. However, he'd been too afraid of what their reaction would be to his having *two* knives in his room. So he'd kept his mouth shut, except to say that he was sorry.

"You have a lot of other nice toys," his mother was saying now. "Are you sure you want to take that?"

"Can't I?"

He looked up into her face. She smiled, and he knew it was okay.

"Sure," she said.

Later, while he ate his Cheerios, milk, and banana slices at the breakfast table, he noticed that his mother seemed kind of upset. He was relieved to hear that it had something to do with the orange juice and nothing whatever to do with him. He didn't want her to be upset with him for a long, long time.

"I bought two half gallons of orange juice last week," she said, holding open the door to the refrigerator, "and they're both gone."

"We drank them," Alex said.

"We drank *one* of them. The other one should be right back here."

"Are you sure you bought two?"

"Pretty sure."

"Well, *I* didn't drink it," Alex said, looking at Brian. "Did you?"

Brian was startled for a moment, thinking his father was accusing him of something. But then he winked, making Brian smile.

"Well, *I* didn't drink it, either," he said, trying to imitate his father's voice.

"Very funny." She retrieved a large cardboard carton from the refrigerator and shut the door. "You'll both just have to settle for grapefruit juice."

"Yuck."

"That goes double for me," Alex said.

After breakfast Alex drove Brian to school. Brian was both surprised and dismayed when his father insisted on walking with him all the way inside the building, something he'd never done before, except on the first day of the school year. Brian expected it had something to do with his having borrowed his mother's knife. No matter the reason, it embarrassed him to be treated like a little kid.

As soon as his father left, Brian saw Eddy Teesdale in the hall. He was eager to show him his Sword of Power, but he kept it down at his side so that he wouldn't attract attention. He didn't want everyone crowding around him and admiring it. Not yet. There would be time enough for that after show-and-tell.

The trouble was, Eddy wasn't alone. He was standing with Charley Brooks. Brian didn't particularly like Charley Brooks. He was a smart aleck.

"Hi, Brian," Eddy said as he approached.

"Hi." He saw that both Eddy and Charley were looking at his sword.

"Did you bring that for show-and-tell?" Eddy asked.

"Yeah. Pretty neat, huh?"

"What is it?" Charley asked in a smart-alecky tone of voice. Brian noticed that Charley always seemed to have a half smile on his face and his head tipped back a little bit, as if he were sneering at everything and everyone around him.

"It's a sword," Brian said.

"It's pretty junky looking."

"It's a Sword of Power," Brian said loudly. "My dad made it, and it's probably better than anything *you've* got."

Charley Brooks sneered.

"Some sword," he said. "It's made out of cardboard. You couldn't cut anything with that, not even a jelly sandwich."

"You don't *need* to cut anything with it, you dodo, it's a Sword of Power. You can just *do* things with it."

"Like what?"

"Like anything you want."

"Anything but *cut* things," Charley Brooks said with a laugh.

Brian clenched his jaw and stepped toward him, ready to make him take back his words. The bell rang. Charley Brooks turned on his heel and walked away.

"You couldn't even cut *jelly* with a cardboard sword," he said over his shoulder.

"I'll show you," Brian said.

I'll show you something that can cut *anything*, he thought.

† † †

Sarah had a difficult time keeping her mind on her work. More than once she temporarily forgot what she was doing and nearly applied the wrong solution to a customer's hair. Kay was watching her closely.

"Are you okay?"

"What? Sure."

"Come on, now," Kay said, "you're among friends. You can tell us."

No, I can't, Sarah thought, not now.

But she had to say something, she knew, because everyone in the shop was looking at her. So she told them about finding the knife under Brian's bed last night.

"Shoot, honey, that ain't nothing," Kay said, pulling a comb through her customer's wet hair. "One time when Joey was about four years old, Rick and I walked into the kitchen and found him playing 'pirate ship' on the countertop. He'd pulled out the drawers to make steps for himself to climb up there, and on the way up he'd picked out a couple of steak knives. He had one of them tucked down into his belt, and he was waving the other one over his head daring us to 'come aboard.' "

"Jesus, Kay, what did you do?" Kay's customer asked. She was a redheaded woman in her mid-twenties, Sarah guessed. She wore designer jeans and an expensive sweater. Sarah had never seen her before.

"I froze, is what I did," Kay said. "All I could do was picture Joey falling off the counter and landing on one of those knives."

"God," the woman said.

Kay pulled her comb through the woman's hair and snipped. She said, "Rick started talking real calm and slow. 'Give me the knife, Joey, give me the knife.' Joey said, 'Okay, Daddy,' as happy as hell, and threw it at him."

"God."

"Rick jumped back, and the knife smacked him in the leg, luckily, handle first."

"So, what did you do to your kid?"

"I carefully took the other knife out of his belt; then Rick gently lifted him down off the counter, calmly explained that he shouldn't be playing with knives, and then paddled the hell out of his behind so he wouldn't forget."

The woman laughed.

Sarah winced, and when she looked in the mirror, she saw that Martha Kellog winced, too. Martha was one of Sarah's longtime customers. She was a soft-spoken woman, and she usually sat quietly all the while she was in the chair. Now she met Sarah's eyes in the mirror.

"Did you spank Brian last night?" she asked.

"No."

"Why not?" Kay's customer said, butting into their conversation.

"Because he's too old to be spanked."

"You think so? Just how old is he?"

"Six and a half," Sarah said.

Kay's customer made a noise somewhere between a laugh and a snort.

"That doesn't sound too old to me."

Sarah glanced at Kay, who gave her a weak smile and a slight shrug of the shoulders.

"He's old enough to understand the English language," Sarah said firmly. "He knew that what he did was wrong even before my husband and I explained it to him. He felt bad about it, and he won't do it again. There was no need for a spanking."

"According to you," Kay's customer said, turning in her chair to face Sarah. "I'll tell you what, if *I* ever have any kids and—"

"Judging by your personality," Sarah said, "I don't think that's something you'll have to worry about."

The woman's head snapped back as if she'd been slapped, and the shop became perfectly quiet.

Sarah had surprised even herself. It wasn't like her to give a customer a verbal shot. On those rare occasions in the past when one of them had said something out of line, she'd let it go in the interests of business, of harmony in the shop. But she wasn't herself today.

She opened her mouth to apologize, more to Kay than to her customer. Then she saw Kay suppressing a grin.

The hell with it, she thought.

She resumed cutting Martha's hair, and her thoughts returned to last night.

After she and Alex had had their talk with Brian about the knife and then put him to bed, they'd discussed their options concerning Christine. Assuming that she was here in Colorado Springs, what should they do? Should they lock themselves in their house and not go out until Christine was captured? And if she wasn't captured right away, how long should they remain locked in? A few days? Weeks?

"Assuming she's even alive," Sarah had said.

Because the more she'd thought about it, the more uncertain she'd become about whether the woman who'd called herself Mrs. Green was really Christine Helstrum. The woman had resembled the old newspaper photograph, to be sure—dark, thick eyebrows and wide nose. But, Sarah had to admit now, that's all it had been—a resemblance, not a certainty.

Mrs. Green aside, the question was whether they should make themselves prisoners in their own home.

They'd both decided the answer was no. After all, the police had been informed. If Christine, or for that matter an innocent Mrs. Green, showed up, they'd be quick to respond to a call from Sarah or Alex and apprehend her. The most that Sarah and Alex could do was stay alert.

However, there was another, greater concern: Brian.

What should they do about ensuring his safety? They could come up with only three options.

One, they could leave Brian with someone while they both were at work. However, that someone would have to be a neighbor, since neither of them had any relatives in Colorado, much less in town. And they both felt that there were no neighbors with whom they could leave Brian and feel comfortable.

Two, one of them could take Brian to work for the day. But they quickly decided that this would be too much of a strain both on the adult and on the boy, who'd be forced to spend most of the day basically alone in the corner of an office or the shop. Moreover, if Mrs. Green returned to the shop or if Christine attempted to get to Alex at work, Brian would be placed in the path of danger.

Three, they could take Brian to school. They'd decided on this option not because it was the least disruptive to their normal lives, which it was, but because they both felt Brian would be safest there. He'd be surrounded by classmates, who would certainly camouflage his presence. More importantly, he'd be surrounded by teachers.

Alex had talked to several of them this morning when he'd taken Brian to school. He'd given them a story about a fictitious ex-wife who might try to contact Brian.

"If you see anyone unusual hanging around the school," he'd said, "phone the police immediately and then phone me. In no case is Brian to leave school with anyone but me or his mother."

Sarah felt they'd made the best decision under the circumstances. Still, she was worried.

19

BRIAN TOOK THE BOX CUTTER from his toy chest.

He'd been thinking about it since this morning. Charley Brooks had made him so mad that he'd planned on bringing it to school the next day. If Charley wanted to see something that could *cut*, well, boy, he'd show him something.

But then had come his turn before the class at show-and-tell. And what do you know? His Sword of Power had been a big hit. Not everyone shared Charley Brooks's scorn over a cardboard sword. Just the opposite—most everyone thought it was *neat*. So, impressing Charley Brooks had promptly been forgotten.

However, the box cutter had stayed on Brian's mind.

He was afraid his parents might find it. He didn't think that they'd dig clear down to the bottom of his toy chest. But what if they did? He'd already promised them that he wouldn't take any more knives—and he wouldn't. But what if they found *this* knife. How could he explain it?

Brian shook his head.

I'd be in *really* big trouble, he thought.

But what to do with the box cutter? He couldn't hide it, not where it would be completely safe. And he couldn't just throw it away, because what if his dad saw it in the trash?

There was only one thing to do. He'd have to put it back where he'd found it. In the basement.

That wasn't an appealing idea. The basement was scary. It was big and cold and kind of dirty, and there were lots of rooms, rooms where people used to live. His dad had said so. But no one lived down there now. Except it looked like someone *should* be living down there, with the furniture and everything.

Brian turned the box cutter over in his hand. The blade was dull and rusty except for a thin line along the edge, where it shone sharply in the light. Brian touched it with his thumb. It was sharp, all right, and he wished he could keep it. But he couldn't. He had to put it back.

He loosened the screw, slid the blade into the handle, and slipped the box cutter into his jeans' pocket. He moved to the head of the stairs. Someone was knocking on the front door. Brian sat on the top step, leaning over so that he could just see the door. His father answered it. There were two men in long coats, and his father let them in. Then he and his mother went with the men into the living room.

Brian crept down the stairs and crossed the foyer. He stood just outside the doorway into the living room, out of sight. He could hear the men talking to his parents, talking about someone named Christine.

Brian tiptoed quickly through the short hall and the kitchen to the laundry room. He stood before the basement door. He hesitated, then reached up and tried to slide the bolt. It seemed to be stuck, until he saw that he had to rotate it first in order to free the small knob from its slot. Then the bolt slid easily.

Brian pulled open the door.

The light from the kitchen cast his shadow onto the half-dark landing. He hesitated, afraid to go even *that* far into the dark. Then he reached high around the doorframe, searching blindly for the light switch, waiting to yank his hand back at the first feel of anything with spidery legs or pointed teeth or gnarled hands.

He found the light and clicked it on.

He stepped onto the landing and looked down the old wooden stairs. The dusty hallway at the bottom appeared to be a mile away. Brian wondered how fast he could run back up the stairs if he had to.

He swallowed once, then cautiously started down.

Brian stopped on each step, feet together, right hand clutching the banister, eyes focused on the empty floor below, ears straining for the slightest sound.

The trouble was, there were lots of sounds. A creak. A tick. A soft thumping. He realized the latter was his own heart. But the other sounds— He didn't know what they were.

He continued down.

When he'd gone about halfway down, one foot in mid-descent to the next step, the air suddenly was filled with an explosive, monstrous roar.

Brian was frozen with fear, unable to move. His eyes were glued to the bottom of the stairs and the open doorway on the right. It was from here that the wild noise had come. The roar continued, but now it sounded tamer.

The furnace, Brian thought, trying to slow his pounding heart, it's just the furnace.

He stood there for long minutes until his entire body was convinced that the roar was not coming from a boy-hungry monster. Then he continued his descent.

Brian stepped off the last step and held perfectly still. The long, dusty hallway stretched before him, then disappeared in a distant left-hand curve. He'd been frightened when he'd been down here before with his parents, but it was nothing compared with what he felt now—a tingling that went clear out to the ends of his fingertips.

He strained his ears, trying to hear beyond the muffled roar of the furnace.

Suddenly, the furnace clicked off.

The silence seemed to press around him, punctuated only by an occasional tick.

But now there was another sound. A new sound. A rustling. It came from the open doorway to his right. Something was in that room. And it was moving. The rustling was tiny, slight, but it was distinct. It was getting closer to the doorway.

Then Brian saw something—movement at the bottom of the doorway. A gray mouse looked up at him and twitched its tiny pink nose.

Maybe it was the mouse that had made the rustling sound, or maybe not—Brian didn't wait around to find out. All he knew was that there was something down here and it was *alive* and he wanted no part of it.

He turned and fled up the stairs.

The detectives' names were Yarrow and Keene. They sat in chairs, one on either side of the Christmas tree. Sarah and Alex sat together on the couch.

Detective Yarrow asked all the questions. He was a good-looking man, Sarah thought, about forty years old, with soft brown eyes and a touch of gray in his hair. Detective Keene was younger, with horn-rimmed glasses and stringy black hair. He sat with an open notebook and a ballpoint pen.

"I know you've already talked to our men," Yarrow said, "so a few of my questions may seem redundant. First, though, I'd like you to look at some pictures."

He opened a large manila envelope and removed several eight-by-ten prints. He stood, and Alex stepped over to him and looked at the photographs. He nodded grimly.

"That's her," he said. "That's Christine Helstrum."

"Yes, it is," Yarrow said. "Four years ago."

Alex handed the photographs to Sarah.

The pictures were in color—a woman's face, straight on and in profile. She had thick, dark eyebrows and a wide nose.

"Mrs. Whitaker, is that the woman who approached you in your shop?" Yarrow asked. "The woman who called herself Mrs. Green?"

"I . . . I'm not sure."

Sarah studied the photographs of Christine Helstrum. Her hair was cropped close to the skull, shorter than Mrs. Green's had been. And Christine's face looked fuller, more round. The biggest difference, though, was the makeup. Mrs. Green's face had been caked with it, and Christine's face was colorless. And her facial expression in the photo was dull and lifeless—different from Mrs. Green and much different from the old newspaper photo. In fact, Sarah thought, looking more closely at the photo, she looks drugged. Then she realized it was because Christine's right eyelid drooped slightly lower than her left. Sarah tried to remember if Mrs. Green had that feature.

"I just don't know," she said to Yarrow.

"Are you sure, Sarah?" Alex asked. "Look again."

She glanced at the photos and shook her head.

"There's *some* resemblance," she said.

Yarrow removed a notebook from his overcoat. Both he and Keene had unbuttoned their coats but had left them on. Now Keene stepped over and took the photos from Sarah.

"Would you describe Mrs. Green," Yarrow asked.

As Sarah did so, Keene took notes. Yarrow seemed to be checking his own notebook, but he wrote nothing. When Sarah had finished, Yarrow said, "That fits with the description you gave to the officers yesterday."

"It fits Christine," Alex said.

"It certainly could, and we're not ruling her out as a possibility."

"She's more than a possibility," Alex said loudly.

"Of course she is," Yarrow said. "I didn't mean to imply otherwise. We've contacted the Albany police and the New York

State police, and they're giving us their complete cooperation. They've already supplied us with these photographs, background information, and even some medical records from . . ."

Yarrow glanced at Keene.

"Wycroff State Hospital."

Yarrow looked back at Alex. "So we're proceeding on the assumption that this woman could be Christine Helstrum."

"She is," Alex said.

Yarrow flipped a few pages of his notebook.

"Mr. Whitaker," he said, "I understand that Christine Helstrum once threatened your life. Is that right?"

Alex nodded yes.

"Could you give me the details, please? Exactly what she said, and so on."

"I've been through that with your officers," Alex said. There was a pained look on his face, as if an old wound had been touched. "And besides, didn't you just say that the Albany police sent you their files?"

"That's true, sir. However, sometimes things get inadvertently left out of files. Also, I'd like to hear your impression of this woman and of what happened. So, if you wouldn't mind . . ."

Alex sighed. "Yes, of course."

Sarah held Alex's hand while he related the tragedy of his past life. Detective Keene wrote furiously to keep up. When Alex was finished, he seemed drained, as if he'd relived the events not just verbally but emotionally as well.

"Mrs. Whitaker," Yarrow said, "would you tell us exactly what happened when Mrs. Green came in your shop. I know you've gone through this before, but if you wouldn't mind . . ."

"Of course," Sarah said, and told them everything.

When she was through, Yarrow asked, "How do you suppose Mrs. Green found out where you worked?"

Sarah shrugged her shoulders. "The shop is listed in the telephone book."

"With your name?"

"Well, no. Then I don't know how she found it. Except . . ."

"Yes?"

"I remember now. I asked her who'd recommended me, and she said a name I'd never heard before. An odd name, at that. Ettle. She said she'd gotten my name from Mrs. Kay Ettle."

Yarrow frowned, then flipped through his notebook. He wrote something in it.

"You called the police here Monday also, is that correct? The day before yesterday?"

"Yes . . ." Sarah felt warmth on her cheekbones.

"Something about a teakettle?"

"Yes."

"Would you mind telling us about that?"

Sarah felt embarrassed to describe how she'd been startled by the kettle on the burner after she'd been certain she'd removed it.

"I was probably just being forgetful," she said.

"Hmm." Yarrow frowned at his notebook.

Alex sat forward on the couch. "What is it?"

"Maybe just a coincidence," Yarrow said. "The name, Kay Ettle. 'K' plus 'ettle' equals 'kettle.' "

Sarah looked from Yarrow to Keene.

"It may mean nothing," Yarrow said.

"Or maybe," Keene said, "this Mrs. Green was in your house on Monday and she wants you to know about it."

"You can stop calling her 'Mrs. Green,' " Alex said. "The woman is Christine Helstrum."

Yarrow said, "Not necessarily. Unfortunately, there are a lot of nuts running around. Mrs. Green might be one of them."

"She's Christine," Alex said firmly.

"We don't think so," Keene said.

"What?"

"Let me rephrase that," Yarrow said. "The New York police don't think so. They have serious doubts that Christine could have left the area surrounding the hospital, much less the state. She escaped the building with no money and no clothes other than a hospital gown and slippers. It was below freezing and snowing heavily on the night of her escape and—"

"Yes, yes," Alex said impatiently.

"—and it's doubtful that she survived the storm."

"We've heard all that before," Alex said. "What I want to know is what are you going to do now?"

Yarrow paused and breathed out through his nose.

"We've alerted the patrol cars in your neighborhood and in the neighborhood of your shop to keep an eye on things."

"What about Brian's school?" Sarah asked.

"We'll watch it, too. Which school is it?"

Sarah told him, and Keene wrote it down.

"Is that it? Is that all you're going to do?"

Yarrow glanced at Alex, then stood. So did Keene.

"There's one more thing we'll do, Mr. Whitaker," Yarrow said. "We'll be waiting near your wife's shop tomorrow when Mrs. Green shows up for her appointment."

There were no more questions, so Alex and Sarah showed the two men to the door. Alex closed it, and Sarah put her arms around him.

She sighed. "Maybe they're right. Maybe Mrs. Green is just some nut."

"I hope not," Alex said seriously.

"Why?"

"Sarah, when this woman comes to your shop tomorrow, the police will question her, right? What if she really is just someone named Mrs. Green? Then we'll still have Christine to worry about."

Sarah hugged him tighter.

"On the other hand," he said quietly, "if Mrs. Green and Christine are the same person, then after tomorrow our worries will be over."

"God, Alex, I hope you're right."

"Come on," he said, and rubbed her back. "Let's go build a fire."

Sarah nodded, her cheek against his chest. "Brian would like that, too."

Sarah climbed the stairs, trying to force thoughts of Christine from her mind. We're a family, she told herself. We're together. That's all that matters.

She found Brian on his knees, digging in his toy chest.

"Hi, pumpkin."

He turned around quickly and closed the lid of the chest.

"Hi."

"Dad's going to build a fire."

"Really?"

"Yeah. Why don't you bring your checkers?" She made what she thought was a tough-looking face. "I challenge you."

"Okay."

He turned tentatively, opened the lid of his toy chest just enough to reach in, then dug out the box of checkers.

Alex was putting a match to wadded-up sheets of newspaper as Sarah and Brian came into the family room. The flames danced around the log on the grate. Soon the log began to crackle.

Alex reclined in one of the chairs and flipped through the current issue of *Time,* while Sarah and Brian sat cross-legged on the floor in front of the fireplace and played checkers. Brian picked up a black king and slapped it on the board beyond one of her red kings.

"Gotcha!" he said.

Sarah smiled. She was still aware of Christine waiting in some corner of her mind. But she had a stronger awareness now, one that overpowered any images of Christine—the awareness of home and family.

She'll never take them from me, Sarah thought. She may cause me anxiety and even fear, but she'll never take away my home and my family.

And then Sarah was struck by an odd notion. The more she considered it, the more it disturbed her:

Christine Helstrum had helped create this home and this family. If she had not brutally murdered Laura and Timothy Whitaker, then Alex would never have moved here. He would have remained in Albany, New York, a happy father and husband.

And me? Sarah wondered. I'd still have Brian. But I wouldn't have Alex. And I probably wouldn't be living in this house or sitting in this room.

Sarah tried to push these thoughts from her mind.

They preoccupied her, though, and she idly moved her last king into the path of certain death.

20

SHE STARED OUT THE WINDOW and thought about her son.

He was born early in the morning, she thought, just like this, cold out and barely light enough to see the black trees and the snowy ground.

She shivered and hugged herself. She never took off her coat anymore, because she felt cold most of the time. And what made it worse, she ached. The dull pain had begun in her back because of the awkward position in which she slept. But now her hips and legs hurt, too. And her neck was always stiff.

She pictured the face of her son and smiled.

I wish he were with me, she thought. Then I could leave this place. We could leave together. We'd go someplace far away from here, someplace where no one would find us, someplace where we could be together forever. Someplace warm.

Her breath had fogged the window. She started to wipe it with her hand, then changed her mind.

If only he weren't dead, she thought, then everything would be all right.

She turned her back to the window and walked a few steps into the room. Then she stopped as suddenly as if someone had struck her. She'd had a thought that was so staggering, so powerful, so *insightful,* that for a moment she couldn't move. It had been a revelation. And it was so simple, so *pure,* that she wondered why it had never occurred to her before.

Her son was alive.

Timothy was alive.

Her mouth hung open in amazement.

They've lied to me all along, she thought. They've made a fool of me.

She considered her facts. She examined them like a jeweler examining the facets in a stone—looking for a flaw but hoping none would be found. After the fight with Alex's wife, she and Timothy had gone to her apartment and she'd put him to bed. Then the police had come in and taken him away. They'd *told* her that he was dead. But they'd never let her get close to him after that, never let her *touch* him. In fact, she'd never seen him at all after that night. She'd never even seen his body.

Had they even told her where he was buried? No. All during the time she'd been locked up, they'd never told her that. Never even *hinted* at it.

And what if I had demanded to see his grave? she thought. Oh, they'd have shown me one, all right, but it would've been empty. Or if there *had* been a body inside, it would've been some other two-year-old boy, not Timothy.

No, he's alive, she thought. Except he's not two years old anymore.

She tried to remember how long it had been since she'd seen him. What does he look like now? she wondered. And where is he? She began pacing the room to help herself think. Then she stopped, stunned by another thought.

They've got him.

Now it became clear to her, the full depth of their plan and the cleverness of it. They'd made her believe that her son was dead so that they could lock her up. Then Alex and his wife had been free to take him away to another state.

She turned toward the window and the gray morning light.

It's early, she thought. They're probably still asleep. I could go into their house right now and kill them both for what they've done. Then I could take Timothy with me. Except . . .

She was thinking that Timothy might not recognize her. In fact, he might be afraid of her and not want to go. Of course, she could *force* him to go with her, but that wouldn't be right.

I'm his mother, she thought, and I shouldn't have to force him. He should go with me because he loves me. Because he *trusts* me.

She frowned.

Wait, now, wait. They've probably lied to him. They've made him trust *them.*

She paced back and forth, her hands jammed deep in her coat pockets, her head bent in concentration.

I'll show him how weak they are. I'll show him that I can do whatever I want to them. Then he'll see that *I'm* the one who's strong. *I'm* the one he can trust.

She let her pacing take her out of the room and into the bathroom. Leaning over the sink, she studied her dim reflection in the mirror. She touched her hair.

And I'll make sure he's not afraid of me, she thought. I'll make myself pretty for him.

She smiled broadly.

She'll make me pretty for him.

21

THE NEXT MORNING, BRIAN wanted to know why Sarah was riding with him and Alex.

"It's, ah, the other car won't start," Sarah said.

Even though it was a small lie, it made her uneasy. She'd never lied to Brian before. She'd always tried to answer truthfully—although not necessarily in complex detail—every question he'd asked. Until now she'd never consciously kept anything from him.

But how could she tell him about Christine Helstrum? How could she explain the fear that she and Alex felt?

"You see, Brian," she'd have to say, "a very bad lady may try to see me today, so some policemen will be hiding outside my shop ready to arrest her. But if she somehow sneaks past them, your father will be there to protect me. It's nothing to be concerned about."

She couldn't say any of that, she knew. Nevertheless, she felt uncomfortable lying to her son.

When they got to Brian's school, Sarah walked him inside. She spoke for a few minutes to his teacher, reaffirming another lie, the one Alex had told the teacher about an ex-wife. Back outside, she saw Alex standing across the street next to a police car. He leaned over to speak to the officer inside, then crossed the street and climbed in the Celica.

"All set?" he asked.

"Yes, I . . . yes."

He put his hand on her leg and squeezed it gently through her coat.

"Everything's going to be okay."

Sarah nodded but said nothing.

They drove to the shop in silence. When they got there, Kay Nealy was unlocking the front door. Alex parked beside her car. Sarah scanned the parking lot, looking for the police. There were a number of cars scattered about, but none of them were police cars, and none of them seemed to be occupied.

Kay smiled and waved at Alex, assuming, Sarah knew, that he was merely giving her a ride to work. Then Kay frowned briefly when Alex shut off the engine and climbed out with Sarah.

"Hi, Alex," she said. "Sarah."

"Good morning."

"Are you here to get a quick trim before going off to the blackboard jungle?"

"Not exactly," he said.

Sarah and Alex followed Kay into the shop. Kay switched on the lights, then took off her coat and hung it on a hook. She hugged herself.

"God, it's cold in here," she said.

She turned up the thermostat, then went to the back to make coffee. Alex sat in one of the chairs against the wall and shuffled through magazines in the nearby basket. Sarah stood at the desk and looked down at the appointment book, which was open to today's date: Thursday, December 10. She had Donna Rothman at eight, cut and perm. She'd blocked off three hours, which would give her enough time to get Donna out of the shop before her eleven o'clock appointment with . . . Mrs. Green. She checked her watch: 8:01. Less than three hours now.

Kay came into the room.

"Are you going somewhere this morning?" she asked Sarah, then nodded toward Alex.

"No."

"Oh . . ."

Kay waited for Sarah to say more, and when she didn't, she said, "So Alex just came in to read our magazines, right?"

Sarah gave Kay a brief smile.

"This is . . . awkward," she said. "To explain, I mean. Alex is here to . . ."

She looked at Alex, who had put down his magazine and faced them across the room.

"Alex is here in case there's trouble," Sarah said.

"Trouble?" Kay almost laughed. "You mean like if one of our customers starts to bitch about her perm?"

"No," she said. "It's Chris— It's Mrs. Green I'm worried about."

"Who?"

"She was in here Tuesday, remember? The strange woman with the—"

"Oh, yeah, yeah," Kay said, grinning from ear to ear. "The loony tune with the blow-dried clothes and the permanent-press hair." She looked from Sarah to Alex, expecting a laugh, getting none.

"I'm afraid of her," Sarah said. "We're afraid."

"Are you kidding?" Kay's smile began to fade. "Hey, come on, that woman was weird, maybe, weird *looking*, anyway, but you don't really think she's dangerous, do you?"

"We think she might be," Sarah said.

Kay looked at her carefully.

"You're serious, aren't you?"

"Yes."

Kay swallowed, then glanced at the front door.

"Well, what . . . who *is* she?"

"She—"

Sarah stopped and looked toward Alex for help. He lowered his eyes to his magazine, as if to say that any explanation should come from her. Sarah didn't know how to tell Kay part of it without telling her everything. And she wasn't prepared to describe Alex's traumatic past, not with him sitting right there.

"We think she broke into our house," Sarah said.

"What?"

"Last Monday. Someone came in the back door while I was in the living room."

"My God. Did you see her?"

"No, but . . . one of our neighbors did," she lied. It surprised her how easy it was to do once she got started. "They described her to me and, ah, after Mrs. Green came in the next day, I realized how closely she fit the description."

"Jesus, Sarah. Did you call the police?"

"Yes. They're looking for her."

Kay glanced at Alex, then back at Sarah.

"She has an appointment with you today? You think she might come in?"

"She might," Alex said, and they both looked at him. "That's why I'm here."

Kay started to say something, then stopped when the front door opened and in walked Jerry Calveccio. They all three knew that this wasn't something to discuss in front of customers.

"Hiya, Kay. Hiya, Sarah. Hiya," he said to Alex, then plopped down in the chair at Kay's station.

Jerry was one of Kay's favorite customers because she thought he was funny as hell. He was a salesman—Sarah was never quite certain what he sold—and he tried his best to keep up on the latest jokes, or at least on the latest versions of old jokes. Even Sarah sometimes found him funny, if mildly so.

Not today, though. Today all his supposedly humorous stories sounded silly and insensitive, or even downright cruel. At least they did to Sarah. Apparently, though, Kay thought differently, or else she was covering her tension with loud laughter.

Sarah endured Jerry's wisecracks and forced herself to smile, checking her watch every few minutes. Donna Rothman was already late, and Sarah wanted to be finished with her well before eleven o'clock. She wanted to be prepared for Mrs. Green, prepared for whatever might happen.

Finally, at 8:35 Donna walked in. She was a dowdy young woman who always seemed to be caught up in herself. She did not apologize for being more than half an hour late.

Sarah led Donna to the back room, where she shampooed her hair, then wrapped it in a towel. She brought her out to the front and sat her down at her station. While she combed and cut Donna's hair, she tried to ignore the jokes and laughter coming from Kay and Jerry.

At 8:45, Kay took the smock from Jerry and gently shook clipped hair to the floor. Sarah watched her brush off his neck and shoulders and hold a mirror up for him to admire the back of his head. She was relieved he was leaving except for one thing: It meant that nearly an hour had passed, an hour less to separate her from . . . that woman. And what if she really is Christine Helstrum? Sarah wondered.

Sarah went to the back room for a basket of perm rods and a dispenser of end papers, brought them out front, and gave them to Donna.

"Would you hand me a paper one at a time, please?"

Sarah took an end paper from Donna, placed it around the tip of a strand of her hair, then rolled it up on a small plastic rod and fastened it in place. She took the second end paper, then glanced at her watch: 9:20. Less than two hours left.

Kay's next customer burst through the door, and Sarah winced. When she glanced at Kay, she could tell that her partner felt the same way.

The customer's name was Jane Newhouse, and Kay referred to her—behind her back, of course—as "Jane the Pain." She was a complainer. Nothing was ever right as far as she was concerned, and she made sure that everyone heard about it. Worse yet, she always brought along her sons, Billy and Lenny, one five, one six, both with flaming red hair and big, splotchy freckles. As far as Sarah could tell, the boys never walked or talked—they always ran and yelled.

Today they ran directly through the shop to the back, one chasing the other, both waving large plastic guns, both screaming at the tops of their lungs. One of them stopped at the doorway to the back, turned, and fired his gun at Alex. A Ping-Pong ball flew across the room, barely missing Alex's head.

Kay winced and smiled and invited Jane Newhouse to sit at her station. She began preparing her for a tint.

"Be careful of my ear," Jane said, "because of my infection. Didn't I tell you about that? Well, my doctor says it's nothing, but what does *he* know, I mean, *I'm* the one with sharp pains, not that it hurts *all* the time, you understand, but *sometimes* it's *very* painful, take last night, for example . . ."

Sarah finished rolling Donna's hair in rods. Then she put protective cream and cotton around her neck at the hairline and draped her in towels and a plastic cape. She led Donna to a chair in the back and found Billy tugging at a basket of rods in the open cupboard. Kay was looking over the room divider and saw what was about to happen at the same time Sarah did and said, "Um, Jane, could you tell your son to . . ." just as Lenny yanked on his brother's hair, pulling him back, along with the basket, sending perm rods scattering all over the floor. Billy jumped up crying and banged his sibling across the knee with his gun.

Jane Newhouse yelled at her sons to shut up, which only made them cry louder.

"Sorry about all this," Sarah said to Donna, then began applying the perm solution. When she was finished, she covered Donna's head with a plastic cap, had her sit under one of the beehive-shaped driers, then set the timer for fifteen minutes. Kay and Jane walked past her to the shampoo bowl. Sarah picked up all the rods from the floor and returned them to the basket and the cupboard. She went out to the front and sat beside Alex.

She glanced at her watch. It was 10:14. Sarah was beginning to think that this was not such a good idea, simply waiting for "Mrs. Green" to show up.

Maybe we should just leave, she thought, leave now, get in the car and drive home . . .

"Are you okay?" Alex asked her.

"Those kids," she said under her breath. "I don't know how much more of them I can take. Not today." She glanced at her watch: 10:15.

Alex took her hand in his.

"I'm right here with you," he said, smiling faintly.

But his smile vanished when Billy and Lenny came running into the room, hurled themselves at the basket near Alex's chair, and began pulling out magazines as if they were digging for buried treasure.

Kay trailed Jane into the room, looked at Sarah and Alex, and shrugged her shoulders.

". . . my gallbladder," Jane was saying. "I've had a *lot* of trouble with my gallbladder, and it's hereditary, you know, because my mother had a lot of trouble with *her* gallbladder. She still does. In fact, last week . . ."

Sarah went to the back and got Donna out of the drier. She took off her plastic cap, then removed a perm rod and tested a curl to see if the perm had taken. It had. She rinsed Donna's hair, blotted it dry with a towel, then changed the cotton around her hairline and applied the neutralizing solution. She twisted the dial on the timer and set it for five minutes. Then she checked her watch: 10:34. Less than half an hour left.

At 10:39 she began removing the perm rods from Donna's hair. Then she took off the towels and cape, again rinsed Donna's hair, and applied a conditioner. As she was leading her back to the station, she nearly had a head-on collision with Billy and Lenny, who were making their way to the back, swatting each other with magazines along the way.

10:49.

Sarah began blow-drying Donna's hair. She noticed that Jane had moved the discussion from her gallbladder to the carburetor on her station wagon.

". . . in the garage three times this month," Jane said.

Sarah shut off the blow drier, then held up a hand mirror so that Donna could see the back. Sarah's eyes moved from the back of the mirror to her watch: 10:58.

"Oh, I like it," Donna said. "I do."

Donna followed Sarah to the desk and wrote out a check, which included a five-dollar tip.

"Thanks, Donna."

"Thank *you*," she said. "See you next time."

Donna put on her coat, waved good-bye to Kay, and walked out. Sarah looked down at the open appointment book before her. Near the top of the left-hand page it said, "11:00—Mrs. Green." Sarah checked her watch: 11:00. She looked over at Alex. He glanced at his watch, then put his magazine aside and sat up a little straighter in the chair.

Sarah could feel the tension in her shoulders and back. She tried to relieve it by busying herself around her station, brushing off the chair, sweeping up hair, straightening her combs and brushes. She looked out the window, but no one approached the door, no car drove up to the shop. She glanced at her watch: 11:04. She looked out the window again.

Suddenly there was a scream and a crash.

Sarah spun quickly around, banging her elbow on the back edge of the chair and sending a jolt of pain through her arm. In her mind's eye she saw Christine Helstrum bursting in through a window. But the sounds had come from the back room.

"You boys better calm down in there!" Jane Newhouse yelled from her chair.

Sarah was startled by the loud voice. She held on to the chair to calm herself, squeezing so hard that it hurt her fingers. She noted that Billy and Lenny were dead quiet in the back room.

"What's going on back there!" Jane yelled.

Sarah saw that Kay had stepped back to allow Jane to get up and go see to her sons. But Jane made no move other than to turn to Sarah.

"Would you mind taking a peek back there," she said, "since you're not busy?"

Sarah stared at her for a moment, her mind still filled with violent images.

"Well?"

"Oh, of course."

Sarah went to the back room and saw Billy and Lenny busying themselves with a pile of perm rods that they'd dumped out of a basket and were now arranging on the floor in cryptic patterns. Nearby lay pieces of a shattered coffee mug. Kay's favorite mug, Sarah saw with dismay. She opened the closet and got out a whisk broom and dustpan and swept up the pieces.

She was dumping the remains of the shattered mug in the wastebasket when she heard the front door open.

Sarah froze, waiting for the sound of a voice, a cry, a scuffle. There was nothing. She went out to the front.

Kay was still trimming Jane's hair and listening to her complaints.

Alex was gone.

22

"WHAT HAPPENED?" SARAH asked, her voice tight.

Kay and Jane Newhouse both stared at her in the mirror.

"Where's Alex?"

"He went outside," Kay said, and suddenly she looked worried.

Sarah rushed to the front door and pulled it open. Alex was standing just outside. He turned and stepped in, bringing with him a cloud of chill air. His eyes met Sarah's, and he shook his head no.

"It's a quarter after eleven," he said.

They sat down and waited.

Kay finished with Jane Newhouse. The woman wrote out a check, gathered up her sons, and left. Sarah checked her watch: 11:32.

"Maybe she's not coming," Sarah said.

"Or else she's just late."

They were still waiting at noon, when Alex phoned the school to arrange for someone to fill in for his afternoon classes. And at one, when both Sarah and Kay had their next customers. At two-thirty, with still no sign of Mrs. Green, Sarah and Kay and Alex went out for a late lunch, returning an hour later. Sarah and Kay were both cutting hair when Alex phoned Brian's school at four to say he'd be late picking up his son and to make sure that at least one teacher would be there with him for the next few hours. Kay left for the day at six, and at six-thirty Sarah finished with her last customer. Still no Mrs. Green. Sarah locked up the shop and walked out with Alex.

The parking lot was awash with cold yellow light. Sarah and Alex both noticed a car parked under a nearby light standard. There were two men in overcoats standing beside it. One of them, Sarah saw, was Detective Yarrow.

"I'm going to talk to them," Alex said.

Sarah got in the Celica and watched Alex walk over to the two men. She couldn't hear what they were saying, but she could see that Alex was getting upset. Finally, he waved his arm in disgust and stalked back to the Celica. He swore under his breath as he started the engine.

"What's the matter?"

"Those cops," he said. "They're ready to dismiss the idea that Christine was ever in your shop."

"What?"

He nodded, backing the car away from the curb.

"They're not dropping the case," he said, "but they think this Mrs. Green was just a nut. They think that if Christine Helstrum had had the nerve to walk in your shop two days ago she would've done it again today."

"But there could be a *hundred* reasons why she didn't come."

"That's what I told them."

"What did they say? What are they going to do?"

Alex slowed the car, then turned out of the parking lot onto Nevada Avenue. The headlights from oncoming cars glared on the windshield.

"I don't know," he said. "I walked away when Yarrow started to give me some bureaucratic bullshit."

Sarah could see the anger in Alex's face. She put her hand on his coat sleeve. He didn't respond, but stared straight ahead, as if fiercely concentrating on his driving. Sarah turned from him and looked out her window at the black night and the passing lights.

Maybe Mrs. Green really *was* Mrs. Green, Sarah thought, just another oddball, as the police believed, who'd come in off the streets, made an appointment for a haircut, and then promptly forgotten about it.

It was a distinct possibility, Sarah knew. But it didn't put her mind at ease. Christine Helstrum was still out there somewhere. And Sarah and her family would not be completely safe until Christine was caught.

Sarah wasn't very hungry that night, and she definitely wasn't in the mood to spend time preparing dinner. Tuna salad would have to do, she decided.

She got three eggs from the refrigerator and put them in a pot of water to boil on the stove. Then she opened the cupboard and reached up for a large can of tuna fish. She stopped, frowning. There was only one can of tuna on the shelf. She thought she'd bought three cans just last week, and she was certain that she hadn't already opened two of them. In fact, she couldn't remember having opened any.

"Maybe I didn't buy that many," she said to herself.

"That many what?"

Alex had come into the kitchen. He'd changed from his slacks, sports coat, and loafers to jeans, a flannel shirt, and fleece-lined leather slippers.

"Cans of tuna. I thought we had more."

"Is that what we're having tonight?"

"If it's okay with you."

"Sure."

"If not . . ."

"It's fine," he said. "Can I help?"

"You can set the table."

While he did so, Sarah looked through the silverware drawer for the can opener.

"Well . . ."

"Now what?"

"I can't find the opener," she said.

Alex held up his hands in a mock-defensive gesture. "I swear, I didn't take it."

Sarah smiled wryly and shook her head. "I guess my memory is shot."

She pulled open a lower drawer, then dug around until she found another opener. She started to shut the drawer, then stopped. She reached in and moved a few knives and utensils around.

"Oh, no." There was sadness in her voice.

"What's wrong?"

"The butcher knife's missing. The one Brian used to draw his cardboard sword."

Alex sighed and stood next to her, looking down into the drawer.

"Are you sure?"

"It's not in here, Alex, and this is where I put it."

"I thought we made it clear to him."

"So did I."

"Do you want me to—"

"No," Sarah said. "Let me talk to him first."

She followed the sounds of the television into the family room. Brian was sitting cross-legged on the floor, watching an ancient rerun of *I Love Lucy.*

"Brian?"

He looked up at her, his eyes wide with innocence.

"What, Mom?"

"Did you take the butcher knife again?"

"What?"

"You heard me," she said, more sternly than she'd intended. "Did you take that knife again?"

"No." He shook his head quickly from side to side.

"Are you sure?"

"No, Mom."

Sarah didn't know what hurt worse—that Brian had disobeyed her and Alex or that he was lying to her now.

"Brian, it's not in the drawer where I put it."

"I didn't take it." There was fear in his voice.

"Are you certain you didn't borrow it again to draw another sword?"

Tears formed in his eyes. "Honest."

"Brian, please . . . don't lie to me."

"I *didn't,*" he said. He stood up and faced her, his tiny fists clenched at his side, his bottom lip quivering. "I *didn't.*"

"Well, it's not there, so somebody—"

"I *didn't*!" he yelled, and ran past her.

Sarah stood unmoving, listening to Brian's running footsteps fade down the hallway, across the foyer, and up the stairs. She heard the muffled slam of his bedroom door.

"Oh, God," she said softly.

She met Alex in the foyer. He looked from the stairs to Sarah.

"What happened?"

She held on to him, her head on his chest, the sting of tears in her eyes.

"I don't know, Alex," she said. "Either I'm losing it, or else he . . ."

"Did he admit it?"

She shook her head. "I don't think he took it. But I pushed him. I accused him." She looked up into Alex's face. "I've never done anything like that before."

"We're both on edge," he said, as if that were explanation enough.

"I know, but still . . ."

Sarah gently disengaged herself from Alex's arms, then climbed the stairs alone. She found Brian in his room, sitting on the side of his bed. His back was to the door, and he was looking down at the floor, crying softly. Sarah sat beside him and put her arm around his shoulders.

"I'm sorry, baby," she said quietly.

"I didn't take the knife, Mom." His voice caught on the words.

Sarah gently wiped the tears from his cheeks. "I know you didn't, baby," she said.

"Honest."

"I know. I was wrong to think that you took the knife. It was my fault, Brian. You see, lately I've been . . . upset, and little things that shouldn't even bother me seem to make me, well, nervous." She looked down into his upturned face. "I promise I won't do that anymore. Okay?"

Brian put his arm around her waist and leaned his head against her side.

"I'm sorry," she said.

"It's all right, Mom," he said seriously.

Later, they all sat in near silence at the dinner table. No one had an appetite for either food or conversation. Alex tried one humorous story about an incident yesterday at school involving the janitor, a bucket of soapy water, and Miss Horst. But Sarah could only manage a weak smile, and Brian didn't even lift his eyes from his untouched food.

Sarah was thinking about the knife. There were only three explanations for the knife's disappearance, none of them satisfying, each of them disturbing in its own way:

One, she'd misplaced the knife, along with the can opener, all because her mind had become preoccupied with Christine. Or two, Brian had taken the knife and was continuing to lie about it. That thought made her sick at heart. Or three, someone *else* had stolen her largest butcher knife. But why would—

"Can I go upstairs?" Brian said.

Sarah blinked, coming out of her thoughts.

"Sure, honey," she said.

Brian started to get off his chair when suddenly the lights went out, plunging the kitchen into blackness. A second later, they came back on. Sarah and Alex and Brian stared at each other across the kitchen table. Then the lights went out again.

This time they stayed out.

"Son of a bitch," Alex said.

Sarah saw Alex's dark shape rise from the chair and move to the counter, where he fumbled in the drawer, looking for the flashlight. She sat still, nearly as disturbed by the failure of the lights as by his brief outburst—she'd never heard him swear in front of Brian.

Alex clicked on the flashlight, indirectly illuminating them in a pale yellow glow. He moved through the kitchen to the laundry room. Sarah heard him throw the bolt and open the basement door. A moment later, the lights came on, and Alex returned to the kitchen.

"The main breaker tripped again," he said. He put away the flashlight. "I'll call the utility company tomorrow. Maybe it's an outside line."

Sarah hoped he was right.

Sarah awoke in her bed with a start.

Someone was standing in the hallway outside their bedroom. It was too dark for Sarah to see, but she could sense someone out there.

"Brian?" she called softly.

Alex stirred beside her and mumbled something in his sleep.

"Brian, honey?"

Sarah stared at the doorway. She saw movement in the dark

hall. Or perhaps her eyes were playing tricks on her. Then she heard the faint whisper of fabric. A large silhouette, black against the darkness of the hall behind it, filled the doorway.

Sarah lay perfectly still, afraid to move, afraid to breathe. The figure in the doorway came forward and stopped just inside the bedroom.

As Sarah stared at the silent visitor, details began to appear. It was as if the vague light from the window were adhering to the figure, gradually accumulating like a mist of luminescent paint, until Sarah could clearly see.

It was a woman.

Her hair was wild. She wore a hospital gown, and her feet were bare. She made no sound, no movement.

Sarah could not clearly see her face, but she felt the woman's eyes on her, studying her. She had the desperate notion that if she just lay there and pretended to be asleep, the woman might go away.

Then she thought of Brian, helpless in his room. Had the woman already been in there?

The woman came forward and moved toward the bed, slowly, one measured step at a time, her arms hanging loosely at her sides.

Now that she was closer, Sarah could see that she carried something in her right hand, something long and pointed. It reflected the faint light from the window.

The missing butcher knife.

Sarah tried to move, to shake Alex out of his slumber, to get up and run, to do something—but she could only lie there, as frozen as a mouse staring into the eye of a snake.

The woman walked slowly around to Sarah's side of the bed, her eyes never leaving Sarah's face. Sarah tried to cry out, to scream for help, but her throat was constricted in terror. She tried to move again but couldn't. She was tangled in the sheets, and her arms were pinned to her sides as effectively as if she'd been bound in a straitjacket.

Now the woman stood directly over Sarah, close enough to reveal her face, twisted in a devilish grin. She leaned over and put her left hand firmly on Sarah's shoulder to hold her still. Then she slowly raised the knife high overhead until it was poised directly over Sarah's left breast. With a terrible force, she brought the knife plunging down. . . .

"Sarah."

Sarah jerked awake, her heart pounding. Alex's hand was on her shoulder.

"You were having a nightmare," he said.

"Oh, my God." She rolled over and buried her face in his chest. She felt cold with sweat. "God, Alex, it was horrible," she said, her voice partially muffled by his pajama top. "It was Christine."

"Shh." He stroked her hair as if she were a child. "It was only a dream."

Sarah hoped it was only a dream. She prayed it wasn't a premonition.

23

SARAH WAS NERVOUS ALL MORNING. She jumped every time someone came in the shop's door, expecting it to be Christine Helstrum.

She'd wanted Alex to be with her at work today, but he'd told her that it was impossible for him to miss classes two days in a row. "Besides," he'd assured her, "the police will be outside the shop. They're not going to simply forget about us." Sarah had searched the parking lot when she'd arrived at work, hoping to see plainclothes policemen crouching in unmarked cars. She'd seen none. She'd hoped that was because they were good at hiding.

It wasn't only the apparent absence of the police and the possible proximity of Christine Helstrum that made her edgy. Something else troubled her: the items missing from the kitchen. She could imagine herself misplacing the can opener, and even the knife—although she doubted it. However, she could not believe that she'd misplaced food.

And so at one o'clock, when she went home for lunch, she'd already devised a simple plan, one that would at least resolve the question of the food.

Sarah parked the Wagoneer in the garage, then walked back to the curb. This morning before leaving for work, Alex had dragged the large plastic trash barrel here from the side of the house. Today was pickup day.

Now Sarah pulled off the lid, and to her relief the barrel was nearly full.

She knew that their trash was picked up on Fridays, but she hadn't been able to remember whether it was mornings or afternoons. What she still couldn't remember was on which days she'd emptied the kitchen wastebasket into this barrel.

Now she wrinkled her nose from the stale smell and began digging into the trash. At first she dug tentatively, afraid of getting gunk on her hands, afraid one of the neighbors might drive by and see her. But then she worked with greater energy, determined to find what she was looking for.

She noticed that the contents of the barrel were not mixed in a totally haphazard fashion. They were more or less arranged according to rooms: Here was a concentration of pale green Kleenex from the wastebasket in the master bedroom; there was an accumulation of crumpled-up notes and typed pages from Alex's den. When she began turning up kitchen waste, she knew she was close.

She dug through sticky eggshells and soggy vegetable scraps and dripping soup cans. At one point she came across the shriveled body of a headless mouse, one of the three she'd found in her car last Saturday. She made a face, flicked the body aside, and continued to burrow through the trash.

She'd nearly reached the bottom of the barrel when she found it: last Thursday's cash-register receipt from the grocery store.

It was folded and crumpled and stained yellow with some unknown liquid that had long since dried. Sarah picked off a few crusty scraps from one corner of the four-inch-wide, foot-and-a-half-long receipt. Then she straightened and flattened the paper as best as she could. Thankfully, it was still legible, containing a detailed computerlike printout of each item purchased. Sarah replaced the lid on the barrel and went into the house.

Patches greeted her at the door and followed her into the kitchen.

Sarah decided she was no longer hungry; she felt too much anticipation for what she might find. She heated water on the stove for coffee, then brought a notepad and pencil to the table. She began searching her memory and writing down as completely as she could the description of each meal that she and Alex and Brian had had since last Thursday.

Patches circled her feet a few times, rubbing his tail against her leg. When no caresses were forthcoming, he marched haughtily away.

By the time Sarah finished her cup of coffee, her list was as complete as she could make it.

She spread the grocery receipt flat on the table beside her list and began drawing a line through each item that had been consumed, or partially consumed, since last Thursday. When she was finished, more than half the items on the grocery receipt had been crossed off.

Now she took the receipt to the cupboards. She carefully arranged the cans and boxes on the shelves, checking them against the receipt. There were some items on the shelves that were more abundant than her receipt would indicate. This didn't concern her. She was only interested in those items that she *knew* she'd purchased last Thursday and that now were either on the shelf or on her list of meals.

When she'd finished with the cupboards, she checked the refrigerator, crossing off more items. And then she was done. Theoretically, every item should have been crossed off the receipt, having either been consumed during the week or located on the shelves. Of course, there were exceptions, such as apples, for which she didn't have an accurate count.

However, she did have an accurate accounting of *these* items, and they had not been crossed off the receipt: one 32-ounce can of beans, one loaf of whole wheat bread, two large cans of soup, one package of sliced ham, one box of saltine crackers, one package of cheddar cheese, one box of chocolates, one large can of fruit cocktail, one half gallon of orange juice, and two cans of tuna fish.

There may have been more things missing, but she was absolutely certain about *these* things. They were gone. Definitely gone.

She had a sudden, disturbing mental image of Christine Helstrum sitting here at the kitchen table, alone in the house while they were all at work or school, calmly fixing herself a sandwich.

Sarah checked the back door. It was tightly closed, and its heavy snap-latch lock was solidly in place. She opened the door and examined the lock, not quite certain what she was looking for. However, it did not look damaged or even tampered with. She was remembering last Monday, when she'd found this door open.

She must have gotten in another way, Sarah thought, then went *out* through the back door, leaving it open behind her.

Sarah walked back through the kitchen to the front of the house. She checked the front-door lock but could find nothing wrong with it. Then she began a thorough inspection of the ground floor, going from room to room and carefully examining every window. Each one was closed tight and securely latched. She knew that the second-story windows were too high to reach without a ladder. She tried to think of how else someone could get into the house.

The basement windows?

She walked through the kitchen to the laundry room. The door to the basement was bolted shut. She turned the bolt and slid it completely into its housing on the door. Then she pulled open the door, slid the bolt out as far as it would go, and bent down to examine it closely.

She frowned.

There were scratches and nicks on the bolt, some of them

relatively deep. Most of the scratches were shiny, as if they'd been made recently. Sarah wondered how scratches like that could have been made. She closed the door, slid the bolt, and rotated it into place. Then she rotated it the other way, away from her. The scratches seemed to line up with the direction of rotation, but she couldn't yet see what was causing them.

Something brushed the back of her leg, making her jump.

"Damn it, Patches," she said, feeling her heart thump.

The big cat meowed and rubbed his body against her.

Sarah opened the door again and slid out the bolt to take another look. Suddenly, Patches darted past her onto the landing.

"Patches, come—"

The cat ran down the stairs into the dark basement.

Sarah hesitated, then reached around the doorway, found the light switch, and flipped it on. When she stepped onto the landing, the harsh overhead light cast her shadow halfway down the wooden stairs. She could see partway along the hallway below. It was empty.

"Patches!" she called.

There was a muffled roar from below. She knew it was only the furnace, but it brought goose bumps to her arms and neck.

She checked her watch. Her next customer was due at the shop in less than twenty minutes, so she'd have to leave soon or be late. But she didn't want to leave the house with the basement door open. She had a very bad feeling about that. And she didn't want to lock the door and leave Patches in the basement all afternoon—it was too cold for him down there.

She started down the stairs slowly, reluctantly. She had a nagging sense of uneasiness, as if she shouldn't be doing this, as if she shouldn't go down there alone.

That's ridiculous, she scolded herself. You're being childish.

However, there was an uncharacteristic tightness in her chest. She stopped halfway down.

"Patches," she called, though not as loudly as before.

She waited a moment for the cat to appear, and when he didn't, she descended the stairs to the bottom.

The low-ceilinged hallway stretched before her, cold and empty. Sarah held perfectly still, listening. The only sound was the low, muffled roar of the furnace coming from the room to her right. The door was partly open. Sarah pushed it completely open, surrounding herself with the noise from the furnace.

Light from the hall spilled through the doorway, forming a narrow path leading into the dark room. Yellow and blue lights, like alien animal eyes, flickered from beneath the small furnace in the corner of the room.

"Patches, come on out of there."

Sarah reached around the door, feeling for the light switch, afraid to step into the dark room, afraid that her hand might encounter a spider or something worse.

She found the switch and flipped it on, filling the room with sick yellow light. The huge, old iron furnace dominated the room and reached up to the ceiling with cylindrical air ducts. In Sarah's mind the abandoned furnace became a leechlike parasite that had attached itself to the underbelly of the living, warm-blooded house.

More realistically, it looked like a good hiding place for a cat. She stepped around the giant furnace and peered into the shadows, wishing she'd brought a flashlight. She could see just well enough to discern that Patches was not crouched there.

He's been back there before, she thought, wrinkling her nose from a stale, rancid odor.

She backed away from the furnace.

Something grabbed her.

She panicked and started to yank free. Then she saw that she'd merely caught the sleeve of her sweater on the latch securing the furnace's iron door. Sarah carefully unhooked herself. She noticed with dismay that she'd smudged her sleeve with rust—reddish brown, like old blood.

Sarah switched off the light and started across the hall toward the old canning room. A movement caught her eye. She spun around in time to see Patches trotting toward her with something hanging from his mouth.

A dead mouse.

He dropped it at Sarah's feet and sniffed it. Sarah scooped up the cat in her arms, nudged the mouse carcass against the wall with the toe of her shoe, and quickly climbed the stairs.

After she'd slammed the door and thrown the bolt, she allowed herself to relax. But only slightly. There was still the matter of the missing food. She wondered if she should call Alex now or wait to tell him after work.

Before she'd decided, the phone rang.

"Mrs. Whitaker? This is Frank O'Hara."

"Yes, hello." Sarah wondered if he was calling to get news or to give it.

"I tried to reach you several times this morning," he said.

"We were both at work. Is there . . . something?"

"Is your husband home?"

"No."

"Well . . . I suppose I can tell you. I mean, it's good news, if somewhat morbid. Or perhaps the Colorado Springs police have already informed you."

"Informed us about what?"

"Christine Helstrum is dead."

Sarah was stunned. For a moment she didn't speak.

"Mrs. Whitaker?"

"Yes. Yes, I'm here. It's just that . . . she's dead? Are you certain?"

"I'm positive."

Sarah felt her shoulders slump as the tension drained from her body.

"They found her yesterday," O'Hara said. "I just heard about it myself, and I wanted you to know right away. I can imagine the anxiety you must have suffered these past days."

"Yes, but . . . are you *positive*?"

"Absolutely. Some hikers found her body in the woods a few miles from the state hospital," O'Hara said. "It was partially buried in the snow. Apparently, she, that is, her body, had been there for a few weeks, since the night of her escape."

"What happened? I mean, how . . . ?"

"They don't know yet. An autopsy will be performed today, or perhaps tomorrow. But the police think she froze to death."

"And they're certain it's her?" Sarah was afraid to let herself believe it—it seemed too good to be true.

"Yes," O'Hara said, "even though her face was—it's difficult to be delicate about this— Small animals had been at her. Her face was mostly gone. But everything else fits exactly—same-size body, same hair color, same hospital clothes, right down to the underwear. It's her, all right."

"Thank God," Sarah said. "Thank God it's over."

But it *wasn't* over, she knew. Someone had been in their house. She considered telling him about Mrs. Green but decided against it. After all, what could he do about that?

"My husband may want to talk to you," she said. "Will you be home today?"

"Yes."

"I'll have him call you, and, well, I want to thank you, Mr. O'Hara. Thank you for everything."

"It's no problem. Take care."

He hung up.

Sarah immediately phoned Jefferson High and had Alex paged. He was as stunned as Sarah had been, but more skeptical. As she'd guessed, he wanted to talk to O'Hara. She gave him the number, then glanced at her watch.

"I've got to run," she said. "I'm really late for my next appointment. See you tonight. Love you."

Sarah was twenty minutes late for her two o'clock appointment and nearly twenty-five minutes late getting started on her four o'clock. She tried to work faster, but her mind wasn't on her job.

Christine was dead, and she should have felt relieved. But there was still the missing food. A burglar? She smiled to herself. A hungry burglar whom she'd surprised and scared away last Monday.

Stranger things have happened, she thought.

She also thought it ironic that the idea of a burglar in their house had once frightened her terribly and now it was almost a relief.

At six o'clock Kay left for the day. Sarah finished with her last customer half an hour later. After the woman had gone, Sarah went into the back room to make certain everything was straightened up and ready for tomorrow. She turned off the coffee machine, rinsed out the cups, and dried her hands on a towel. She turned from the sink and walked to the doorway.

She stopped dead still.

A woman stood in the middle of the front room. She wore a plaid scarf and a rumpled brown coat.

It was Mrs. Green.

24

MRS. GREEN SMILED.

Sarah felt her blood turn to ice.

She's *Christine.*

But she can't be. Christine is dead. O'Hara said so. She's *dead.* This woman . . . *resembles* the photos, but . . .

"Hello, Sarah," Mrs. Green said pleasantly. "I'm sorry I'm late."

"What—" Sarah's voice caught in her throat. Her impulse was to run, to get away from this woman, whoever she was. But the shop had no back door, and Mrs. Green stood between her and the only entrance. "What . . . do you want?"

"What do you think? I'm here for my hair."

Mrs. Green untied her scarf and removed it, revealing limp, dull brown hair. She casually dropped the scarf onto a chair.

"No," Sarah said, trying to find strength in her voice. "No. I'm sorry, but we're closed."

Mrs. Green stood unmoving, her hands hanging loosely at her sides.

"But *I* have an appointment," she said.

"No," Sarah said firmly. "That was for yesterday. I'm sorry, but I said we were closed."

"AND I SAID," Mrs. Green yelled, making Sarah take a step

backward. The shop was deathly quiet. "And *I* said," Mrs. Green continued, her voice very low and mean, "that I have an appointment."

"No," Sarah said, fighting to maintain control.

She moved forward along the edge of the room, intending to get to the front door, to run if she had to.

Mrs. Green stepped directly in front of her.

Sarah stopped.

She knew that the only way to get out was to fight. And she didn't know the first thing about fighting. Even if she did, she would've been reluctant to fight this woman, who was noticeably larger than she was.

"You can't leave, Sarah," Mrs. Green said in a commanding tone of voice. "Not until you do my hair."

She wanted to shout for help. But there was no one to hear; the shops on either side had closed at six. And the blinds were shut, so no one could see in from the parking lot, even if anyone were looking this way.

Sarah watched helplessly as Mrs. Green unbuttoned her coat and carelessly tossed it aside. She wore a pleated skirt and a pink sweater. Cashmere, Sarah guessed, and somewhat familiar. However, it was smudged with dirt and at least one size too small for Mrs. Green. It stretched tightly across her shoulders and chest, partly flattening her breasts. She wore no nylons. Sarah saw that her legs were white and muscular.

"Well?" she said, for Sarah hadn't moved. "Shouldn't we get started?"

"I . . . I can't," Sarah said, her mind frantically searching for a way out. "I have to leave. My husband is expecting me. If I don't get home on time . . ."

Mrs. Green moved toward her, wagging her forefinger as if she were a teacher lecturing a stubborn student, wagging it so close to her face that Sarah could see that the nail was chewed down to the quick. Sarah looked beyond the finger to the woman's eyes.

They were dark gray. Expressionless. Doll's eyes. And they were an inch or two higher than Sarah's, further reminding her how big this woman was. Sarah guessed that Mrs. Green outweighed her by more than thirty pounds.

"Oh, no, you don't," she said, smiling impishly.

"No, it's true. If I'm not home soon, he'll worry. He'll . . . he'll come here."

"Oh." Mrs. Green blinked once, thinking. Then she moved forward, forcing Sarah backward to the desk. "Call him and tell him you'll be late."

Sarah hesitated, then picked up the phone. Mrs. Green moved beside her.

"And Sarah," she said, "we don't want anyone to get excited. So let's don't mention any names."

As she said this, she picked up the letter opener from the desk. The opener had been a gift from Kay Nealy's husband to both Kay and Sarah. It had an ivory handle carved in the likeness of a seabird with its head bowed and its beak resting along its neck. The blade was stainless steel, six inches long and tapered to a dull point. Mrs. Green held the opener in her right hand, her fingers wrapped tightly around the bird's neck.

Sarah tapped out her number, then listened to the rings.

"Hello?" Alex's voice sounded small and distant.

"Hello, Alex? It's me."

"Hi. What's up? Don't tell me the Jeep won't start."

"No, it's . . . not that."

Mrs. Green was now drawing the flat of the blade slowly across the palm of her hand, as if it were pleasurable to feel the cool steel against her skin.

"Sarah?"

"Yes."

"Is something wrong?"

She nearly said yes. But then what would she say when he

asked her to explain? What *could* she say with this woman standing beside her?

"No," she said. "No, nothing's wrong."

Mrs. Green smiled at Sarah, as if she'd heard Alex's question.

"I'm . . . just running late, that's all. I have . . . one more customer."

Mrs. Green slowly turned the letter opener in her hands, carefully examining the blade.

"Oh," Alex said. "Well, how long before you get home?"

"How long?"

Sarah glanced at Mrs. Green.

"Don't you remember?" Mrs. Green whispered, as if she didn't want Alex to hear. "We need time to change the color and then cut it real nice."

"About . . . two hours," Sarah said helplessly.

"Okay, well, I guess Brian and I will have to eat without you. By the way, I talked to O'Hara."

"Yes?"

"He told me pretty much what he told you," Alex said. "The hospital people positively identified the body as Christine. I guess it's really over."

Sarah said nothing, but clamped her jaws shut to keep herself from crying for help—help that was miles away.

"Sarah?"

"Yes. Yes, you're right."

"Okay, then, I'll see you later. Good-bye, hon."

"Good-bye," she said. "Alex—"

But he'd already hung up. Sarah slowly replaced the receiver in its cradle.

"Now, then," Mrs. Green said, leaning close enough for Sarah to smell her sour breath, "may we begin? I don't have all night, you know."

Mrs. Green held out her arm toward the doorway.

Sarah hesitated. Her eyes fell to the letter opener, still clenched in Mrs. Green's hand.

Go along, she thought fearfully. Don't upset her.

Sarah led Mrs. Green to the back room. The room seemed brighter than Sarah had ever seen it—as bright as an operating room.

"What's first?" Mrs. Green's voice was filled with glee.

Sarah noticed that she'd brought along the letter opener. She was afraid to ask her to put it down, afraid to draw her attention to it.

"We, ah . . ." Sarah's mind went blank. It was as if she were doing all this for the first time. "We . . . need to choose a color for you."

She opened a cabinet and took out the color chart—a large book with thick pages to which were attached rows of small hair swatches. Each swatch was subtly different in color from the ones on either side. Sarah motioned to the padded hydraulic chair.

"If you'll sit down, we—"

"I'll stand," Mrs. Green said, smiling. "Let's have a look."

Sarah opened the book and turned to the page of browns, which ranged from fawn through chestnut to chocolate. She glanced at Mrs. Green's hair, which appeared to be a medium brown. It also appeared to be quite dirty—it even *smelled* dirty—and Sarah guessed that after it was washed and dried it would be at least one color level lighter.

"Perhaps one of these," Sarah suggested, trying to keep her voice calm, trying to pretend that this was normal, that this was a normal customer. "Did you want it lighter or darker?"

"Oh, lighter, I think. Don't you?"

Sarah nodded and wondered if she could escape now, just run for the door. She imagined Mrs. Green grabbing her from behind, perhaps by the hair, pulling her over backward, slashing down with the letter opener. . . .

"Perhaps this one," Sarah said. She pointed to a light golden-brown swatch. Her finger trembled only slightly.

"Hmm. Yes, well, if *you* think it's best."

"It's a nice color," Sarah said. Then she added, almost apologetically, "I'll have to wash your hair first."

"Oh?" Mrs. Green reached up and touched a strand of her hair. She twisted it between a thick thumb and forefinger. "I suppose so."

"Please." Sarah indicated one of the chairs that was tilted back under a porcelain shampoo bowl.

Mrs. Green frowned.

"We have to wash it," Sarah said, suddenly seeing a chance to escape. "Otherwise, the color won't hold."

Mrs. Green nodded, eyeing Sarah and then the chair.

"All right. Go stand on the other side of the chair."

Sarah's hope faded—the chair would be between her and the door.

"But I need to—"

"Over there."

Mrs. Green motioned at Sarah with the letter opener. Sarah got a cape from the closet, then stood on the far side of the chair. Mrs. Green eased into it, letting her right arm hang loosely over the chair so that her hand brushed Sarah's pant leg. Sarah draped the cape around her. Mrs. Green put her left hand—the one with the letter opener—in her lap above the cape, then leaned back until her head rested against the edge of the bowl. She looked up at Sarah and smiled.

"I'm all yours," she said.

Sarah turned on the water, testing its temperature on her hand as it sprayed out of the flexible showerlike head. When it was warm enough, she began wetting down Mrs. Green's hair. Then she squeezed shampoo into her hands and rubbed it into her hair.

Her hair felt at once greasy and gritty, as if it hadn't been washed in days, perhaps weeks. Sarah had difficulty working up a lather. She had to rinse the hair and then apply shampoo a second time before the foamy suds began to build. All the while, Mrs. Green kept her eyes on Sarah's.

At one point she moaned with sensual pleasure, making Sarah's skin crawl.

Sarah again thought of escape. She didn't think she was fast enough to run around the end of the long chair, especially not with Mrs. Green's hand brushing against that side of her leg.

But maybe the window . . .

There were windows behind the counter and the shampoo bowls. They were closed and covered with venetian blinds. Sarah remembered that the few times during the summer when she and Kay had opened the windows it had been a difficult task, for the wood frames were slightly warped and the windows often stuck. And she wasn't certain if the screen could be removed from the inside.

I could jump up on the counter, she thought, yank open the window, kick out the screen . . .

"Sarah." Mrs. Green's voice was a stern warning.

"What?"

"Why did you stop?"

"I . . . we're through."

Sarah rinsed Mrs. Green's hair, then hastily blotted it with a fluffy white towel. Without thinking, she moved toward the doorway. Mrs. Green leapt from the chair. Sarah froze.

"I . . . I need to get the tint," she said.

"I want to see." Mrs. Green's voice was as bright as a child's.

She followed Sarah across the room to the large cabinet near the doorway, then peered over her shoulder as Sarah selected the proper bottles. Mrs. Green looked on with rapt attention as Sarah mixed the chemicals in a plastic bowl, then poured the mixture into an applicator bottle and screwed on the top.

"You'll have to sit down," Sarah said, indicating the hydraulic chair.

"Fine. But don't you dare get any of that in my eyes."

Mrs. Green turned the chair so that it faced the doorway, so that Sarah would have to stand behind her.

Sarah wrapped her in a plastic cape. Then she combed her hair into four sections, parting it front to back and side to side. She put on plastic gloves and began squeezing the foamy coloring agent onto Mrs. Green's hair, working it first to the roots. The mixture had a faint smell, not altogether unpleasant, but it seemed now to be overpowering to Sarah. She tasted bile in her throat and feared she might vomit.

She clenched her teeth and finished applying the solution.

Sarah set the timer for twenty minutes. She also glanced at her watch: 7:00. She wondered if Brian and Alex were eating dinner yet. Maybe they were finished already. She pictured Alex washing the dishes while Brian . . .

"Now what?"

Mrs. Green swiveled the chair, nearly pinning Sarah against the counter.

"We have to leave it on for twenty minutes," she said.

Sarah moved away from her, into the room, and rinsed out the bottle, washed off her gloves, and laid them near the sink to dry. Mrs. Green watched her every move, her hair partially plastered to her skull.

"Tell me about your family," she said from across the room.

"What?"

"Your *family,* Sarah," she said, sarcasm dripping from her voice like venom from a fang. "Tell me about them."

"I . . . I don't know what you want."

"I mean *describe* them, Sarah. *Describe* them."

"What are you . . . why are you doing this?" she shouted, no longer able to hold back. "Please. You know all about us. Why can't you just leave us alone?"

Mrs. Green was on her feet.

She walked slowly toward Sarah, the overhead light glimmering on her slick hair. The plastic cape hung over her hands, and Sarah could just see the shiny tip of the letter opener.

"I don't know what you mean, 'Leave us alone,' " Mrs. Green said. "I just want you to tell me about your family. Your husband. Now what was his name?"

"You *know* his name." Sarah drew back until she was against the far wall.

Mrs. Green walked right up to her.

"Sarah." There was scolding in her voice.

"His name is Alex," she said softly, looking down.

"Alex. That's right, I heard you call him that on the phone. That's a nice name. A strong name. Do you love him?"

Sarah looked up at her. Mrs. Green's face was neutral, expressionless.

"Yes," Sarah said firmly. "Yes, I love him very much."

Mrs. Green nodded.

"And your children?"

"I have a son," she said, hearing the pride in her own voice. "Brian."

Mrs. Green nodded.

"I have a son, too," she said.

A bell rang. Mrs. Green spun around.

"It's just the timer," Sarah said. "I need to comb the tint through your hair."

She followed Mrs. Green back to the chair. She was so tense that her joints ached. Mrs. Green sat down, and Sarah pulled a wide-toothed tint comb through her hair, then reset the timer for ten minutes.

"That's why I'm getting my hair done," Mrs. Green said.

"What?"

"For my son. I haven't seen him for . . . for a long time."

Sarah swallowed hard and looked more closely at her face, afraid of what she might see.

"We were separated some years ago," Mrs. Green said. "But we're getting back together. A reunion. And I want him to see me in my best light."

Mrs. Green's eyes were aimed at Sarah, but they'd lost their focus. Neither she nor Sarah spoke or even moved until the timer rang again. Mrs. Green snapped out of her trance.

"Now what?"

"We wash off the tint."

When this was done, Sarah removed the plastic cape, wrapped her hair in a towel, and followed her out to the station. She could hear the faint sounds of traffic coming from the distant street. Mrs. Green turned the chair toward the front door, so Sarah was forced to stand behind her with her back to the shelf and the large mirror.

Sarah draped a clean cape around her, then ran a comb through her hair. She guessed it had once been squarely cut above the shoulders, but now it hung with ragged ends.

"Make it look real pretty," Mrs. Green said.

"How much should . . . would you like taken off?"

"I'll leave it up to you."

"I . . . think a light trim."

"Oh, well, *you're* the boss."

Sarah picked up her scissors from the shelf. Suddenly, Mrs. Green turned and grabbed her wrist, so quickly that Sarah saw her hand only as a blur. Mrs. Green's grip relaxed almost at once, but Sarah could still feel the bite where the woman's fingers had dug into her flesh.

"What an interesting pair of scissors," Mrs. Green said. "May I see them?"

She took the scissors from Sarah and held them up, testing the points with her forefinger.

"They're small, but they're terribly pointed, aren't they? Just like cats' teeth."

She handed the scissors back to Sarah.

"Please be careful, won't you? I wouldn't want you to accidentally stick me in the neck."

That was something that Sarah never would have considered doing. But she considered it now, stabbing the woman in the neck and running out of the shop, shouting for help.

Sarah swallowed hard.

No, she thought. She'd jerk away from me at the last second and I'd miss. Or I'd only wound her slightly, just enough to enrage her. Or maybe I *would* hit her solidly and the scissors would crunch through her neck and the blood would spurt and . . .

No, she thought, I can't.

She began to trim Mrs. Green's hair. Her hands trembled so badly that she could barely hold on to the comb.

"Did you ever see a cat catch a mouse?" Mrs. Green asked suddenly, startling Sarah.

"I . . . no, I . . ."

However, she now remembered early this afternoon, when Patches walked toward her in the basement, a dead mouse dangling from his jaws.

"That's too bad," Mrs. Green said, "because it's something to see. It's instructive. It's all about life and death. You see, the cat doesn't kill the mouse right away. He has some fun first. He plays with it. He takes his time and enjoys it. He's in no hurry. And the mouse, well, the poor little mouse can do nothing but let it happen. It knows it's going to die." Mrs. Green paused. "Of course, we're all going to die."

Sarah felt a chill go through her.

"Sometime," Mrs. Green said. "Sometime."

She said nothing more, and Sarah finished trimming her hair in silence. Then she blew it dry and carefully brushed it. Mrs.

Green swiveled in her chair and looked past Sarah to the mirror, admiring her newly styled golden-brown hair.

"It's very nice, Sarah," she said, pulling off the cape.

She stood almost nose to nose with Sarah.

And for the first time Sarah noticed something about the woman's eyes. More specifically, her eyelids. Her right eyelid drooped slightly lower than her left.

Two days ago, in her living room, Sarah had been shown a police photograph of Christine Helstrum. In that photo, Sarah recalled as clearly as if she were looking at it now, Christine Helstrum's right eyelid drooped lower than her left.

"Good-bye, Sarah," Mrs. Green said, and raised the letter opener.

Sarah jerked backward, the shelf jabbing her in the back. Mrs. Green leaned forward, quickly reached around Sarah, and placed the opener on the shelf beside the scissors. Then she turned on her heel, crossed the room, picked up her coat and scarf, and pushed out through the door.

25

SARAH COULDN'T MOVE.

She felt paralyzed, leaning back against the shelf, staring at the front door, expecting Mrs. Green to walk right back in.

Except it *wasn't* Mrs. Green.

It was Christine.

There was no doubt now in Sarah's mind—Mrs. Green was Christine Helstrum. Somehow O'Hara was wrong. The people at the hospital were wrong. Christine wasn't dead. She was alive, and she was here, right here.

Suddenly Sarah pushed away from the shelf and ran to the front door. She savagely twisted the metal knob, throwing home the lock.

Fully expecting Christine to come into view at any second, Sarah backed away from the heavy glass door and stopped only when she'd reached the desk. She picked up the phone and then nearly dropped it because her hand was shaking so badly.

She started to tap out her home number, then stopped. Alex could get to the shop in twenty minutes, she knew. But that meant twenty minutes of sitting here alone. What if Christine came back? What if she became enraged by the locked door and smashed through the window?

No, Sarah thought wildly. I've got to get out of here.

She yanked out the bottom drawer, tore open her purse, and grabbed her keys from it. She ran to the front door, then stopped, her hand on the metal knob.

Maybe she's waiting right outside, Sarah thought.

She pressed her face close to the cold glass and tried to see if anyone was standing against the building. Her breath fogged the glass. She wiped it with her sleeve. She could see a light snow falling through the lights from the shop. The sidewalk and the parking lot were already dusted white. Far away, across the lot, cars were clustered near the department store. But in this corner of the shopping center, all the shops were closed, and the parking lot was deserted. The Jeep Wagoneer looked cold and abandoned.

Again Sarah pressed her face against the glass. She didn't *think* anyone was out there, but she couldn't tell for certain.

She took a deep breath, as if she were preparing to swim underwater. Then she twisted the knob, pushed open the door, and ran to her car, almost falling on the slick pavement. She dropped her keys, bent down, and nearly kicked them under the car. They were wet from dirty snow, making her fumble with them for a few maddening seconds before she found the right one. All the while, her shoulders were hunched against the blow from behind, which could come at any moment.

She shoved the key in and opened the door, then scrambled into the Wagoneer, slammed the door, and locked it.

Sarah started the engine with a roar and flipped on the windshield wipers, then yanked the lever to "R" and spun the tires in reverse, suddenly realizing that a thin layer of snow covered the rear window, blocking her vision.

She blindly whipped the car around in a tight circle in reverse, barely missing a concrete-anchored light pole. When the hood was pointed toward a distant driveway, Sarah jammed the gear shift to "L" and flattened the accelerator pedal to the floor. The tires spun, making a whirring noise on the slick asphalt. The

Wagoneer began to move forward, slowly at first, and then with greater speed.

By the time Sarah reached the entrance to the parking lot, she was going thirty miles an hour. The entrance led out onto Nevada Avenue, which Sarah suddenly realized was busy with traffic. She slammed on the brakes, throwing the Wagoneer into a sideways skid. She slid across one lane of traffic, barely missing a small sports car, which swerved wildly to avoid her. Sarah managed to regain control of the Wagoneer and hold her place in traffic as cars around her honked like angry geese.

She was shaking with adrenaline and with cold, and for the first time she realized that she'd left the shop without her coat or her purse. She turned on the heater and then—seeing something else she'd forgotten—the headlights.

Sarah drove for several blocks before she felt the heat from the blower. It was comforting, something warm and familiar. She began to calm down. She even allowed herself a dark smile: Christine had stiffed her for a color and a cut—she'd left without paying.

Then Sarah saw a shape move in the rearview mirror.

She slammed on the brakes, evoking more angry honks, before she realized that the shape was the top of a large truck that had changed lanes behind her. For a brief moment, though, she'd thought the movement had come not from behind the Wagoneer but from inside it. And she was seized with a new panic.

She swerved the vehicle to the side of the road and slid to a stop. Quickly, she shifted into neutral, set the emergency brake, and climbed out.

The engine's idle made a low rumble as Sarah stood beside the car, hugging herself from the cold. Tiny snowflakes, whipped into currents by the passing cars, whirled around her. The drivers gave her curious looks, but none of them stopped or even slowed down. Sarah walked completely around the Wagoneer—at one point sinking up to her ankles in frigid snow—and peered into every window, assuring herself that Christine was not crouched in hiding behind the seats.

She climbed back into the Wagoneer.

She sat there for a moment, shuddering from the cold. Her eyes were pressed tightly closed to keep back the tears—tears of humiliation and guilt. For now that the blinding fear had passed from her, she began to blame herself for what had happened. She knew it was illogical, but part of her mind insisted that she could have done more when she'd first been confronted by Christine. She could have pushed past her and immediately left the shop. She could have fought. She could have done something, anything. But she'd done nothing, merely obeyed. She'd submitted.

Sarah pulled the Jeep back onto the road and moved into the flow of traffic. The heater was still set at maximum, but Sarah shivered all the way home.

Alex met her at the front door.

"Hi, babe. How was— What's wrong? Are you okay?"

"Oh, Alex."

She stood in the doorway, her shoulders slumped, her arms straight down at her sides. Alex reached for her, gently pulled her inside, and closed the door.

"Were you in an accident?"

"Oh, God, Alex, it was her."

"What?"

"I *tried* to get away from her, I *wanted* to, but I was so frightened, I . . ." She shook her head, then clung to him as if her life depended on it. "She came in the shop. She was there when I called you. It was Christine."

"*Christine*? That's impossible. Christine's dead."

"No, Alex, she's alive. She was just in the shop. We've got to call the police."

Alex pushed her slightly away and looked down into her face. "Are you talking about Mrs. Green? Did Mrs. Green come in your shop?"

"She was there, the same woman as before, but it wasn't Mrs. Green. It was—"

"When exactly?" Alex's face was flushed with anger.

"Just *now*." Sarah briefly told him how Christine had held her there with implied threats.

"Goddammit," Alex said, pulling away from her.

He opened the closet door, grabbed his ski parka, and hastily put it on. Then he began rummaging inside the closet.

"Alex, what—"

"Maybe she's still around there," he said. "Goddammit, the police were supposed to have been watching your shop."

He came out of the closet. Brian's baseball bat was clenched in his fist.

Sarah remembered when they'd given the bat to Brian. It was on his birthday last June. After he'd unwrapped it, he and Alex had gone immediately out to the backyard, where Alex began showing him how to hold it, how to stand, how to swing it. And the very first time Alex had tossed Brian the baseball-sized rubber ball, Brian had hit it solidly. It had flown clear over Alex's head, delighting them both. Brian had taken the bat to bed with him that night. Sarah remembered gently prying it out of his hands after he'd fallen asleep.

And now Alex wielded the bat as if it were a deadly weapon.

"I'm going to the shop," he said flatly.

"No, Alex, she—"

"You stay here with Brian and keep the doors locked."

"Alex, no."

Sarah grabbed his arm, wrapping both her arms around it. He tried to pull free, but she hung on tightly.

"No, Alex, please. Don't leave us here alone. Please, call the police. Let them—"

"The police." Alex spat the words. "We already know how effective *they* are."

"Alex . . ." Sarah pressed her forehead to the shoulder of his coat. "I . . . I'm frightened. I don't want you to go. I don't want you to leave us here alone."

Alex took a breath and let it out through his nose.

"All right," he said. "If you want to, get Brian. You can both go with me and stay in the car."

Sarah looked up at him.

"Either way, Sarah, I'm leaving now."

Alex drove the Wagoneer in silence, his face grim, his shoulders hunched forward.

The snow had increased. Large, puffy flakes flattened themselves on the windshield and were swept aside by the wipers. Sarah looked out the side window, away from the occasional glare of oncoming headlights. There was little traffic. She saw a city truck spreading sand near a street intersection.

She hugged Brian closer. He was bundled up in his coat, hat, scarf, boots, and gloves. When Sarah had told him they were going for a ride, he'd been excited, but now he seemed tired. She realized it was past eight, close to his bedtime.

By the time Alex turned into the shopping-center parking lot, Brian was asleep in Sarah's arms.

"The lights are on," Alex said, as if that might mean something.

"I left them on. And the door open. My purse is in there, my coat. I just ran . . ."

Alex parked in front of the shop. The blinds were drawn, glowing faintly from the lights inside. Alex stared at the front door of the shop, but he made no move to turn off the headlights or the engine. The wipers ticked rhythmically from side to side.

"Sit tight," Alex said softly. He glanced down at Brian, then reached behind the seat and came up with the baseball bat.

Alex climbed out and quietly closed the car door. He motioned to Sarah, and she pushed down the lock button. She watched him walk warily to the front of the shop, looking to his left and right. He held the ball bat with both hands, resting it on his shoulder, as if he were waiting his turn at bat. Then he pulled open the door, paused for a moment, and stepped inside, letting the door close behind him.

Sarah could see Alex's faint silhouette against the drawn blinds. His shape moved to the right, into the shop. Brian stirred beside her. Sarah gently moved his head so that it rested more comfortably against her side, and when she looked up, Alex's silhouette was gone.

Sarah stared at the front window of the shop. There was no movement. The only sound was the low, rhythmic rumble of the Wagoneer's engine and the steady ticking of the wipers.

Minutes passed.

Sarah considered locking Brian in the car and going into the shop.

Then a light went out behind the blinds. Then another, and the shop was dark. Sarah held her breath, and a moment later Alex stepped outside, pulling the door closed and locking it with a key. Sarah's purse was in his left hand, and her coat was draped over his arm. He walked toward the car, ducking his head from the snow, looking defeated.

When he climbed into the car, Brian woke up.

"Can we go home now?" he said sleepily.

Alex faced Sarah, snowflakes clinging to his hair and eyebrows. "Yes," he said. "Let's go home."

He turned the Wagoneer around, crunching snow beneath the tires, and pointed the hood toward Nevada Avenue.

"I was wrong to drag you out here," he said softly.

Sarah put her hand on his arm.

"I should've known she wouldn't still be here. I . . . lost my head."

"It's all right," Sarah said. But she had a frightening image of him, standing in the foyer, clenching the baseball bat, ready to kill. "We must call the police."

Alex nodded.

By the time they got home, it was snowing heavily. Thick white flakes filled the air, obscuring vision. Their house seemed unsubstantial, made up of dots of pale light behind the black evergreen trees.

Alex turned into the driveway.

They all left deep tracks in the snow as they walked from the garage to the house. Brian led the way, fully awake now, his face turned up to the white-speckled black sky, trying to catch snowflakes on his tongue. As he approached the front porch, he called to them over his shoulder.

"Hey, tomorrow can we build a snowma—"

Brian stopped abruptly, one foot on the porch. Alex and Sarah came up behind him. Sarah sucked in her breath, then pulled Brian back to her.

Yellow-white light was spilling onto the porch.

The front door stood wide open.

26

ALEX STEPPED AROUND SARAH and Brian and walked through the open doorway.

"Alex . . ."

He stood in the middle of the foyer, head cocked, as if he were listening for something, holding the baseball bat slightly out from his side. Sarah entered the house with her arm around Brian. Patches strolled out from the kitchen, then arched his back against the cold air, turned, and went back.

"Alex."

Alex looked around at her. His mouth was a straight, firm line, and his eyebrows were pulled down in a frown. He glanced past her toward the door.

"I was in a rush," he said. "I might not have shut it all the way. The wind could have blown it open."

He turned away from her and faced the interior of the house.

"Stay here with Brian," he said.

Before Sarah could respond, he'd gone down the short hallway to the kitchen. She felt cold air behind her and closed the door. In a moment, Alex returned to the foyer.

"The back door's locked, and so is the basement," he said, moving toward the living room, the bat raised before him.

"Alex, let's call the police."

"No," he said firmly, stopping to face her. "The wind blew open the door. That's all. I'm just going to check the house to make sure. You and Brian just stay here for a few minutes."

Sarah felt anger stir inside her.

"Alex, don't be stupid. We—"

"This is my house," he said loudly. "Our house. I can deal with this, Sarah. Now please."

He did not wait for a reply, but walked directly into the living room. After a few moments he came out, crossed the foyer without looking at Sarah, and stepped into the "music room."

Sarah remembered how they'd named the room right after they'd moved in. The previous owner of the house had left them one piece of "furniture": a baby grand piano. Neither Sarah nor Alex played, although she'd taken lessons as a child. But they'd paid to have a man come to the house and tune it. It had seemed so civilized. Now Alex walked out of the room carrying the baseball bat.

He walked down the hall toward the dining room and the family room.

"What's Dad doing?"

"He's . . . he'll be through in a little bit, Brian."

"Can I go up to my room?"

"No," she said quickly. "No, honey." She squatted down next to him. "Let's just wait here until your father is finished, okay?"

Brian shrugged. "Okay."

Sarah watched Alex reappear in the hallway, then climb the stairs. Five minutes later he came back down, walked past her, tossed the bat in the closet, then hung up his parka.

"Nothing's been disturbed," he said. "I even looked under the beds and in the closets. It was just the wind." He put his arm around her shoulder. "I'll call the police now."

They all climbed the stairs. Alex went into his den, and Sarah took Brian to his room. She helped him undress and put on his pajamas, then tucked him in bed and kissed him good-night.

When she walked back to the den, Alex was sitting with his elbow on the desk, the phone in his hand.

"When *will* he be on duty?" he said into the receiver. "Then you tell him that I want to talk to him. . . . Alex Whitaker." He gave their phone number. "You tell him that Mrs. Green came into my wife's shop today and—"

"Alex, no, it was—"

Alex shook his head at Sarah. "—and he was supposed to be there to apprehend her. . . . You're damned right. . . . That's right. . . . No, we don't need any policemen coming to our house tonight. . . . Yes, I'm sure. Good-bye." He hung up the phone.

"Why did you say it was Mrs. Green? I told—"

"Because it was her."

"It was Christine."

"No."

"Alex, I'm telling you that—"

"Christine is dead!" he shouted, then glanced past her to the hallway leading to Brian's room. "She's dead."

Sarah was shaking her head, remembering.

"The hospital people identified her body, Sarah." Alex sounded as if he were trying to convince himself as much as convince her. "The Albany police identified her. She's dead, stone-cold dead."

"No. She was there in the shop."

"The same woman as before."

"*Yes,* Alex, she—"

"The same woman who you thought resembled Christine's photograph. *Resembled.*"

"This time I'm certain."

Alex stood and shoved his chair under the desk. He faced her, his arms folded across his chest.

"How so?"

"Her eyelid. It drooped, just like in the picture."

"What are you talking about?"

"Christine's right eyelid droops lower than her left one, remember?"

Alex shook his head no. "I don't remember anything like that, and believe me, I've seen that woman up close."

"Alex, for God's sake . . ."

"Okay," he said soothingly, "okay." He stepped forward and put his hands on her shoulders. "Let's take it easy. We're both upset. But there's nothing the police can do about it tonight. Detective Yarrow will call us tomorrow, and you can tell him what happened."

"Alex, it wasn't Mrs. Green. It—"

"It *was* Mrs. Green. Christine is dead. And by now she's been cut open on an autopsy table."

Sarah said nothing. She wished she could believe that he was right.

Alex put his arm around her, and they stepped into the hall. He stopped abruptly, his eyes focused on the ceiling beyond the stairwell.

"What is it?"

"The lock on the attic door," he said, taking his arm from around her.

Sarah followed him around the head of the stairs until they neared the sitting room. Alex pointed up at the attic door, and Sarah saw what he meant.

The hasp of the lock was hanging down. It was about an inch wide and four inches long, with a hinge at one end and a vertical slit in the other. If the hasp were pushed up into place, the slit would accommodate a thick U-shaped staple fastened to the ceiling beside the trap door. But now it hung down, open.

"Has it always been open like that?" he whispered.

"I . . . don't know."

"That's one place I didn't search," he said, keeping his voice low.

Then he hurried down the stairs. In a minute he was back with the flashlight and Brian's baseball bat.

"Get the pole for the trapdoor," he whispered.

"Alex, shouldn't we—"

"No," he said firmly. Then his look softened. "Please. Get the pole."

Sarah hesitated, then stepped into the sitting room. She could see the blurred top halves of the pine trees in their front yard through the wide front window. It wasn't snowing as hard as before, and the light from the window was pale and cold. Sarah walked around a pair of overstuffed chairs to the closet in the corner. The pole was leaning against the rear wall. She took it to Alex.

Alex used the blunt metal hook on the end of the pole to snag the metal loop set into the trap door. He pulled the door open. It swung downward, releasing a folded wooden ladder, which slid soundlessly down, stopping four feet from the floor. Alex set the pole aside, then unfolded the ladder so that the side pieces rested firmly in the carpet. The opening in the ceiling gaped above them like a black mouth.

Alex climbed the ladder awkwardly, the flashlight in his left hand and the ball bat in his right. He stopped on the fourth step, his head just below the empty black rectangle, then raised the baseball bat into the hole, like a cowboy in an old movie testing for the presence of Indians.

He went up one more step and poked his head into the attic, then took another step up and raised the flashlight. Sarah watched him swivel slowly from left to right, apparently sweeping the light across the attic floor. He stopped moving. She guessed that he was finished, satisfied that the attic was empty, and was switching off the flashlight, ready to come down.

But instead of coming down, he went up.

"Alex?"

"There's something up here," he said, his voice sounding hollow.

He disappeared into the attic.

"Alex, what is it?"

Sarah could hear the ceiling creak as he moved slowly through the attic. She put her right foot on the bottom rung of the ladder, then stopped, glancing across the stairwell to Brian's bedroom doorway, wondering if she should stay down here with her son. Then she looked up at the empty hole in the ceiling. She strained her ears for a sound, any sound. There was nothing.

She hesitated, then began climbing the ladder.

When Sarah was halfway up, she raised her head through the opening in the ceiling. At first it was too dark to make out anything other than the two small, pale windows, one at each end of the attic. Sarah had been up here only once before, soon after they'd moved in. All she remembered of the large room was its peaked rafters and empty floor.

Suddenly one of the windows winked out. Sarah realized that Alex had moved in front of it. She saw the sickly yellow beam from his flashlight play on something lying on the floor near the far wall at the rear of the house. It was a foot and a half high and as long as a human body.

"Alex?"

"Wha—?"

He spun toward her. The flashlight beam stabbed at her eyes, making her squint.

"Is everything all right?" she asked, holding her hand up to the light.

"Yes."

He moved the light away from her, then began walking toward her in a crouch. His head was directly beneath the peak of the rafters, and his arms dangled like an ape's, the flashlight in one hand and the ball bat in the other.

"What is that? What's back there?"

"It's nothing," he said. "An old rolled-up carpet."

Sarah climbed down the ladder, and Alex followed. Neither of them spoke as Alex folded the ladder, pushed it up into the ceiling, then used the pole to flip up the hasp over the staple in the ceiling. He tapped it once, and it clicked home. Then he pried at it for several seconds before he could get it open. He tapped it closed again, then set the butt end of the pole on the floor and shook his head.

"There's no way that could have fallen by itself," he said.

"Do we have a padlock for it?"

"I don't know. But I'll get one tomorrow."

Later that night, Sarah looked in on Brian before she went to bed. His top blanket had partly slipped off, as if he'd been tossing and turning. He lay still now, deep in sleep. Sarah pulled the blanket over his shoulders and gently kissed him on the brow.

Sarah heard Alex in their bathroom, brushing his teeth. She pulled her sweater up over her head, folded it, and opened the large drawer in the bureau. Her sweaters were neatly lined up, shoulder to shoulder, one row on top of another. Sarah laid her sweater in place, started to shut the drawer, then stopped. She was remembering something from this afternoon. Now she scanned the top row, then bent down and lifted each sweater, looking at the one beneath.

Her pink cashmere was gone.

She remembered the sweater she'd seen today on Mrs. Green. It had been a pink cashmere, and she'd thought at the time that it looked familiar.

Sarah straightened up slowly, drawing in a deep breath, trying to remain calm, trying to remember the last time she'd seen her sweater. Had she taken it to the dry cleaner's and forgotten about it? Not likely. Perhaps she'd lent it to someone. Yes. Now she remembered. Kay had borrowed the sweater several months ago. But hadn't she returned it a few days later? Perhaps not.

Obviously not, Sarah thought. We both must have forgotten about it. I'll ask her tomorrow.

Sarah closed the drawer and climbed into bed.

Much later that night Sarah was awakened by a disturbing dream. She tried to recall what it was, but the harder she concentrated, the farther away from her it receded.

She got out of bed and moved slowly to the bathroom, giving her eyes a chance to adjust to the dim light. She fumbled in the dark medicine cabinet for the plastic drinking glass. After she'd taken a drink of water, she walked out to the bedroom, then passed through it to the hallway, deciding to look in on Brian while she was up.

He was sleeping soundly. However, the covers had partly fallen away from him. Sarah gently pulled them up to his chin.

She moved quietly away from his bed to the window. She stood there for a few moments, looking up at the sky. The snow had stopped, and the sky had partially broken, leaving small openings where cold stars shone through. The moon, however, was almost completely obscured and only faintly lit up the covering clouds.

Sarah's gaze fell to the dimly lit, snow-covered yard at the side of the house.

The garage was dark and silent, and the trees and bushes were almost uniformly black against the white background of the lawn. Sarah started to turn from the window when something caught her eye. It was in the yard almost directly below her.

A patch of yellow light.

Sarah knew immediately what it was: light falling on the snow from a window in the house. She estimated that it was coming from a kitchen window.

Alex had been the last one down there, she thought. He must have forgotten to turn it off.

But something was wrong. The patch of light was small, much too small to be falling from any of the large kitchen windows. It had to be coming from a smaller window, one closer to the ground.

A basement window.

27

She lay uncomfortably in the dark. At least she was warmer than before, now that she had the sweater. The memory of stealing it delighted her. She giggled. The sound echoed in her small space, and for a moment she imagined that she was not alone.

"Hello-o," she sang softly, then giggled again.

All things considered, she felt good. Oh, her back and joints ached horribly, but that was to be expected, given her sleeping arrangements. And besides, it was a temporary condition. Soon she'd be out of here. The main thing was she was warm.

And pretty, too.

She smiled in the dark and reached up to touch her newly styled hair. In the process she banged her elbow on the cold, hard wall. She cursed once, a bark, and felt the pain spread quickly from her elbow up to her shoulder and down to her fingers.

She lowered her arm and focused on the pain, exploring it with her mind, aware that it was touching something deep within her. The pain began to fade, so she banged her elbow again, harder this time and with purpose.

Now her joint was on fire, and the pain spread across her back and through her chest. It began to stir the emotion she'd sought—hate. She embraced it and considered the people in the house.

Not her son, Timothy, but the people who'd taken him from her. Alex and his wife.

They thought they were so damn smart, so goody-goody, rich and fancy and everything nice. Well, it was time to show them who the smart one was. Who the strong one was.

It was time to hurt them.

Timothy would have to wait. Besides, she could take him away from them whenever she wanted, now that she looked pretty. He wouldn't be afraid of her. He'd come with her gladly. And once she left with him, she'd never come back. So if she was to hurt them, she had to do it first, before she took her son.

She thought about exactly what she would do, what she *could* do, to them. So many things, so hard to choose.

No matter. She'd think of something just right. She'd sneak back into the house and decide then.

Improvise, she thought, smiling, tenderly rubbing her elbow.

28

SARAH HURRIED INTO HER BEDroom and shook Alex awake. "Alex," she said in a loud whisper. "Alex, wake up."

"Wha—?" He blinked open his eyes.

"There's a light on in the basement. I think someone's down there."

He sat upright in bed. "What?"

"I saw the light from Brian's window."

Alex hesitated a moment, then quickly got out of bed. Sarah followed him out to the hall. He flipped on the light and quickly went down the stairs. She started after him, then turned and walked quickly back to Brian's room. When she saw that he was still asleep, she closed his door and went after Alex. She found him in the kitchen removing something from a drawer. When he turned, she saw that he'd armed himself once again with the flashlight and the baseball bat.

"Maybe you should stay upstairs with Brian," he said, keeping his voice low.

"He's okay. He's asleep. If you're going down there, I'm going with you."

Alex paused. "All right," he said, "but stay close."

Together they moved through the laundry room to the basement door. Alex pressed his ear to it and listened for a few moments. He looked at Sarah and shook his head. Then he handed her the flashlight and quietly slid back the bolt, unlocking the door.

Sarah stood back as he pulled open the door, stepped out onto the landing, and stared down the stairwell. She leaned around the doorframe. The stairs were dark, but the floor below was partially lit. Light spilled from the open doorway of the furnace room. Sarah remembered having gone in there earlier in the day, looking for Patches.

She told Alex, adding, "But I think I turned off that light."

Alex switched on the overhead light and started down the stairs, holding the bat before him as if it were a sword. Sarah stayed one step behind. When they reached the bottom, they walked cautiously to the open door of the furnace room.

The room was harshly lit by a bare bulb. The huge iron furnace stood cold and silent, its ducts reaching outward and upward like the heavy branches of a petrified tree. From the corner of the room came the soft hissing of the small heater. It winked at them with a wavering blue eye. Alex moved quietly toward the large furnace, as if he were afraid he might awaken it. He bent down under a duct and looked behind the furnace, ball bat at the ready, then stepped back and stood up.

"It stinks back there," he said quietly.

Sarah remembered smelling the same faint stench.

Alex followed her from the room, and they crossed the hall, looking into the old canning room. It was empty except for its vacant shelves. They quickly searched the kitchen and the bath, finding both rooms dusty and silent and empty. In the bedroom Alex looked into the closet, then yanked open the door of the wardrobe, releasing a faint odor of cedar.

Back in the hallway, they checked the outside door, then walked into the living room. Sarah was the first to notice the broken window.

It was in the corner of the room, beyond the last of the stacked cardboard boxes. One of the window's small glass panels had been broken along a roughly diagonal line. Half of the pane was still in its frame, and the rest of the glass lay in shards on the dusty carpet.

Alex checked the window latch. It was locked.

"Someone broke in here," Sarah said.

Alex shrugged. "This could've happened months ago, for all we know. Maybe I bumped it with the lawn mower."

"Or maybe someone broke in. Alex, listen, there's something I was going to tell you, but so much else happened that I forgot, and I know it's going to sound crazy to you . . ."

"What is it?"

"There's food missing from the cupboards."

"What?"

She explained how she'd first suspected and then confirmed her suspicions by digging out last week's grocery receipt.

"Lunch meat and tuna fish and crackers . . . lots of things."

Alex stared at her for a moment, worry lines deep in his forehead. He took the flashlight from her and more closely examined the window's latch. Then he shone the light outside, scanning the beam across the snow-covered lawn, which was nearly level with the bottom of the window. He switched off the flashlight and handed it to Sarah. Then he tore a flap from a nearby box and wedged the piece of cardboard into the window pane.

"That'll have to do until I get a new piece of glass."

"Alex, I think you should nail these windows shut."

He looked at her.

"I'm serious," she said.

He nodded. "Okay. I'll do it tomorrow."

"What about tonight? Someone could get in here."

"Sarah, it's late, my tools are in the garage . . ." He shrugged his shoulders in exasperation. "Look, if anyone got in, they'd get no farther than the basement door upstairs. I'll search down here again tomorrow before I nail everything shut."

She gave him a brief smile. He put his arm around her.

They walked back along the hallway, turning off the room lights as they went. When they reached the furnace room, Alex paused, then walked into the room. He stood before the old furnace for a moment before he turned to Sarah.

"Bring the flashlight."

She saw now that he was standing next to the furnace's small door. It was about eighteen inches square—large enough, Sarah suddenly realized, for a person to squeeze through. And the furnace itself was large enough for several people to stand in.

Alex lifted the latch and pulled open the door. Sarah shone the light inside.

The furnace was empty. Its curved inside wall was a sickly gray splotched with red. There were four large black holes evenly spaced around the circular wall—openings for the abandoned air ducts. Sarah pointed the light at one.

She saw something in the duct.

"What's that?"

Alex took the flashlight from her and leaned into the furnace. Standing where she was, it looked as if he were being eaten, headfirst, by a giant iron spider. Alex backed out.

"The ducts are plugged, that's all," he said. "I think the men who installed the new heater did it to prevent drafts."

He closed the furnace door and brushed dirt from his hands.

"Come on," he said, "let's go to bed."

They left the room, switching off the light and shutting the door behind them. Sarah followed Alex up the stairs. He closed the basement door and solidly slammed home the bolt.

† † †

On Saturday morning Sarah awoke to the sound of Alex going down the stairs and out of the house. She climbed out of bed, stretched, then stood for a few moments at the window.

The sky was blue gray over the mountains and light blue overhead. The smooth colors were broken only by a few stray clouds, stragglers from the storm that had passed in the night. Below her, the lawn was evenly white, and the trees and bushes looked as if they'd been dolloped with whipped cream.

Like a scene from one of Brian's books, she thought, smiling.

But her smile quickly melted as the memories of yesterday began to flood into her mind:

Christine in her shop. Or had it really been Christine? The woman calling herself Mrs. Green looked like Christine's photographs. But not exactly. And everyone said Christine was dead—Alex, Frank O'Hara, the Albany police, even the hospital.

The missing food. On this matter there was no room for doubt. Food had been taken from the cupboards, perhaps by the same person who'd broken into the basement window—the same person who'd been in the kitchen while Sarah was in the living room wrapping Christmas presents. Mrs. Green?

Last night's hunt. That's what Alex had been doing—and she, too, she realized—hunting. First at the shop, then throughout the house, and finally in the basement. Hunting for whom? Mrs. Green again?

Sarah didn't know which reality upset her more: that Mrs. Green was really Christine, a madwoman bent on revenge; or that the woman in her shop was someone else, a complete stranger, with thoughts and plans totally unknown to them.

She turned from the window, trying to clear her mind. After she'd washed and dressed in faded jeans and a baggy sweater, she looked in on Brian. He was still in bed, but awake.

"Good morning, pumpkin," she said. The cheer in her voice sounded false.

"Morning."

"I'm going to make breakfast pretty soon. Will you be up and ready?"

"Okay."

When Sarah got down to the kitchen, she heard the muffled thud of hammering coming from below. She put water on for coffee, then set the table. She was pouring orange juice into three glasses when Brian came into the kitchen.

"What's that noise, Mom?"

"It's your dad."

"What's he doing?"

Sarah wondered when she'd be able to explain all of this to Brian. Perhaps when he was older. Perhaps never.

"He's fixing some of the windows in the basement," she said.

"Oh. Can we make a snowman today?"

"Hey, good idea."

Sarah shook cereal into a bowl, then sliced half a banana on top and added milk. While Brian ate, she got things ready for her and Alex. Then she remembered that she had to call Kay. She picked up the phone but hung it up at once, deciding to talk first to Alex. One thing was certain, though: She wasn't going to the shop today.

The thudding from the basement stopped, and a few minutes later Alex came into the kitchen carrying a hammer and a coffee can filled with nails. He set them on the end of the counter.

"Are you finished?" She noticed that his hairline was damp with perspiration.

"Yes, for now." He washed his hands in the sink, then dried them on a dish towel. "It's a pretty crude job," he said, "but no one will be coming in through the basement windows. Or the door, for that matter."

"You nailed the door shut?"

He looked at her and smiled.

"No, I just wedged a length of two-by-four against it."

"Oh."

"I'm going to build a snowman, Dad," Brian put in.

"You are?"

"Well, me and Mom."

"What about me? Can't I help?"

Brian grinned. "Sure."

After breakfast, Brian bundled up and went outside to find some branches and stones for the future arms and face of the snowman. Sarah and Alex began clearing the table.

"I'm not going to work today," Sarah said.

"I don't blame you."

"I was going to call Kay and have her cancel my appointments, but I didn't know what to tell her."

"Tell her you're sick."

"That's not what I mean. I mean about Christine. Or Mrs. Green, or whoever the hell she is. What if she comes back while Kay's there?"

Alex called the police—specifically, Detective Yarrow. He was put on hold for a few minutes, and when Yarrow came on the line, Alex told him how Mrs. Green had terrorized Sarah in her shop yesterday.

He listened for a moment, then said angrily, "Where were you? Where were your men? . . . Right, well they'd better be there *all* day today. . . . No, my wife isn't going in, but her partner is. . . . Yes, we'll be home. . . . Fine." He hung up. "He's coming here this afternoon to get a statement from you."

"Why not this morning?"

"Who knows. He's busy. And he said he'd make sure someone was watching the shop all day today, so I don't think you have to worry about Kay."

Sarah was worried, though. So when she phoned Kay, she told her about her encounter with Mrs. Green.

"Oh, my Lord, honey, are you all right?"

"I'm still a little shaken, but otherwise okay. I'm not coming in today, though." Sarah told her how the police would be watching the shop all day. Then she suggested that Kay might feel safer if she stayed home, too.

"Are you kidding? I need the money too much. Besides, I hope that bitch *does* come back. I'll show her a thing or two."

Kay said she'd call all of Sarah's customers for today and reschedule them. Sarah thanked her and hung up. Alex was standing by the sink, staring out the window.

"The electric company's here," he said.

Sarah stood beside him and saw a van parked in their driveway. A moment later there was a knock on the back door. Alex opened it.

"I've been checking your outside electric lines, sir," the man said. He wore a heavy sweatshirt under his jean jacket, and his wide leather belt was weighted down with tools. "Everything's okay on the main line and on the feeder to your house. I'd like to take a look at your breaker box, if I could."

"Sure," Alex said, unlatching the screen door. "Come on in. I thought maybe you people had forgotten about us."

"No, sir," he said a bit uncomfortably. He nodded hello to Sarah, then followed Alex across the laundry room, tracking melted snow on the floor.

The man stood on the basement landing for fifteen minutes, flipping switches and taking readings on a hand-held meter. Finally, he shut the metal door on the box and stepped into the laundry room.

"No problem there," he said. "Didn't you report that the main switch had tripped?"

"Twice this week," Alex said.

"Were you running a lot of appliances at once? Or maybe a couple of space heaters? Sometimes that can cause an overload."

"No," Alex said. "Nothing out of the . . . ordinary." He looked at Sarah, and she knew what he was thinking: someone had gotten into the basement.

The man raised his eyebrows as if in apology. "Well, then," he said, "I hate to tell you this, but you might have internal wiring problems. This is a pretty old house, and if it still has the original wiring . . ."

He looked at Alex questioningly. Alex nodded yes.

"Then you might have to hire an electrician to check it out. And the sooner the better."

"Sure," Alex said. "I appreciate your coming here."

The man left, and Alex closed the door behind him.

"The lights, Alex. Do you think it could have been—"

"Nobody's getting in the basement now, Sarah," he said firmly. "Nobody's down there, and nobody's getting in."

"I know, but—"

She was interrupted by a knocking on the back door.

"Did he forget something?"

Alex opened the door, and they were both surprised to see Brian standing on the steps, his stocking cap down to his eyes.

"Are you guys coming out?"

Alex and Sarah and Brian packed together a beach-ball-sized mound of snow in the backyard. Then they pushed it across the snowy lawn, rolling it from side to side to keep it round until it grew to nearly three feet in diameter, a giant snowball speckled with bits of brown grass and dead leaves, too large finally for them to budge. They patted down the rough spots with their gloves, smoothing the ball as best as they could.

An hour later, after some serious building and an impromptu snowball fight, the backyard was a maze of ruts and footprints in the snow surrounding a larger-than-life snowman. He had sticks for arms and stones for eyes, nose, and mouth. His round head was topped with a wide-brimmed straw cowboy hat that Sarah had bought last summer for Alex as a joke and that he'd ended up wearing whenever he did yard work.

"That's you, Dad," Brian said, his face flushed from excitement and exertion. They'd all removed their coats and wore only sweaters and gloves under the warm, bright sun. "Now let's make one for me and Mom."

"How about we take a break first?" Sarah said.

They picked up their coats and walked through the wet snow to the back door, leaving their boots in the laundry room. Sarah made hot chocolate, emptying the can. She looked in the cupboard and shook her head.

Brian said, "Let's make one in the front yard, okay?"

"I think you two will have to work without me," Sarah said. "We need groceries."

It was almost one when Sarah returned from the grocery store. She was surprised to find Alex's car gone from the garage. She assumed, though, that he and Brian wouldn't be gone for too long—Alex had said that Detective Yarrow was coming to the house that afternoon.

Sarah hugged a heavy sack of groceries in each arm and carried them along the walk, giving herself a mental kick for not remembering to unlatch the side screen door. She walked around the front of the house and smiled when she saw a snowman in the front yard. A snow boy, she corrected herself, noticing that it was wearing one of Brian's baseball caps.

As she passed the front window, something caught her eye.

She stopped and turned to look up. The drapes were open, offering a wide view of the upper walls and the ceiling of the living room. But that was wrong. The Christmas tree should have been filling the entire window.

The tree was gone.

29

SARAH STARED FOR A MOMENT at the empty window. The heavy grocery bags began to slip from her arms. She carried them to the porch and set them down, then rummaged through her purse for her keys.

She could think of only two reasons why the tree was no longer in the window. First, Alex and Brian had taken it somewhere. Ridiculous. They'd gone off on an errand, and whatever had happened to the tree had happened after they'd gone. The second reason—in fact, the only probable one—was that the tree had fallen over.

Sarah knew it was possible for the tree to have been slightly off center in the stand. It may have been tipping farther off balance, a fraction of an inch a day, until it toppled, pulled down by its own weight. She remembered that her parents' Christmas tree had once fallen over when she was a child. She'd cried her eyes out until her father had righted it in its stand.

She unlocked the front door and went in, leaving the grocery bags behind her on the porch.

Patches strolled into the foyer from the living room, tail erect. He padded across the tile floor to Sarah, purred loudly, and bumped against her leg. Sarah bent down and briefly scratched his head, then stepped to the doorway of the living room.

"Oh, my God," she said under her breath.

The Christmas tree had indeed fallen. It lay in a heap, sprawled across the middle of the floor in a tangle of tinsel and strings of lights and broken ornaments. But Sarah could see that the fall had been no accident.

Every Christmas present had been ripped open, and wrapping paper was strewn about the room.

Sarah walked into the living room, dazed, as if she were a survivor of a train wreck, unharmed but surrounded by destruction.

Pants and sweaters had been slit apart, the pieces tossed about. Alex's robe lay partially beneath a branch of the tree, cut to ribbons. Brian's Parcheesi board was broken in half and the game pieces scattered across the room. His ski parka was slashed in a dozen places, and his radio-controlled VW had apparently been hurled against the wall—it lay broken on the floor below a red-and-black smudge on the wall. In the corner of the room near the base of the tree lay Alex's first-edition history book. The cover was off, and most of the pages were torn out in bunches and lay scattered on the floor.

Sarah's initial shock began to wear off. Now she had a mental image of someone in here, violently and thoroughly ripping things apart, slashing them with a knife.

Damn her, she thought. She had no *right*.

But her anger was chilled by fear—fear that whoever had caused this destruction was still in the house.

Sarah backed out of the room, nearly tripping over Patches. She scooped up the cat, tucked him under one arm, and hurried out the front door.

The very act of fleeing seemed to intensify Sarah's fear, to make it more real. And fleeing from her own home made it that much worse—this was the place she should be able to run *to*.

She ran through the yard and past the grinning, sun-lit snow boy, her feet sliding in the wet snow. When she neared the edge of the yard, the snow was deeper, old and crusty beneath the shade of the pines, and it slowed her progress. But not much, for a panic had seized her, forcing her on. Still carrying Patches, she pushed her way into the high, leafless lilac bushes that separated the yards. The big cat struggled under her arm, clawed her wrist, then broke free and ran back toward the house. Sarah fought her way through the bushes. And they fought back with stiff, dry branches, pulling her hair and scratching her face and neck.

At last she broke through into the neighbor's yard. She half-ran, half-stumbled through ankle-deep snow to the house.

Sarah rang the bell, then pounded on the door, until it was opened by Jack Dahlquist.

He was a middle-aged man with a balding head. Sarah had spoken to him at length only on one occasion, during a backyard barbecue she and Alex had hosted on the Fourth of July. Other than that, she'd only waved to him and said hello from a distance. She was better acquainted with his wife, Denise. Even so, Sarah had expected Jack to recognize her. Clearly, though, he did not.

He frowned and kept his hand on the inside knob, as if he were ready to slam the door in her face.

"Yes?" he said with disapproval.

"Jack, it's me, Sarah, from next door."

His eyebrows went up. "Sarah? Oh, yes, of course. Are . . . are you all right?"

"I need to use your phone," she said hurriedly. "I have to call the police."

"The police?"

"Jack, *please*."

"Yes, of course." He stood aside for her to enter. "You can use the phone in the hall," he said, extending his arm and then following her across a small foyer and around the base of a staircase to a long, narrow hallway. There was a telephone sitting on a fragile-looking antique table.

"Are you sure you're all right?" he asked.

Sarah nodded. "Someone's been in our house," she said, lifting the receiver. "She may still be there."

Sarah dialed 911. She looked up from the phone and gave a start at the small oval mirror on the wall. Staring back at her was a wild-eyed stranger with messed-up hair and a long red scratch on her forehead.

A woman answered the phone, and Sarah blurted out that she needed the police. The woman calmly asked Sarah for her name, her address, the reason for the call, if anyone was injured, if she'd seen anyone in the house . . .

All the while Sarah was clenching the phone in her fist, trying to force herself to calm down but realizing that Alex and Brian might drive home at any minute.

Denise Dahlquist came down the stairs.

"Sarah's house has been vandalized," Jack told her. He'd obviously been listening to Sarah talk on the phone.

Denise's carefully made-up eyes grew wide. "Oh, dear," she said, and reached out a hand toward Sarah.

Sarah told the woman on the phone that she'd wait in the driveway for the police, then hung up.

"I've got to go," she said, brushing past them.

"But, Sarah . . ."

She hurried outside, hoping to intercept Alex and Brian. She didn't want them to walk into the house before the police got there. She prayed they hadn't already returned.

Sarah started toward the bushes, then changed her mind and ran down the driveway to the street.

The pavement was wet with melted snow. Ghostly wisps of vapor snaked along its surface, wiggling under the warm sun. Sarah ran along the edge of the street toward her driveway, stopping when she heard a car approaching from behind.

It was Alex's Toyota.

Sarah waved frantically, getting his attention. Alex nosed the car into the driveway and stopped. As Sarah ran toward the car, she saw Brian staring wide-eyed at her through the passenger-door window. He moved away from her and toward Alex when she climbed in.

"Sarah . . ." Alex looked alarmed.

"Someone's been in the house again."

"What?"

"Who, Mom?"

"The Christmas tree, the presents, everything's been destroyed."

Alex held her eyes for a moment. His face hardened.

"Wait right here," he said evenly, and started to get out.

"No, Alex, she might still be in there. I've—"

"*Who*, Mom?"

"I've already called the police. They'll be here soon."

Alex paused, then steered the car down the driveway to the garage, shut off the engine, and set the emergency brake.

"Did you see anyone?"

"No, I just got home and walked in and—"

She stopped when she saw the police car pull into the driveway behind them. Two policemen climbed out. Sarah recognized them from last Tuesday—overweight and red-faced Officer Bauer and tall, black Officer Eastly.

"You and Brian wait in the car, okay?"

Without waiting for a reply, Alex got out and went back to the officers. Sarah watched them talk for a moment, then walk toward the front of the house—Bauer first, followed by Eastly and Alex.

"What are they doing?" Brian looked confused and afraid.

Sarah put her arm around him. "They're . . . just seeing if it's safe for us to go in."

"Why isn't it safe?"

"We . . . had a burglar, honey, but I'm sure it's okay now. No one's going to hurt us or—"

"But Patches is in there," Brian said in a panic. He turned and reached for the door handle. Sarah stopped him, holding him close to her.

"No, honey, Patches is okay. I took him outside with me."

"Where is he?"

Sarah remembered her last image of Patches, leaping from her arms, running back toward the house. She tried to remember whether she'd left the front door open.

"He's . . . okay, honey. He's just playing outside."

Sarah held on to Brian and waited.

After a few minutes Brian said, "Did you see me in the front yard?"

"What, honey?"

"The snowman in front. That's me."

"Oh . . . Yes, I did. He's pretty neat."

"I made him all by myself. Well, mostly by myself. Dad helped some."

"You did a good job."

Brian explained in detail how they'd done it. Sarah only half-listened, staring through the window toward the house, wondering what was going on in there. Now she asked Brian where he and his dad had gone.

"To the store to buy a lock."

"A lock?"

"For the attic," Brian said.

Sarah saw Alex walking toward them from the house. She and Brian climbed out of the car.

"We searched the whole house," Alex said. "There's no one. The back door was ajar."

"You saw the living room," Sarah said. It wasn't a question.

Alex nodded yes. "Also . . ."

"Was there more?" Sarah asked.

Alex glanced down at Brian. "She'd been upstairs, too," he said. "Let's go inside."

The three of them walked around to the front of the house.

"They're in the kitchen," Alex said. "Maybe you should take Brian upstairs first."

Sarah helped Brian off with his coat and hung it in the closet. When she turned around, she saw him standing in the doorway of the living room. His mouth hung open, and his arms were out from his sides, elbows bent.

Quickly, Sarah went to him and put her arm around him.

"Mom, the tree." There were tears in his eyes.

"It's all right, baby, we'll fix it."

"What happened to it?"

"It just fell over, honey. It's okay. We can fix it."

She gently pulled him out of the doorway before he could focus on the other, more violent destruction. As she led him toward the stairs, she glanced down the hallway to the kitchen. Alex was sitting at the end of the table next to Officer Bauer, who appeared to be filling out a form with a pen. Officer Eastly was not in sight.

Sarah walked Brian up the stairs.

Her legs were heavy, and it was an effort for her to climb the steps. She realized now how tired she felt, drained by her earlier rush of adrenaline.

As they reached the top of the stairs, Sarah hesitated, remembering something.

"She's been upstairs, too," Alex had said.

Sarah knew he'd meant there was more damage. But she didn't know exactly what. Obviously, he hadn't elaborated because Brian had been standing next to her. Was it something that would be particularly upsetting to Brian? she wondered. Surely it wasn't in his room, or Alex wouldn't have suggested that she take Brian up there.

Then she saw that the door to their bedroom was closed.

She walked Brian past it to his room.

"Come here, Mom, I want to show you."

He led her by the hand to the window. The last time she'd stood there had been last night, when she'd seen the light from the basement window. Now she looked down on the snowy side yard, blindingly white under the hungry sun, which had already eaten most of the snow from the concrete driveway and the peak of the garage roof. Although the sun hadn't been able to get at the north side of the garage.

"See, over there," Brian said, pressing his nose and index finger against the glass.

Sarah had to lean close to the window to see where Brian was pointing, beyond the corner of the house and behind the garage. Another snowman. This one wore a scarf on its head.

"That's you, Mom. Neat, huh?"

"It sure is." She put her hand on his head. "I have to go downstairs and talk to the policemen now. But when I'm through I'll come back up here and get you, and then we can go outside for a closer look. Okay?"

"Okay. Mom?"

"What, honey?"

"Is Patches still outside?"

"I . . . believe so." Sarah was thinking of the closed bedroom door.

"Can I go out and look for him?"

Sarah shook her head no. "I'll be back in a little while, honey."

She stepped out and softly closed the door behind her. Then she walked down the hallway to the master bedroom. She paused for a moment, her hand on the knob, a sick feeling in her stomach.

Then she opened the door.

The bedspread and blanket had been pulled from the bed and lay on the floor. There was a huge dark-red stain in the center of the sheets. The brass headboard and the white wall behind it were splattered bloodred. Protruding from the center of the stain in the sheets was the handle of a kitchen knife. The entire length of its blade was buried in the mattress.

Sarah stood there, stunned, unable to move. All she could think of was Patches, jumping from her arms and running back toward the house.

30

SARAH WALKED SLOWLY INTO the bedroom, afraid of what she might see, afraid of finding Patches.

She stopped at the foot of the bed. The knife handle looked obscene, protruding from the red-stained sheets. She was fairly certain that the knife was one of her own, and she shuddered to think of how it had been used.

Now Sarah noticed an odor in the room. She recognized the smell, but it seemed totally out of place. Then she looked more closely at the red-stained sheet and the red spatters on the wall. They were *too* red.

"Sarah."

She turned as Alex came into the room. He took her by the arm and gently pulled her toward the doorway.

"I didn't want you to see this," he said, "until I had a chance to prepare you for it."

"Is it paint?"

"Yes." He closed the bedroom door.

"I thought it was blood," she said with disgust.

"So did I." He put his arm around her. "I guess that was the idea."

"I mean, I thought she'd— I thought it was Patches."

"Patches is in the kitchen," he said.

The big cat was under the table. Officer Bauer was politely trying to push him away.

"I'm allergic," he said in apology as Alex and Sarah entered the room. He brushed cat hairs from his pant leg.

Sarah took Patches upstairs to Brian's room, happily squeezing him until his green eyes nearly bulged out of his furry head. Brian seemed even more happy than Sarah.

"Can I take him outside? He likes to play in the snow."

"No, honey, not now."

"Why not, Mom?"

"Just wait for a little while, Brian, okay? Then we can all go out together."

Sarah was thinking about the knife stuck in the bed. It *had* to have been Christine, she thought. Except Frank O'Hara had told them that Christine was dead. Well, *whoever* had done that could still be in the neighborhood. Sarah was beginning to feel as if they were prisoners in their own home. First she'd been afraid to go to her shop, and now she was afraid to let Brian outside alone.

"You can take Patches downstairs and watch TV if you like," she said.

Sarah left Brian in the family room and found Alex and the two policemen waiting for her in the kitchen. She saw that Alex had brought in the sacks of groceries and set them on the counter. Alex told her that Officer Eastly had contacted Detective Yarrow on the police radio and had let him talk briefly to Yarrow.

"I told him we'd been vandalized and that Mrs. Green had terrorized you in your shop yesterday. He said he already knew about Green. I also told him that, well, that you still thought this woman was Christine."

Sarah gave him a brief smile. She knew that he was standing up for her, even in the face of his conviction—and the conviction of the authorities—that Christine Helstrum was dead.

"I'd like to ask you a few questions," Officer Bauer said to Sarah. He straightened the form in front of him and clicked open his pen.

Sarah sat at the table and told him what had happened after she'd returned home from the grocery store.

"Did you notice anyone in the neighborhood as you drove up to the house? Anyone unusual."

"No."

"Any strange cars parked in the street?"

Sarah shook her head no.

"Did you open the back door when you came in?"

"No."

"And as I told you before," Alex said, "it was locked when I left the house."

"Then it looks like whoever did this picked open the lock. We didn't see any signs of forced entry, no scratches around the lock or the doorframe."

"Is it that easy to open a lock?" Sarah asked.

"For some people, yes," Officer Eastly said. "Especially a lock like that."

He was standing against the counter. Sarah had to turn in her chair to face him.

"What do you mean, 'a lock like that'?"

"A spring lock. What you want is a dead bolt. Much tougher to open."

Sarah looked at Alex.

"They're not too difficult to install yourself if you're handy with tools," Eastly added.

"I'll call a locksmith," Alex said.

Officer Bauer had a few more questions for Sarah. Then he said that he and Eastly were going to look around outside while they waited for Detective Yarrow. Alex phoned several locksmiths, but all of them were either closed on weekends or too busy to install any locks today. He found one, though, that could do the job tomorrow, Sunday, if Alex didn't mind paying double time.

"I don't care what it costs," Alex said. "Just get out here as soon as you can." He hung up and looked at Sarah. "Not till tomorrow."

"What about tonight? Are we safe in here?"

"I'm sure we are," Alex said. He turned away from her toward the doorway, but not before she'd read the uncertainty in his face. "I guess we should start cleaning up the living room," he said. Then he closed his eyes and shook his head. "And the bedroom."

"Why don't we eat lunch first," Sarah said. "It's getting late in the day."

"I'm not very hungry."

"Neither am I, but I'll bet Brian is. Anyway, we should try to eat."

While Sarah made toasted cheese sandwiches, Alex went upstairs, pulled the sheets from the bed, and brought them down in a bundle. He set the knife on the counter and took the sheets outside to the trash. Sarah saw now that it was a boning knife, exactly like one of hers. Then she searched through the drawers until she was certain that the knife *was* hers. She wondered if perhaps Alex shouldn't have touched it, in case the police wanted to take fingerprints.

Or maybe they only do that for serious crimes, she thought with a grim smile. After all, we've only been vandalized.

They finished lunch just before the arrival of Detectives Yarrow and Keene.

Almost immediately Alex released his pent-up anger and directed it at Yarrow. He blamed him for what had happened in Sarah's shop and in their home.

"If your men had stayed at the shop as they were supposed to," Alex said bitterly, "they could've arrested Mrs. Green and she'd be in jail now and none of this would've happened."

"Not necessarily." Yarrow spoke calmly, almost gently. "First of all, the officer staking out your wife's shop left to answer an emergency call less than two blocks away—an armed robbery in progress. As a matter of fact, he interrupted the robbery and arrested the—"

"I don't give a damn about that," Alex said.

"Alex . . ." Sarah put her hand on his arm.

"I'm just trying to explain to you, Mr. Whitaker, that yours is not our only case."

Alex ground his teeth and said nothing.

"And even if Mrs. Green had been stopped before she entered your wife's shop," Yarrow went on, "we could've brought her in for questioning, perhaps, but that's all. We certainly couldn't have arrested her."

"Why not?"

"Because we have no proof that she's committed a crime." He turned to Sarah. "Now, Mrs. Whitaker, I understand that you still believe this woman, Mrs. Green, may be Christine Helstrum."

"Well, yes, except . . ."

Yarrow raised his eyebrows and waited.

"Except," Sarah said, "she's supposedly dead, isn't she?"

"We're still waiting for positive confirmation."

"What do you mean?" Alex was incredulous. "I thought her body had been positively identified."

"I talked to the Albany police today," Yarrow said. "They're ninety-nine percent sure the body is Helstrum's. However, they weren't able to get a positive ID on her fingerprints because of the condition of the body. Right now they're trying for a match with her dental records."

"So this woman could be her." Alex's anger had left him. Now his face was pale. "Christine could be alive."

"It's doubtful," Yarrow said, "but possible. Mrs. Whitaker, I'd like you to look at these photos again."

He turned to Keene, who handed him a manila envelope. Yarrow withdrew two photographs and gave them to Sarah. They were the same pictures she'd seen several days ago: Christine Helstrum, front and profile, blank expression, close-cropped hair, droopy eyelid. However, the eyelid seemed less noticeable in the photo than it had when she'd stood face-to-face with Mrs. Green. Sarah tried to imagine this face with longer hair and heavy makeup. She shook her head slowly.

"I . . . I don't know," she said. "I *think* it's her. I just can't be certain."

Yarrow nodded and took the photos from her.

"Now what?" Some of the bitterness had crept back into Alex's voice.

"I've got Officers Bauer and Eastly canvassing the neighborhood," Yarrow said. "Maybe one of your neighbors saw something that will lead us to Mrs. Green, or whoever this woman is. Also, I'm putting a twenty-four-hour watch on your house. That's about all we can do for now."

After the detectives had left, Sarah and Alex went to work in the living room.

They tipped the tree upright and secured it in the stand. Then they got down on hands and knees and began sorting through the demolished presents, which were sprinkled with pine needles, strands of tinsel, and pieces of broken ornaments.

"This may take a while," Alex said, trying to keep his voice light.

Sarah smiled. "We've got all weekend."

They found precious little that was not damaged. When Alex uncovered a batch of ripped pages from the rare history book, he knew immediately what they were. He hugged Sarah and thanked her for buying him the book, as happily as if it were Christmas morning and the book were whole. And they both smiled when he held up an undamaged pair of lavender bikini briefs.

Their smiles did not last long, though, as they began gathering up slashed clothing and smashed toys, stuffing it all into plastic trash bags. They picked up the ornaments that had survived the crash and replaced them on the tree. Then Alex straightened the strings of lights and the dangling tinsel while Sarah vacuumed the carpet. When they were finished, they plugged in the lights and stood back.

"As good as new," Alex said.

"Not quite. No presents."

"Only temporarily. Look, tomorrow or Monday I'll give our insurance agent an estimate for all of this, and then we'll all go out on a shopping spree. We'll make this a Christmas to remember."

"It's already one I'd like to forget," Sarah said.

Alex put his arms around her. "We're safe and we're together. That's all that matters."

They brought Brian down to the living room. When he saw the tree, his eyes lit up like blue-colored lights.

"All right! It's just like it was!"

He walked up to it and touched a shiny ornament, a strand of tinsel, the tip of a branch—just to make sure it was real. His face fell, though, when he stepped back and looked under the tree. It was bare now except for the cotton snow.

"Don't worry, pumpkin," Sarah said, coming up behind him and crossing her arms over his chest. "There will be more presents under there than before."

He tipped his head back into her abdomen and looked up at her, smiling.

"Really, Mom?"

"Really."

Later Sarah and Alex went upstairs to the master bedroom. It smelled of paint. Alex opened the windows, letting in cold air.

Sarah examined the mattress and saw that the red paint had soaked through the sheets, leaving a plate-sized stain. In the center of the stain was a small slit where the knife had been thrust, giving the illusion that the mattress had bled after it had been stabbed.

"What are we going to do about this?"

"The mattress?" Alex said. "Junk it, I suppose. And we can paint the wall. And the headboard?" He touched the paint spatters on the brass work at the head of the bed. "I think I can find something that will remove this without harming the brass. But let's deal with it tomorrow, okay? I've had enough excitement for one day."

"*You've* had enough?" Sarah said, and they both laughed.

Later that night Sarah took Brian up to his room and read with him from Frank L. Baum. When his eyes began to droop, she tucked him in bed, kissed him good-night, and left him with Patches curled up on the end of his bed. She left his door ajar in case the cat might want out later. Then she went down the hallway to prepare the guest bedroom for herself and Alex.

Brian was dreaming that someone had come into his room, and when he opened his eyes, there really *was* someone in his room, standing just inside the doorway.

Or is this still part of my dream? he wondered.

"Timothy?" the woman said softly.

Brian could tell that it was a woman even though the room was dark. He could see her outline in the doorway. She was *shaped* like a woman, and she had long hair. Not as long as his mother's, though. And her voice—when she'd said that one word—had been deeper than his mother's voice, so he knew for sure it wasn't she.

"Are you asleep?" she whispered, and walked quietly toward his bed.

I *am* asleep, he thought, and he almost said so.

He knew he was asleep, because he knew that some stranger couldn't just walk right into his room like this. Still, he was afraid. He knew that even in his dreams bad things could happen if you weren't careful. So he closed his eyes almost all the way and held still and pretended to be asleep.

"Are you ready to come with me?"

The woman stood now at the foot of his bed. He saw her only as a shadowy figure, her arms at her sides. From one hand dangled a long, narrow object that glinted dully in the meager light.

"The cat," she whispered. "They let the *cat* sleep in here?"

Brian watched her shake her head from side to side.

"Cats smother babies," she said quietly, viciously. "They strangle babies with their tails."

She reached down and touched Patches. Brian could feel the big cat purring, even through the sheet and the blankets.

"Bad kitty," the woman whispered, and began to stroke the cat. Then she slowly raised her other hand, the hand holding the long, narrow object.

Brian could see the object more clearly now—his mother's butcher knife. He nearly asked the woman if she would please give him the knife so he could return it to his mother, because he knew she'd been looking for it—in fact, she'd even blamed *him* for taking it. But he said nothing. He was certain now that he must be dreaming, and he thought that if he spoke to the woman then the dream would become real. And he knew—although he wasn't quite sure why—that he didn't want this dream to become real. He held perfectly still and kept his mouth closed.

The woman raised the knife to chest level, then tucked it under her left arm. She leaned down and gently lifted Patches from the bed.

"Bad kitty," she said softly.

She held the cat to her chest as if it were a baby. And then, petting the cat with long, gentle strokes, she turned and walked from the room.

Sarah awoke to a scream.

She sat up in bed, the high-pitched wail still echoing in her brain. She strained to hear more, but the room was dark and silent. Alex snored softly beside her.

It must have been a dream, she thought.

She got out of bed, pulled on her robe, and stepped into the hall. For a moment she was disoriented—the head of the stairs was straight ahead instead of to her left as it should have been. Then she remembered that they'd been sleeping in the guest bedroom.

She walked around the dark stairwell and past the master bedroom to Brian's room.

The door was slightly ajar, just the way she'd left it. She peeked in and saw her son stir once in his sleep and then lie still. Sarah walked back toward the guest room. She stopped at the stairwell. With one hand on the railing, she peered down into the darkness and listened.

Silence.

She stood there for several minutes, until she was certain that nothing was moving downstairs.

31

IN THE MORNING SARAH BANGED her elbow getting out of bed.

It was the first time she'd slept on the fold-out couch, and she'd forgotten about the metal braces running along the sides. She sat on the edge of the bed, rubbing her elbow and muttering under her breath, careful not to wake Alex. Since this was Sunday, she thought he might want to sleep in.

She walked down the hall to the master bedroom and opened the door. The room was cold, but Sarah decided to leave the window open because she could still smell paint. She examined the mattress and wondered if they would have to junk it, as Alex had said. She wondered if they would even *want* to keep it.

After she'd showered and dressed, she looked in on Brian. He was just waking up.

"Good morning, pumpkin."

She went over and kissed him on the forehead.

"Morning."

"How are you this morning?"

"I had a bad dream."

"You did?" She sat beside him on the bed.

"A woman came in my room and took Patches away."

Sarah glanced around the room. The cat was not in sight.

Of course he's not in here, she thought; that's why I left the door open.

She smoothed the hair on Brian's head.

"I peeked in on you last night," she said. "Maybe I walked into your dream."

"Can you do that?"

"Maybe."

"Did you take Patches?"

"No, honey. He's probably downstairs. And he's probably hungry for his breakfast."

"I'm hungry, too, Mom."

"Then why don't you get up and get dressed and we'll all eat together, okay?"

"Okay."

Sarah met Alex in the hallway.

"Aren't you going to sleep in?" she asked.

"On that torture device? I feel like I've slept on a bag full of auto parts."

Sarah laughed. "Tell me about it," she said; then, "I'm going to start breakfast."

"Sounds great. I'll take a quick shower and be down in ten minutes."

Alex kissed her on the cheek, then went into the master bedroom. As Sarah reached the head of the stairs, she heard the phone ringing. She heard it in stereo—from the stairwell in front of her and from Alex's den to her right. She answered in the den.

It was Frank O'Hara.

"I hope I'm not calling you too early," he said. "I dialed your number before I thought about the two-hour time difference."

"It's okay. Is . . . there something wrong?" Sarah guessed that he wasn't calling just to be sociable.

"Yes." His voice sounded hollow in the receiver. "Perhaps I should talk to your husband first."

"He's in the shower. Please. What is it?"

O'Hara paused before he spoke.

"A friend of mine with the Albany police just called me. He said they've now compared the dental charts of Christine Helstrum with the body found in the woods near the hospital."

Sarah held her breath, afraid of what he might say.

"The body was not Christine's," O'Hara said.

Sarah's breath came out in a rush, as if she'd been slammed against a wall.

"Are you— I mean, are they certain?"

"I'm afraid so. When the dental charts didn't match, the police ran a computer check of missing persons. They found a very close match, a housewife from Glens Falls who'd been missing for over two weeks. They brought the husband in early this morning, and he positively identified the body by a birthmark on her back. Her name was Patricia Ann Green."

"Green," Sarah muttered. "Mrs. Green."

"The autopsy revealed that she'd been strangled. The police believe that Christine murdered her, exchanged clothes with the corpse, then took Mrs. Green's car."

O'Hara continued to talk—something about the Colorado Springs police and an APB on the car—but Sarah heard only a jumble of words. All she could think about was that Christine was alive and somewhere nearby. And she'd murdered a woman to get here.

It's Alex she wants, Sarah thought. She could've murdered me in the shop, but she was just playing . . .

"Mrs. Whitaker? Are you still there?"

"I'm . . . yes. Please, hold on. I'll get my husband."

Sarah hurried down the hall to the master bedroom. Alex was coming out of the bathroom with one towel wrapped around his waist and another draped around his neck. He stopped abruptly when he saw the look on Sarah's face.

"Christine is alive," she said. "It's been her all along."

"How . . . ?"

"Frank O'Hara. He's on the phone."

Alex held her eyes a moment longer, then brushed past her. Sarah followed slowly and slumped in a chair in the den. She wondered what she and Alex and Brian should do. Should they move out of their house? Should they try to hide until Christine was caught? *Could* they hide?

Alex said good-bye and hung up the phone.

"Where will we go?"

Alex turned to face her. "What do you mean?" Then he seemed to notice for the first time that he was draped only in towels. He folded his arms across his chest for warmth.

"I mean, we've got to get out of here," she said.

"We're not going to run away, Sarah. This is our *home*."

"But, Alex—"

"We're staying," he said firmly, then gently pulled Sarah to her feet and held her. "Look, the police are watching the house around the clock. We're safe here . . ." He paused. When he spoke again, his voice was weak. "That is, you and Brian are safe. It's me she's after. Maybe I should leave, draw her away from you two until—"

"No," Sarah said, "absolutely not." She stood up and put her arms around his waist. "We're a *family*, Alex, and leave or stay, we do it together."

He started to protest, but Sarah put her finger to his lips.

"We stay together, Alex, and that's that."

He smiled briefly.

"Now I'll go down and get breakfast started."

Alex went to the bedroom to get dressed, and Sarah walked down the stairs. She passed through the foyer and the short hallway to the kitchen. Sunlight was streaming in at an angle from the window. It fell across the countertop and the floor, and it just barely touched the corner of the kitchen table.

Sarah stopped dead still.

There was something lying in the center of the table, something that shouldn't have been there, something that Sarah didn't recognize. At least for a moment. But when the realization finally struck her, she felt her stomach twist, and she nearly vomited.

The table was smeared with blood. The ropelike thing lying in the center was about a foot long, orange and white. And furry.

It was the tail of the cat.

Sarah clamped her jaws and forced back the bile in her throat. She remembered what Brian had told her this morning—his "dream" about a woman coming into his room and taking Patches. She yelled for Alex.

Seconds later he was behind her, his hands on her shoulders.

"What's the matter? What—"

His eyes followed her shaky finger to the table.

"Oh, my God."

He let her go and stepped around her to the table. She saw that he'd had time to put on a shirt and pants, but not socks. He stared at the severed tail, then reached down, but did not quite touch it. When he lifted his head to look at Sarah, his face was twisted in pain.

"Brian told me he had a dream last night," Sarah said. "A woman came into his room and took Patches. Alex, she was up there while we were asleep. She could have—"

"Keep Brian out of here," he said, his voice trembling with rage. He started to walk past her, then stopped and held her by the shoulders. "I swear to you, Sarah, this is where it ends."

He stomped down the hall and across the foyer and threw open the front door. He stood for a moment, as if he couldn't decide whether to shout for the police or go out and look for them. Then he slammed the door and stalked back to the kitchen to use the phone.

Sarah started up the stairs and met Brian coming down.

"Hi, baby. Let's—"

She stopped herself from saying, "Let's go in the family room and watch cartoons." What if they walked in there and found Patches . . . ?

"Let's go back up to your room," she said.

"Why?"

"Just because," she said. "Because we'll do something special today and have breakfast right in your room and, um, and we'll bring in the TV set from your dad's den and watch cartoons together. Okay?"

"Why, Mom?"

"Brian, please, let's go upstairs."

Sarah led him up to his room, sat him on the edge of the bed, then brought in the small color set from Alex's den. She made room for it on Brian's desk, plugged it in, and turned it on.

"Which channel?" she asked, trying to keep her voice light.

Brian was staring down at his shoes. "I don't know," he mumbled.

Sarah flipped the dial until she found what appeared to be a blurry Big Bird. She fiddled with the built-in antenna until the image was fairly sharp.

"There," she said. "Now I'll go down and get our breakfast, and you stay up here and wait for me, okay?"

"Mom?"

"What?"

"Did I do something wrong?"

"Oh, no, baby." She sat beside him on the bed. "We're just going to have breakfast up here today, that's all. I'll be back in a few minutes."

She heard Alex talking loudly, almost shouting, even before she reached the stairs. She started down and saw him leading Officers Bauer and Eastly toward the kitchen.

"I already searched down here," he shouted. "There's no sign of her *or* the cat."

When she got to the kitchen, she saw that Alex had covered the table with a large towel. He was standing in the laundry room with the two policemen.

"I found the back door open," Alex said. Some of the volume was gone from his voice, but Sarah could tell that he was still very angry. At least he was displaying anger. She guessed that he probably felt as sick as she did. "And it was closed and locked when we went to bed last night. Where the hell were you guys?"

"There was a car out front all night," Bauer said. "Whoever did this—"

"We *know* who the hell did it," Alex said. "Christine Helstrum."

"—probably slipped through one of the neighboring yards," Bauer finished.

The men came into the kitchen. Eastly went to the table and began to lift the towel. Sarah turned her back, not wanting to see again what lay beneath it. She stared out the window over the sink, then gave a start.

"Alex!"

He rushed to her side and looked out the window.

There on the driveway was Patches. The big cat was curled up in the sun, hard against the garage door, dazedly licking his stub, which was all that remained of his tail.

Sarah and Alex hurried out the back door, leaving the two policemen in the kitchen.

They tried to approach Patches without startling him, but when the cat saw them, he moved weakly across the driveway toward the front of the house. Sarah and Alex followed, calling his name. The cat stopped several times, curling up to lick his wound. But each time they came near, Patches moved away.

Finally, after they'd nearly circled the house, Patches let Sarah touch him, then pick him up. She could see that only an inch or two remained of his tail. There was little blood. The fur around the end of the stub was matted, wet with saliva. The tip of the tailbone poked through the fur like a tiny white eye.

"We've got to get him to the vet," Sarah said.

"I'll do it. You stay here with Brian."

They took Patches inside, where Bauer and Eastly were waiting patiently. Alex put some towels in the cat carrier, and Sarah laid the cat inside. She held open the back screen door and then the garage door as Alex carried the cat out to the car. He drove away, and Sarah went back inside.

"Cats are pretty tough," Eastly said. "I'm sure he's going to be okay."

Sarah nodded a thank-you. Her eyes fell to the towel covering the table.

"Perhaps we can talk in another room," Bauer said. "We just need to ask you a few questions."

"Please," Sarah said. "I have to fix breakfast for my son."

They stood aside while she made up a tray for Brian—an apple turnover, milk, and orange juice—and carried it upstairs.

Brian was so engrossed in his cartoon that he hardly noticed her enter. Sarah saw that he'd changed the channel from *Sesame Street*—the TV screen was now filled by an ominous black figure waving a sword. Brian was holding his cardboard sword. He pointed it at the screen.

"Lord Doom," Brian explained. "And that's the Sword of Power."

"I see," Sarah said, wondering how she was going to explain about Patches. She handed him the glass of orange juice. "It's sort of like yours."

"Sort of," Brian said.

Sarah remembered that his sword had been traced from her butcher knife. The missing butcher knife. She wondered if it had been used to butcher Patches. She set the tray on the bed next to Brian.

"Have you got everything you need?" she asked.

"Uh-huh." His attention was on the TV set.

"I'm going downstairs for a while, but I'll be back up in a little bit, okay?"

Brian nodded without moving his eyes.

Sarah sat in the living room with Bauer, while Eastly went outside to look around the house. Bauer squatted uncomfortably on the edge of a stuffed chair and used an end table for a writing surface. Sarah told him everything that had happened since last night—waking to a scream, hearing about Brian's "dream," getting the phone call from Frank O'Hara, and finding the cat's tail on the kitchen table. She was interrupted by the phone ringing. She glanced at her watch. It had been nearly half an hour since Alex had left.

"Excuse me," Sarah said to Bauer.

She went in the kitchen and answered the phone.

"I'm at the vet's," Alex said. "He says Patches will be okay."

"Thank God."

"He's lost a lot of blood, but the vet says it's not critical. He's giving him a shot to fight infection and another one to help him build back his blood."

"Does he have to stay there overnight?"

"I don't know yet. In any case, it will take me an hour or so to get home. There's something I . . . I have to do something first."

"What?"

"I'll explain later. Good-bye, hon."

He hung up.

32

SARAH REPLACED THE RECEIVER just as Officer Eastly came in the back door.

"Where does that lead?" he asked, motioning with his head across the laundry room.

"The basement."

"I'd like to take a look down there."

"Please, go ahead."

Eastly unbolted the basement door, and Sarah went back to the living room, where Bauer was waiting. She finished telling him about this morning, and then they sat and waited for Eastly. Bauer looked uncomfortable. He cleared his throat.

"You did a good job fixing the Christmas tree," he said.

"Thank you."

"It looks very nice."

"Thanks. Oh, would you like some coffee? I didn't even think to ask."

"No, thanks."

They sat in awkward silence until Eastly returned.

"Nothing down there," he said. "Who nailed the windows shut?"

"My husband."

"When?"

"Yesterday."

He nodded. Bauer stood.

"I'm going to put in a call to Detective Yarrow," Bauer said. "He may want to come out here today. In any case, we're going to be right outside, at least until your husband gets home."

"Thank you," Sarah said. She walked them to the front door, then looked back toward the kitchen. "What should I do with . . . that?"

"You can dispose of it," Officer Eastly said gently. "Or if you'd like, I'll do it for you."

"No," Sarah said. "But thank you."

After they'd left, Sarah stood at the kitchen table for a moment, then scooped up the towel and its contents and carried it out the back door. She stuffed the bundle in the trash barrel. Back in the kitchen she used a can of cleanser and a damp sponge to wash the dried blood from the table. She noticed a deep scratch in the table's surface. She felt a brief wave of nausea, realizing that the gash must have been made as the cat's tail was chopped off.

"Mom?"

Sarah turned to see Brian standing in the doorway.

"Can I go outside now and play?"

She went to him. "Honey, let's wait until your dad gets home, okay?"

"Where did he go?"

Sarah searched for a lie.

Enough lying, she thought.

"Come into the living room with me," she said gently.

They sat together on the couch, and for the first time this morning Sarah noticed the smell of the Christmas tree. She inhaled deeply, drinking in the scent of pine. It soothed her, at least momentarily. Then she saw the remnants of a shattered ornament dangling from a lower branch.

"I need to tell you something about Patches," she said.

Brian looked up at her, worry on his face.

"What's wrong?"

"Patches got hurt, and your dad took him to the cat hospital."

Brian opened his mouth to cry out, but Sarah spoke before he could.

"It's going to be okay," she said. "He called me from the hospital to say that Patches is all right and they'll both be coming home soon."

"What happened to Patches?" Brian's eyes were filled with tears.

"Someone . . . we don't know exactly, Brian. His tail, part of his tail got cut off, but he's—"

"No!"

"He's going to be okay and he won't feel any pain and he'll play with you just like—"

She stopped because Brian had buried his face in her sweater and was sobbing. Sarah held him tightly and stroked his hair.

"It's okay, baby. He's okay now."

"That woman did it," Brian said between sobs, and Sarah felt herself stiffen. "She took Patches out of my room and cut off his tail."

Sarah hugged Brian tighter. "She'll never do anything like that again, baby. If she ever comes near this house again, I'll . . . take care of her."

What exactly would I do? Sarah wondered.

"Come on," she said, "let's wipe away those tears. When Patches gets home, he'll need an extra lot of love."

An hour later Sarah heard Alex's car in the driveway.

She and Brian stood at the door as Alex carried in Patches. The cat looked drowsy, and he could barely manage to meow when Brian petted him. His stub of a tail was wrapped in a white bandage.

"There, there, Patches. You'll be okay." Brian looked up at Alex. "He will be okay, won't he, Dad?"

"Sure he will. He's just tired now."

"Can he stay in my room?"

"Okay, but he needs to rest."

"I won't bother him, honest."

"Sarah, would you?" Alex asked. "I have to get something from the car."

Sarah took Patches upstairs, with Brian carefully monitoring her every move. When she went back down, Alex was going into the kitchen carrying a small, heavy-looking paper sack. He set it on the table with a thunking sound.

"We need this, Sarah," he said, opening the sack.

She remembered now that a locksmith was supposed to come to the house today.

"Are those locks?"

"No," he said, and pulled out a gun.

Sarah stared as if there were a live snake in his hand. Alex set the gun on the table.

"Where did you get that?" She did not hide her disgust.

"At a sporting-goods store," he said evenly. He reached in the sack and lifted out a small, heavy red-and-white box. Sarah saw the words ".38 Caliber—Super-X" printed in bold letters.

"A gun, Alex?"

"Yes, a gun. A thirty-eight caliber Smith and Wesson revolver, to be precise, capable of stopping Christine Helstrum."

He folded up the sack and laid it flat on the table.

"I can't believe this," she said.

"Believe it." His face looked grim, almost haggard.

"Alex, what's happening to you? To us?"

"*She's* what's happening, Sarah. And until the police arrest her or until she's dead, this gun stays in the house."

"Do you think you could actually use that thing on someone?"

"Not on 'someone,' " he said. "On Christine. And you're damn right I could. Sarah, she was in Brian's room. She had a knife." He shook his head. "It won't happen again. If she tries it, I'll stop her. And if I have to . . . I swear to God, Sarah, if I have to, I'll kill her."

He picked up the gun and the box of shells and walked out. Sarah started to go after him when the phone rang. It was Janet Teesdale, Eddy's mother.

"We're going to the Cheyenne Mountain Zoo today," she said happily, "and Eddy asked if Brian could go with us. The temperature's supposed to be in the fifties and—"

"No, Janet, we can't, I . . . we just can't. I'm sorry."

She hung up.

We're prisoners in here, she thought.

She went upstairs to find Alex. He was just leaving the guest room. She followed him into the master bedroom. It still looked devastated to Sarah, with red paint spattered on the wall and the brass headboard and the mattress marred by a dark stain and the cut of a knife. The smell of paint, though, was gone.

Alex walked to the window and closed it.

"We need to get rid of it, Alex."

"The mattress? I agree. We—"

"No, the gun."

"Sarah." For a moment he looked angry. Then his expression softened, so much so that Sarah thought he might cry. "There are only two things in this life that matter to me," he said. "You and Brian. This woman, she . . . I don't know if I could stop her without—"

"But the police—"

"The police? What have they done so far?"

He walked past her and stood by the bed, staring blankly down at the ruined mattress.

"Maybe I'm being selfish," he said, not looking at her, "but I know what it feels like to lose a wife and a son. And to lose them to *her*." Now he raised his head and faced her. "I know exactly what she's capable of, Sarah. I won't let that happen again. I'm keeping the gun."

He held her eyes for a moment, then looked down at the mattress.

Neither of them spoke.

Finally, Alex said, "Would you help me with this?"

Together they hauled the big mattress into the hallway. It was heavy and awkward, and it took all their strength to wrestle it down the stairs and out the front door. They dragged it around the walkway and leaned it against the house near the trash barrel. Sarah felt slightly winded from the effort. But she felt good, having worked off a lot of tension.

"I wonder if we have any white paint," Alex said.

They found what they needed in the garage, then carried it all up to the bedroom—paint, brushes, a roller and pan, drop cloths, and masking tape. The room had been painted less than a year ago, so they decided to paint only the one wall, carefully masking it off at the corners. While they worked, they discussed getting a burglar alarm, or even a large dog. Neither of them mentioned the gun.

By the time they were finished painting and cleaning up, it was well past noon and they were both famished.

Alex volunteered to fix lunch while Brian took Sarah outside to show her the snow boy and snow lady they'd made yesterday. When they came in, Sarah was thankful to see that Alex had covered the table with a checkered cloth. They sat down to eat.

They were still eating when Detective Yarrow arrived. Alex invited him to join them.

"No, thanks."

"Some coffee?" Sarah asked.

"Yes, please, if it's no trouble." He sat down next to Brian. "How you doing?"

"Okay. My cat got its tail cut off."

He'd said it almost proudly, and Sarah nearly smiled.

"Brian, maybe you should go upstairs and see if Patches is okay."

After Brian had gone, Yarrow said, "We found her car."

"Christine's?"

"The one she took from Patricia Green, yes. It was parked in the street three blocks from here. We're doing a door-to-door search of the area. Officer Eastly told me he searched your basement, is that correct?"

"Yes," she said.

"How about the attic? Eastly didn't mention that."

Sarah looked at Alex.

"Do you folks have an attic?"

"I bought a lock for it yesterday," Alex said, "but I forgot all about it. I didn't put it on."

Alex got the flashlight, and all three went upstairs. Yarrow climbed the wooden steps. He raised his head into the dark, square hole and clicked on the flashlight.

"There's something back there."

"It's just a rolled-up carpet," Alex said. "I've already checked it."

"Did you look inside? Or unroll it?"

"I . . . no."

Yarrow disappeared into the attic. Sarah could hear him moving toward the rear of the house. A few minutes later he came back down, shaking his head and brushing dust from his suit jacket. Alex raised the steps and closed the attic door, then got a chair from his den. Yarrow steadied the chair as Alex stood on it and fastened the new padlock in place.

"I heard of a case," Yarrow said as they descended the stairs, "that happened right here in Colorado. It was fifty years ago or so. The widow of a murdered man kept hearing noises at night, and she thought it was the ghost of her dead husband. This went on for months after his death. It turned out that the murderer had been hiding in the attic all that time, and what the widow had heard was him sneaking down at night to steal food from the kitchen."

Sarah and Alex exchanged glances.

"What?"

Sarah told Yarrow about the missing food.

"Let's take another look in your basement," he said.

Yarrow and Alex were still in the basement when Sarah answered the doorbell. It was the locksmith, a young bearded man carrying a heavy toolbox. Sarah led him through the house to the laundry room. He asked her to show him the nearest electrical outlet.

"I'll need to do some drilling," he explained. "Also, do you want the old lock left in or taken out?"

"Didn't my husband tell you that on the phone?"

"No, ma'am. But . . ."

"What?"

"The more locks, the better, I always say."

"Then leave it in."

Alex and Yarrow came up from the basement, and Alex bolted the door. Sarah walked with them to the foyer.

"Thanks for coming," Alex said. "And I'm sorry about blowing up at you yesterday. I know you're doing all you can."

"I can understand your feelings. Try not to worry. If Christine Helstrum shows her face again," he said, "we'll get her. We'll get her, anyway."

Yarrow spoke with confidence, but Sarah still felt terrified. Christine had already proved that she could sneak into their house in spite of locks and police.

That night all four slept in the guest bedroom, Brian tucked between Sarah and Alex and Patches curled up in a basket in the corner of the room.

Sarah did not sleep easy. She felt as if she were waiting for something to happen, as if she *knew* something would happen and it was only a question of when. That Alex had insisted they all sleep together proved to her that he felt the same way.

We're withdrawing, she thought. First into the house and now into a single room.

There was something else that made her uneasy—the gun.

She had always hated guns, particularly handguns. To her there was only one purpose for a pistol: to kill another human being. And now they had a gun in their house. She had seen Alex with it earlier this evening. He'd been sitting at his desk in the den with the gun before him. Next to it had been an open box of cartridges. Apparently he'd just loaded the weapon, because the cylinder was open, and Sarah could see six shiny brass disks. She'd watched him slowly close the cylinder until it clicked into place, and then she'd walked quickly away. She remembered how she'd handled a similar gun last Monday at the sporting-goods store and how she'd hurried away from that one, too.

And now she lay awake, the loaded gun less than two feet from Alex's side of the bed, ready for immediate use. She stared up at the darkness and listened to every creak and groan of the old house.

Then she heard a noise.

It had not been loud, but it had been quite distinct—the scrape of a chair downstairs, as if someone had bumped into it in the dark.

Alex sat up quickly, causing Brian to stir in his sleep and move closer to Sarah.

"Did you hear that?" Alex whispered.

"I heard something. I—"

"Shh." He pulled back the covers and swung his feet to the floor. "Someone's downstairs."

Sarah heard him fumble with the drawer in the nightstand.

"Alex, no. Let's call the police."

She could see his vague outline reach for the lamp and click the switch. The room remained dark.

"She's turned off the electricity," Alex whispered.

He pulled open the drawer and took something out. Sarah hurried out of bed and moved to the doorway, blocking Alex's way. She reached down for his hand and felt something hard and cold. The gun.

"Alex, please don't go down there," she said softly. "Let's call the police and—"

"Call them," he said, then gently but firmly pushed her out of his way.

He moved through the dark doorway toward the head of the stairs. Sarah hesitated for a moment, then ran into the den. She flipped the light switch, and when nothing happened, she stumbled over to the desk in the dark, found the phone, then pulled it toward the window. There was just enough moonlight coming in from this side of the house for her to make out the numbers. She hurriedly punched 911. After one ring, a woman answered.

"This is Sarah Whitaker, and we need the police right away. There's someone—"

Sarah stopped when she heard the scream. It had come from downstairs, and it was unlike anything she'd ever heard before. It was not a scream of fright or of pain. It was a scream of rage—insane, bestial rage.

She dropped the phone and ran for the stairs, hearing the sounds of a struggle even before she got to the banister. She shouted into the darkness below her.

"Alex!"

"Mom?"

Sarah turned to see Brian outlined in the doorway of the guest bedroom.

"Brian, get back in there and shut the door!" she yelled, moving toward him.

He stood still. She shoved him into the room, nearly knocking him down. "Stay in here," she said, and pulled the door closed.

A gunshot.

The sound seemed to echo up the stairwell and off the walls and ceiling, and it sent a shock wave through Sarah's body. She ran to the head of the stairs.

"ALEX!"

His name was swallowed up by the darkness below. Sarah held perfectly still, listening. There was no sound, no movement. She started slowly down the stairs.

When she was halfway down, she could see that the front door stood wide open. Moonlight spilled across the cold tile floor of the foyer. In the center of the floor lay a dark, huddled shape.

There was a moan.

Sarah heard her heart pounding in her ears as she hurried down the stairs and across the foyer to Alex. He was lying facedown, with one knee drawn up under him and his hands clutching the base of his neck. His head was resting in an ever-widening pool of liquid, which looked black in the moonlight.

Sarah quickly knelt beside him and pressed her hand to the wound in the side of his neck. She felt his warm blood run through her fingers as she tried to stop the pulsing flow. She heard a woman's voice screaming for help, a desperate, agonizing cry. It was her own.

33

OFFICERS PEARL AND MAESTAS arrived two minutes later; the paramedics, four minutes after that.

They took Alex away in an ambulance. Sarah and Brian followed in the backseat of a police car, with lights flashing and siren wailing. Maestas drove, while Pearl, her cap off and her blond hair catching the passing night lights, sat half-turned in her seat and spoke through the wire mesh, telling Sarah that everything would be all right, that her husband would be at the hospital in a matter of minutes.

Sarah was numb. Brian clung to her and cried, more from the confusing sights and sounds than from knowledge of what was happening.

Sarah could understand how he felt. She'd looked through the rear window as the police car pulled out of their driveway. Their house had appeared to be under siege. There were police cars in the driveway and in the street, sending red and white lights chasing across the black shrubbery and snow-covered lawn and up the front of the house. Every window in the house was ablaze with interior light, and the front door was wide open as policemen moved in and out of the house. Some of Sarah's neighbors were standing on their front porches, shivering in the cold night, straining for a look. Sarah never wanted to return to that house.

They rushed Alex to the emergency room at Penrose Hospital. Sarah and Brian stood awkwardly in the hallway under bright fluorescent lights. Officer Pearl suggested that they all sit in the waiting room.

"Would you like some coffee?" she asked Sarah.

Sarah nodded yes, and in a few minutes Pearl returned with two steaming paper cups.

"One's black and one's with sugar," she said. "I forgot to ask, and I can drink it either way."

Sarah took the one with sugar. She blew on the hot liquid and then sipped it carefully. Just this small, familiar act made her feel better, gave her some semblance of normalcy. She took another sip and set the cup aside. Brian curled up beside her on the couch and put his head in her lap.

"How long do you think my husband will . . . be in there?"

"I don't know," Pearl said, "but he's in very good hands." She sipped her coffee, then changed the cup from her right hand to her left. "I know how upset you must be, and the last thing you want to do now is talk about what happened. But sometimes it's better to get it out of your system right away. Also, there may be things you would remember now that you might not tomorrow."

Sarah looked down at Brian. He had fallen asleep with one hand tucked under his cheek. He looked so innocent and vulnerable to Sarah that she felt like crying. But she refused to allow herself that luxury. When she spoke, her voice was clear and firm.

"What would you like to know?"

Officer Pearl set aside her cup and got out a notepad and a pen. There wasn't much to say, but Sarah told her everything that had happened from the moment she'd awakened to the noise downstairs to the moment Pearl and Maestas had come through the front doorway, service revolvers in hand.

Pearl thanked Sarah, then went out in the hallway to talk to Maestas. They moved out of Sarah's sight. She sat unmoving, with Brian's head in her lap.

Half an hour passed, and Sarah wanted to stand up, to walk around, to do anything but simply sit and wait. But she didn't want to wake Brian. So she sat. And waited.

An hour later, Pearl came into the waiting room with a young man wearing baggy green pants and a loose-fitting, short-sleeved green shirt. His dark hair was damp and pressed to his forehead, as if he'd just removed a cap.

"Mrs. Whitaker?"

"Yes?" Before she stood, she moved Brian from her lap and placed her coat under his head. He whined in irritation but did not come fully awake.

"I'm Dr. Oakman."

"My husband . . . how is he?"

"His wound is serious, Mrs. Whitaker, but not critical." He explained how the knife blade had entered his body on a downward path beside his neck, just missed the artery, grazed his esophagus without puncturing it, and stopped short of the top of his lung. "The main thing is he's out of danger now. He's going to be all right."

Sarah felt her shoulders slump as the tension drained from her body. "Oh, thank God. Can I see him now?"

"He's still out from the anesthetic. He'll sleep through the night. Tomorrow, you can—"

"I just want to see him, Doctor."

Dr. Oakman paused, then nodded his head. Sarah followed him down the hallway. Pearl stayed behind with Brian.

The room had two beds, but only one was occupied. Alex lay on his back. His eyes were closed, and his face was pale, almost as white as the dressing that covered his neck. Thin plastic tubes snaked around his face and into his nostrils. Beside the bed was a tall metal stand from which dangled a plastic pouch. A tube filled with clear liquid hung down from the pouch and disappeared under a bandage taped to Alex's arm.

Sarah watched his chest slowly rise and fall. She started toward the bed to touch him, to hold him.

Dr. Oakman stopped her.

"He'll be awake tomorrow," he said quietly. "You should go home and get some sleep."

Sarah followed him out of the room. Officer Maestas and Detective Yarrow were waiting in the hallway. Yarrow's hair was slightly askew, and he wore no tie under his overcoat. Sarah guessed he'd recently been asleep in bed. She held out her hand to Oakman.

"Thank you, Doctor, for . . . for saving him."

Oakman nodded, then walked away.

"How is he?" Yarrow asked. He sounded genuinely concerned.

"He'll be all right," Sarah said.

She walked with Yarrow toward the waiting room. Maestas stayed behind.

"Did you . . . did you get her?"

Yarrow shook his head no.

"But how could she get away?" Sarah could hear the strain in her voice. "I thought you were watching the house, the neighboring yards . . ."

"We were."

"And how could she even get *in*?"

"Apparently through the front door."

"That's not what I meant." Sarah's voice was hard.

"I know. I'm sorry. We don't know, Mrs. Whitaker. Somehow she was able to slip past us."

Sarah shook her head in frustration. "She's not human." Then she stopped and grabbed Yarrow's sleeve. "What if she comes *here*?"

"We've considered that," he said. "Officer Maestas will stand guard outside your husband's door all night. And from now on they'll be someone with him until the Helstrum woman is in custody."

Pearl was standing just inside the door of the waiting room when they approached. Brian was still asleep on the couch.

"Thank you for staying with him."

"It's no problem," Pearl said to Sarah.

Yarrow said, "I've arranged to have Officer Pearl be with you and your son tonight," Yarrow said. "She can give you a ride home now if you like."

"Home?" Sarah shook her head. "No, I . . ."

"We've searched it thoroughly and locked it up tight," Yarrow said reassuringly. "Officer Pearl will stay inside with you and—"

Sarah was shaking her head no.

"I don't want to go back there. Not tonight." She looked at Pearl. "It's not that I wouldn't feel safe with you there, but I just—"

"I don't blame you," Pearl said. "I wouldn't want to go there, either. Not tonight."

Sarah and Brian slept that night in a Best Western motel near the hospital. Officer Pearl stayed in the adjoining room, with the door between them open.

When Sarah opened her eyes Monday morning, she was disoriented for a moment until she realized where she was. Then the events of last night came rushing back to her, making her feel sick inside—sick and worried and angry. She was worried about Alex's condition and about all of their safety. And she was filled with hate for Christine Helstrum, who had not just physically injured Alex but who had totally disrupted their lives, perhaps altering their lives forever.

She slid out of bed, careful not to wake Brian. She washed her face in the sink, then rinsed out her mouth with water. It was unsettling not to have at least her toothbrush. When she came out of the bathroom, she noticed that the door between the two rooms was closed. Last night it had been open. She felt a brief moment of panic. Wasn't Officer Pearl supposed to be standing guard?

Sarah parted the heavy drapes on the window and peeked outside.

There was a Colorado Springs police car parked directly in front of their motel door. A black man sat behind the wheel—Officer Eastly. Sarah quickly dressed, putting on the same clothes she'd worn last night. Then she got Brian up and washed and dressed, and they went out into the cold, bright morning.

Eastly got out of the car and held open the rear door.

"How are you folks this morning?"

"Okay, I guess."

Sarah and Brian climbed in the car. It smelled a bit stale inside, but it was warm—Eastly had the engine running and the heater on.

"Where's Officer Pearl?"

"She went off duty at midnight. She'll be back with you around noon."

"Were you out here all night?"

Eastly smiled easily, showing straight yellow-white teeth. Sarah noticed for the first time that he was a handsome man, with even features and smooth skin.

"Me and others, off and on," he said. "Are you hungry?"

"Yeah," Brian said.

"Could you just take us to the hospital?"

"Sure," Eastly said, looking at his watch, "but it's only a little past seven. I don't think they'll let you in your husband's room this early. In the meantime, we can get some breakfast. I'll buy. What do you say?"

"I don't know, I—"

"Can I have pancakes?" Brian put in.

Eastly laughed. "You can have anything you want, my friend."

After they'd eaten at a Village Inn, with Eastly insisting on picking up the tab, they drove to Penrose Hospital.

Eastly led them down the busy corridor. When they neared Alex's room, Sarah saw a policeman standing across the hallway talking to a nurse—flirting with her, Sarah thought, from the coy look on her face. When the policeman saw Eastly, he said something to the nurse, and she walked away.

"This is Mrs. Whitaker," Eastly said.

"Ma'am."

"Anything?" Eastly said.

The cop shook his head no.

"Go ahead on in," Eastly said to Sarah.

Sarah squatted down to face Brian.

"Your dad doesn't feel very well, honey. He might be kind of sleepy, so let's be real quiet in there, okay?"

"Okay, Mom."

Sarah squeezed his hand and opened the door. Alex's bed was raised, and he was sitting up. There was a tray in front of him supporting an empty glass with a trace of orange juice in the bottom. The oxygen tubes were gone, but the intravenous tube was still attached to his arm. He looked over at them and smiled.

"Good morning," he said. His voice was weak.

Brian ran to the bed and hugged him.

"Dad, me and Mom stayed in a motel last night, and it was pretty neat! And then we ate breakfast with a policeman! How come there's a bandage on your neck? Are you going to come home with us now?"

"Brian . . ."

"It's okay," Alex said.

Sarah went to Alex's side, leaned down, and kissed him.

"How do you feel?"

"Not great," he said. "The doctor wants me here for at least another day, maybe two."

"What . . . happened last night? When I heard the gunshot, I thought, hoped even, that maybe you'd . . ."

He gave her a wry smile and shook his head.

"I didn't shoot her, but I think I shot a hole in the wall. The gun went off accidentally when Christine jumped me from behind. The noise, though, might have scared her away. Otherwise . . . Anyway, at least she didn't get the gun. The police have it."

Sarah held his hand, then sat on the edge of the bed.

"I was so frightened, Alex. Even afterward, I was too frightened even to go back in the house. That's why Brian and I stayed in a motel."

Alex glanced at Brian, who was now exploring the room.

"I don't want you to go back to the house," he said. "Not until I can be with you."

"I don't know . . ."

"Well, I do." Alex started to sit up farther. He gritted his teeth and lay back against the raised bed. "Detective Yarrow was in here this morning and said they've found no sign of Christine. She's still out there somewhere. He seems to think we're safe because we've got cops for baby-sitters, but I'm not so sure."

"We've got to at least stop by the house and—"

"No, you *don't.*" He winced from the strain on his vocal cords. "You don't have to go there, Sarah."

"We have to feed Patches," Brian said. He was standing across the room, his back to the window.

"You see?" Sarah smiled at Alex. "We have to feed Patches. And we have to change clothes and maybe brush our teeth."

Now Alex managed a smile.

"Besides," Sarah said, "our baby-sitter will be right there with us."

"Okay, okay. But promise me you won't spend the night in the house until I can be with you."

"I promise," Sarah said.

34

SARAH AND BRIAN SPENT THE morning at the hospital.

Sarah phoned Brian's teacher from a pay phone on the first floor, telling her that Brian was staying home, sick with a cold. Then she bought a game of checkers at the gift shop and brought it upstairs so Alex and Brian could play. Alex was no longer attached to the IV. He got out of bed so that Brian could show him something from the window, but he soon felt dizzy and had to lie back down.

At noon Officer Eastly helped arrange to have a nurse's aide deliver three meals instead of one, and the Whitakers ate lunch in Alex's room.

Officer Pearl relieved Eastly at twelve-thirty. She asked if Sarah wanted to go home.

Sarah nodded. "Just for a little while."

"Sarah . . ." Alex held her hand.

"Just to feed Patches, and pick up a few things. And get our car. I'm sure Officer Pearl doesn't want to be driving us around all over town, and I've got *shopping* to do."

Alex smiled. "Okay, but please be careful." He looked at Pearl.

"I'll be with her all day," she said.

Alex kissed Sarah and Brian good-bye, and they left with Pearl, promising to return later in the afternoon.

Pearl drove them home. The streets were dry, the lawns were white, and the neighborhood looked serene. Sarah kept expecting neighbors to come out on their porches and stare as they glided by in the patrol car. There was a new beige, featureless Ford parked in front of their house. Sarah saw a uniformed policeman sitting behind the wheel. It was Maestas.

Pearl turned into the driveway and stopped near the garage. Maestas walked over and leaned down, and Pearl rolled open the window.

"It's quiet," he said.

"Maybe we should have a look inside before Mrs. Whitaker goes in."

Pearl borrowed Sarah's keys; then she and Maestas walked around to the front of the house.

"Can we go in now, Mom?"

"Pretty soon, hon."

Fifteen minutes later Maestas returned.

"All clear," he said, and walked out to his car.

Sarah and Brian went inside as Pearl held open the door.

Patches was waiting for them, his bandaged stub of a tail erect. Brian hugged the big cat, then lifted him up and carried him to the kitchen. Sarah started to follow him, then stopped when she noticed a brown smear on the floor tiles in the middle of the foyer. She felt her stomach tighten when she realized that it was Alex's blood. It looked as if it had been partly wiped up, perhaps inadvertently, when the paramedics had moved Alex onto the stretcher last night.

"I should've taken care of that," Pearl said, standing beside her. "Can I help you?"

"No, I . . . I'll do it. But I think Brian probably needs some help with the cat food."

They went into the kitchen, and while Pearl assisted Brian,

Sarah partially filled a plastic pail with soapy water. She carried the pail and a sponge out to the foyer, knelt down, and began cleaning the blood from the tiles. Her jaws were clamped tightly shut, both from anger and revulsion.

After she'd finished with the floor, she took Brian upstairs to change into fresh clothes. Brian wanted Pearl to come up, too, so he could show her some of his toys.

A short time later Sarah sat at the kitchen table and made out three lists: presents for Brian, presents for Alex, and damaged items for their insurance claim. The last list was the sum of the first two, plus one king-size mattress.

Sarah phoned the insurance company and requested that a claims form be mailed to them. Then she went up to Brian's room. Brian and Pearl were kneeling on the floor beside a complicated arrangement of small plastic objects connected by a zigzag chute. Brian released a ball into the high end of the chute, starting a chain reaction that ended with a cage dropping on a plastic mouse.

"Neat, huh?"

"Pretty neat."

"Anybody want to go for a ride?" Sarah asked.

Sarah and Brian rode in the Wagoneer, and Pearl followed in the police car. Their first stop was the Mattress Factory on North Academy Boulevard. Pearl sat in the patrol car while Sarah went inside to haggle with a salesman and Brian explored the warehouse-like showroom. Sarah found the mattress she was looking for and bought it with her VISA card. She arranged to have it delivered to the house the next day.

Sarah spent the next few hours in several stores shopping for Alex's gifts. Brian and Pearl dutifully trailed behind. Sarah was very nearly retracing the steps she'd taken last Monday. However, she didn't go to the bookstore, because Alex's history book could not be replaced. And she didn't go to Hobby Town; she'd wait until Alex could be home with Brian.

They drove to the hospital at four.

Alex seemed to be in more pain than in the morning, even though he told Sarah that he felt all right. He said that Dr. Oakman definitely wanted him to stay there two more nights. Sarah winced at the thought of spending the next two nights in a motel. But neither did she relish the idea of her and Brian sleeping alone in their house—even with Officer Pearl on guard downstairs. And, of course, Alex was adamant.

"You're not staying in the house until I'm out of here," he said. "Or until they find Christine."

He went on to say that he'd spoken again with Detective Yarrow. Yarrow had told Alex that they were beginning to think that Christine had left the city, having been scared away by the continued presence of police. However, the police were going to maintain their vigil over the house and the Whitaker family. At least for a while longer.

When Sarah and Brian got home from the hospital, the sun had just slid behind the mountains. The western sky was still light blue, but in the east it was purple, nearly black, as night moved toward them.

Sarah was mildly disturbed to see that Officer Maestas wasn't parked in front of the house. However, Pearl assured her that Maestas was nearby. Still, Sarah was hesitant about taking Brian inside. Pearl told them to wait in the Wagoneer while she went in the house and looked around.

Ten minutes later she came back out and helped Sarah carry the packages inside. They left everything in the living room by the tree. Then Sarah plugged in the lights, which greatly pleased Brian. In fact, it pleased them all. They stood back, admiring the glow of the Christmas tree.

Sarah wondered how long it would be before Alex, and not a

policewoman, stood with them and enjoyed the warmth of this room. And how long, she wondered, before she'd feel at ease in her own home.

She took Brian upstairs and helped him load his backpack with a change of underwear, his toothbrush, and a few toys. Her plan was for them to go out to dinner, spend some time with Alex at the hospital, and then go to the motel without coming here again tonight. But now she remembered all the groceries she'd bought just a few days ago.

She went downstairs and asked Pearl if she'd like a home-cooked meal instead of restaurant food.

"Your place or mine?" Pearl said.

Sarah smiled. "Help me set the table."

She turned toward the cupboards just as the furnace roared to life in the basement. She stood still for a moment, tense, listening. Then she glanced at Pearl and forced a smile.

"It's just the furnace. I guess I'm still jumpy."

"I would be, too," Pearl said.

"You did look down there, didn't you?"

"Tonight? No. The door's bolted, though."

Sarah hesitated, then turned toward the cupboard.

"I'll check it now if you like," Pearl said.

"No, it's . . . okay."

"Hey, it's no problem."

Pearl moved toward the laundry room.

"Wait," Sarah said. "I'll go with you." She smiled nervously. "I just want to reassure myself that everything's nailed tight down there."

Sarah followed Pearl to the basement door. Pearl slid open the bolt, then stopped, frowning. She bent and looked closely at it. She rotated the bolt in its hasp, then slid it closed and rotated it again.

"Is something wrong?"

"Scratches on the bolt," Pearl said.

"I noticed them, too. Is it important?"

Pearl shook her head. She ran the tips of her fingers along the doorframe.

"I don't know," she said. "They were probably caused by the bolt turning."

"That's what I thought."

"It wouldn't hurt to put another lock on this door, though."

Sarah gave herself a mental kick for not thinking about that when the locksmith had been here the day before.

"I'll see to it tomorrow."

"Good," Pearl said, opening the door.

She flipped on the light and descended the stairs. Sarah followed. Pearl had not been down here before, so Sarah found herself announcing the rooms before Pearl opened each door. They checked the furnace room first. Pearl did not hesitate to open the grating of the huge, dead furnace and peer inside.

"It looks like there's cardboard or something in the ducts."

"The workmen blocked them off when they installed the new furnace."

Pearl frowned briefly, then clicked off her flashlight. She and Sarah went out to the hall and began searching the rest of the rooms. When they reached the outside door, Sarah saw how Alex had wedged a length of lumber against it, then driven a large nail directly into the floor to hold it in place. He'd also nailed a board over the broken window in the living room. And he'd pounded nails into the frames of all the other windows. It was a crude job, but it looked secure to Sarah.

"Let's go upstairs and eat," she said.

She turned off the light, and they walked back along the hallway. As they passed the furnace room, Pearl stopped and held out her arm.

"I heard something in there," she said softly.

She put her hand on the doorknob and clicked on her flashlight, which Sarah now noticed was as large and heavy as a club. Pearl swung open the door, then gave a start.

"I saw a mouse," she said in disgust.

Pearl stood a moment more in the doorway. Then she reached in, turned on the overhead light, and walked over to the huge furnace. Sarah followed her into the room.

"What is it?"

"I don't know, this bothers me."

She pulled open the furnace door and shone her light inside. Then she put her head and shoulders through the small doorway. She backed out and straightened up.

"You say workmen closed off the ducts?"

"That's what my husband said."

"It looks like it's just cardboard stuffed in there."

She thumped the butt of her flashlight on the nearest duct. It made a dull, flat sound. She began thumping the duct from the furnace outward and upward as high as she could reach, which was not quite to the ceiling.

"What are you doing?"

Pearl ignored her. She moved around to the next duct and repeated her thumping. She didn't stop until she'd checked all of them.

"They all *sound* about the same," she said, more to herself than to Sarah.

"Yes? And?"

"I was just thinking that if Christine had ever been down here, she might have stowed supplies or something up in there."

Pearl went around to the furnace door and leaned in again. Then she backed out.

"I'd like to open up those ducts, but I can't quite reach them without climbing in there."

"Maybe we can use a coat hanger or—"

"I've got something in the trunk of the car that might work," Pearl said. "Be back in a minute."

She walked out and clambered up the stairs. Sarah started to follow, afraid to be down there alone. Then she chided herself for being so paranoid. She moved over to the furnace and touched the nearest duct, feeling the dents where Pearl had struck with her flashlight. She wondered exactly what sound Pearl had expected to hear. She curled her fingers, palm forward, and drew back her hand to thump the duct.

Then she froze.

There was a rustling sound inside the duct. The sound became a heavy scraping and banging.

Sarah stumbled back and stared with horror at the furnace.

It was quiet for a moment.

Then through the open grate came the head and shoulders of Christine Helstrum. Her hair was in disarray, and her pink sweater was streaked with dirt. She turned toward Sarah with a surprised look on her face, as if she hadn't expected anyone to be there.

Then she smiled and began to climb out—clumsily, though, because she was holding the butcher knife.

Sarah heard herself scream as she turned and ran for her life.

35

SHE PUSHED OUT THE CARDboard and wriggled headfirst from the duct into the furnace. When she leaned out the furnace door, she was surprised to see Alex's wife standing there.

No matter, she thought. She can't stop me. I'll take my son and run away from here.

She'd wanted to do it last night, but Alex had surprised her in the foyer. She knew she was lucky she hadn't been shot. Or that the cops hadn't run in and caught her. She'd barely had time to open an outside door to make them think she'd left, just as she'd done before. Then she'd run down here and squeezed into her hiding place.

It had been a good hiding place, too, she thought. Always waiting for me after I'd snuck into the house.

She remembered holding her breath every time anyone came nearby, keeping silent, tucked safely away.

Then that damn woman cop, she thought.

She'd heard the cop tell Alex's wife that she had something out in the car to pull out the cardboard. She'd waited until they'd both left the room. At least she'd thought they'd both left. She'd been wrong, but it didn't matter. Soon she'd be gone from this place.

With my son, she thought.

She was anxious to be with him. She felt excited but good, warm inside.

She climbed out of the furnace and hobbled on stiff legs to the stairs. She heard Alex's wife slam the basement door and throw the bolt. She clomped up the stairs, allowing herself a smile when she saw the familiar breaker box.

She jabbed the butcher knife through the thin crack separating the basement door and the frame. Then she pressed down hard on the bolt and wiggled the knife back and forth, moving the bolt. She'd done this enough times before to have a good feel for it.

Within seconds the bolt was free.

She turned the knob and threw open the door.

36

SARAH FLED FROM THE FURnace room.

She tried to take the stairs three at a time, tripped, and fell forward, banging her left shin and her right elbow on the hard wooden steps. She clambered to her feet, her eyes watery with pain, and scrambled up the stairs. Just as she slammed the basement door, she heard Christine on the stairs. She slid the bolt in place, then turned and leaned back on the door and shouted for Officer Pearl.

Where is she?

"Pearl!" she shouted again.

Don't panic, she told herself. Think. Her car's out on the street. Run out and get her. No. Brian's upstairs. Get him out of the—

Sarah felt a sudden, sharp pain in the back of her right arm, just above the elbow. She cried out and lunged away from the door. When she turned, she saw a few inches of the butcher knife's blade protruding through the narrow slit between the basement door and the doorframe. The tip of the blade, pink with her blood, began to wiggle on top of the bolt. Sarah realized now how the scratches on the bolt had been made.

She reached for the bolt to hold it in place, but it suddenly slid free. Sarah didn't wait for the basement door to open, but turned and ran through the kitchen, yelling for Brian, trying to ignore the painful cut in her arm, and wondering where the hell Officer Pearl was.

She stopped for a split second in the foyer. The front door and safety were a few feet away, and part of her, the part concerned only with self-preservation, urged her to get out of the house now.

"Brian!" she yelled down the hallway toward the family room.

But she'd heard no TV sounds, and the last time she'd seen him he'd been upstairs.

She yelled for him as she ran up the stairs and around the top of the stairwell and burst into his room. He was sitting cross-legged on his bed beside an open coloring book and a shoe box filled with crayons. His eyes were wide in surprise.

"Come on, let's go!"

She grabbed him by the arm, pulled him off the bed, and half-dragged, half-tugged him out the door and down the hall to the head of the stairs. She took one step down, then stopped, her heart in her throat.

Christine stood at the foot of the stairs, one hand on the banister, the other at her side holding the long, wide butcher knife. It rested casually against her leg.

Sarah felt frozen in the moment, intensely aware of everything around her. She could see perfectly every detail of Christine's lined forehead and thickly made-up cheeks, her straggly golden-brown-tinted hair, and her clothing—the scuffed shoes, the limp skirt, the ruined pink sweater stretched tightly across her body. She could feel a rivulet of blood running down her right arm inside the sleeve of her sweater. Brian's hand in hers was warm and small, like a trapped, frightened bird. She could hear the faint whistling of his breathing and the fainter dull thuds of her own pounding heart. There was an odor in the air, an odor that Sarah could almost taste—sharp and bitter. But she couldn't tell whether it was drifting up from Christine or whether it came from inside, whether it was the odor of her own fear.

Christine smiled and tilted her head to one side as if admiring a picture. Sarah saw madness in her eyes. And she saw something else, something that she found even more frightening—love.

"Such a pretty boy," Christine said in a voice as jagged and brittle as broken glass. "Come to me now, Timothy."

She began to climb the stairs.

Brian was coloring the handle of Luke Skywalker's light sword when he thought he heard his mother call his name.

The sound had been muffled because his door was closed, so he wasn't certain that it had been his name he'd heard. He wasn't even certain that it was his mother calling, because the sound had been a high-pitched yell.

Then he heard it again. This time he was sure that it was his name and his mother yelling. He'd never heard her sound like that before. It frightened him.

Suddenly she burst through the door with a look of such wildness on her face that he could do nothing but sit and stare. She reached out to grab him. For a moment he thought she was angry because he'd been sitting on the bed with his boots on. But in the next second he knew it was something else, something far more serious than boots on the bed, because she yelled, "Come on, let's go!" then yanked his arm so hard he thought it would break.

He was pulled off the bed and out the door. He had to run as hard as he could to keep from being dragged down the hallway. When his mother stopped suddenly at the top of the stairs, he bumped hard into her leg.

He looked past her to the bottom of the stairs.

Down there staring up at him was the scariest person he'd ever seen. Her clothes were messed up, and her hair stuck out in all directions. When she smiled up at him, he felt himself shiver, because now he recognized her—the woman from his nightmare, the woman who had somehow become real and taken Patches out of his bedroom and hacked off his tail. And now she'd come back for him.

She said something that he didn't quite understand, and then she started up the stairs.

Brian knew that he and his mom were trapped. There were no good hiding places upstairs, and there was only one way down.

So they'd have to fight.

He pulled free of his mother's grip and ran back toward his room to get a weapon. She yelled at him to stop, but he ignored her, ran into his room, and dove for the corner and his toy chest. He yanked open the lid to reveal its jumbled contents. Lying on top was his Sword of Power, its blade tapered to a dull cardboard point.

He picked it up and threw it aside. He began frantically digging down into the chest, pulling out things with both hands and throwing them right and left. Balls, games, sporting equipment, toys—all of them sailing through the air or bouncing off the walls and piling up on the floor.

Just as he found what he was looking for, an arm wrapped around his chest and yanked him off his knees and into the air.

He was carried out the door and down the hall, bouncing on his mother's hip. He banged his foot on the doorframe of his parents' bedroom and then cried out, not because of the pain but because of what he saw: the woman with the knife coming around the head of the stairs.

His mother didn't stop until she'd run through the room and into the bathroom. She dropped him on the floor, slammed the bathroom door, and punched the button in the knob with her thumb. Now Brian knew why they'd come here: It was the only room upstairs with a lock on the door.

He sat on the floor, feeling more scared than he ever had in his life, and watched his mother press her ear against the door, listening for any sounds in the bedroom while her eyes searched the bathroom.

Her eyes frightened him more than anything, more than her

yelling and running, even more than the crazy lady who was coming after them. There was fear in her eyes, to be sure, and although he'd seen her frightened before, it had always been brief, nothing like this. But it wasn't the fear that scared him; it was something else, something that he'd never seen before—a fierce, wild look. He felt that at this moment she might do anything. She might even do something that would harm him.

His mother gasped, as if she'd heard something outside the door. Then she stepped over him and stood in the center of the bathroom, glancing quickly at everything around her—the bathtub enclosed in its shower curtain, the window, the toilet, the sink and countertop with the cupboards underneath, the mirrored medicine cabinet—as if she were searching for something to fight with.

"Use this, Mom," Brian said.

He stood and held out the box cutter, its thick, scarred metal handle in his hand and its rusty razor blade pointed toward her.

"Where did you—"

The doorknob rattled.

"I know you're in there," Christine said from the other side of the door.

Brian expected his mother to take the weapon from him and fight the woman. But she didn't. She turned away from the door, then practically flung herself at the window, pulled it open, and began yelling for help.

"It's okay, Mom," Brian said firmly. "I'll fight her."

He reached for the doorknob.

Sarah watched Christine start to come up the stairs. She knew they were trapped, and she tried to think if there was something up here that she could use as a weapon. There was nothing. And none of the doors had locks. Except—

Suddenly Brian pulled away from her and ran down the hall toward his room.

"Brian!"

She glanced down the stairs. Christine was a third of the way up now, climbing with purpose, a faint smile on her lips.

Sarah ran after Brian.

When she got to his room, she expected to find him hiding in the closet or perhaps squeezed under the bed. She was surprised, almost shocked, to see him kneeling before his toy chest, throwing out things right and left. She hurried over, scooped him up with one arm, and ran out of the room and down the hall to the master bedroom.

She saw Christine climb the last step and turn toward them.

Sarah hurried into the bathroom, let go of Brian, slammed the door, and locked it. She hoped it was locked; there was no way to test it—if she turned the knob, the button of the lock would pop open.

She looked frantically around the room, mentally searching behind every closed drawer and door for something, anything, that could be used to defend herself. But there was nothing more lethal than a fingernail file.

"Use this, Mom," Brian said, as if he'd been reading her thoughts.

He was holding something out for her—Alex's box cutter. The last time she'd seen it had been when Alex was opening boxes of Christmas-tree ornaments in the basement. She started to say something when she heard Christine's voice just outside the door. It went through her like an electric current. She jumped at the window, reached up for the shoulder-high latch, then slid the window horizontally in its aluminum frame. She began yelling into the cold darkness.

"Help us! We're upstairs in the bathroom! Help!"

The window faced south, overlooking the side yard and the garage. Sarah had no idea whether her voice would carry along the side of the house to the street.

Where's Pearl? she thought.

She wondered if Officer Maestas had been parked in the street when Pearl went out there. She could picture them now, idly chatting, perhaps both sitting in Maestas's patrol car with the windows rolled up against the cold.

She was about to yell again, yell her lungs out because there was nothing else to do, when she heard Brian say something. She turned in time to see him put his hand on the doorknob.

"Brian, no!"

He looked back at her, his face set in determination, his small hand still resting on the knob.

"She hurt Patches, Mom, but we can beat her."

He was beyond her reach, too far for her to physically stop him from turning the knob and popping open the lock-button, unlocking the door.

"No, Brian," she said quickly. "If you let her in, she'll hurt us both."

He hesitated, then dropped his hand from the doorknob.

Christine pounded on the door.

"It's time to come out now, Timothy. It's time to go home with Mommy."

Sarah glanced at Brian, who now stood petrified in the middle of the bathroom. She turned to the window and twisted the clasps that held the screen in place. She tried to pull the screen out, but it wouldn't budge, so she pounded its frame with the heel of her hand. The screen and frame came free and sailed down to the snowy yard.

Sarah leaned out the window. From this height, the screen looked no bigger than a postcard lying in the moonlit snow. There was no ledge below the window, nothing but a straight two-story drop to the ground. Sarah had hoped that there would be a way to climb down. But there was none. And it was too far to jump. If it were just her, she'd risk it. But there was Brian, and he might not survive the fall.

She thought of the mattress that she and Alex had hauled outside only yesterday, but it was leaning against the house, not flat on the ground. If only—

The bathroom door shook under a solid thud, as if a heavy weight had been thrown against it.

Christine swore from outside the door. She was quiet for a moment. Then she grunted, and immediately there came another thud, this one stronger, making the door shudder in its frame.

Sarah doubted that the fragile lock could withstand more.

She leaned back out the window and looked up. The sky was dark enough now to reveal the brightest stars, except where their light was washed out by the quarter moon or blocked by the overhanging edge of the roof. Sarah reached up for the roof's edge, stretching as far as she could. It was just beyond the tips of her fingers. She put her hands on the window ledge and hoisted herself partially out the window, holding on with one hand and reaching up and back with the other.

Now she could feel the roofing tiles. They felt dry and rough enough to grip. She slid back down into the room just as the bathroom door shook under a tremendous blow, moving it slightly inward, splintering the old wooden frame.

"Brian, come here quick." Her voice was a loud whisper. "We're going up on the roof."

Brian stared at her as if in shock. She pulled him over to the window, took the box cutter from him so that both his hands would be free, and jammed it in her pocket. Then she lifted him up to the window.

"Mommy, no."

"Don't be afraid, Brian, I won't let you fall."

She held him so that he was sitting on the windowsill, his feet inside, his back to the void, his face to the house.

"Climb up there, Brian. Hurry."

She lifted him, then felt him pull up out of her grasp. She gave the bottoms of his boots one final shove and then looked up. He was out of sight.

Now Sarah hoisted herself through the window and tried not to stare at the distant ground below her. She was only halfway through when she heard the crack of splintering wood, the slam of the door banging open against the bathroom wall and the thud and tumble of someone falling into the room. She reached up, grasped the eave, and began pulling herself out of the window as if she were climbing out of shark-infested waters, waiting for the strike that could come at any second to her hip, her thigh, her calf . . .

She felt a sudden blow to her ankle that hurt even through the thickness of her boot. And then she was out of the window and up on the sloping roof.

A cold breeze stung her eyes. To her right she could see the soft glow of Colorado Springs in the night sky. To her left were the Rockies, blacker than night, spotted here and there with lights, faintly outlined by a deep purple glow. Above her sat Brian, knees up, feet flat, hands palms down at his sides. He looked at her with wide, frightened eyes, and he shivered—whether from fear or cold, Sarah couldn't tell.

She moved toward him in a crablike walk. His mouth opened, and he raised his arm and pointed. Sarah looked back and saw two hands gripping the edge of the roof. Then Christine's face rose into view, as pale white as the moon.

"Help us!" Sarah yelled toward the street, which was hidden from view by the length of the house. "Help us! We're on the roof!"

"Leave my son alone," Christine said. "Give him back to me." She pulled herself onto the roof, the knife handle protruding from the waist of her skirt.

"Turn around and climb, Brian," Sarah said, her voice desperate, and together they scrambled up toward the peak of the roof.

We can climb down the other side, Sarah thought. I can hang from the eave and kick in a window, then we can get back in the house and run out the front door, and . . .

They'd reached the peak of the roof. The roofing tiles there were as dark and dry as they were on this side of the roof, the south side. But on the other side the roof was white with unmelted snow.

Sarah realized that if they tried to climb down they'd slide uncontrollably to the bottom and over the edge.

She turned and looked back.

Christine was making her way toward them—slowly, though, slipping slightly in her leather-soled shoes. When she was a dozen feet from them, she stopped and turned to rest on her hip. Sarah enjoyed one wild moment of hope, hope that Christine, for whatever reason, was unable to climb to the top. But her hope vanished when she saw Christine draw the long-bladed knife from her skirt, then turn to face them. She moved upward, more slowly now, because only one hand was free for climbing.

One hand free for climbing, Sarah thought.

She'd taken something from Brian so that both *his* hands would be free for climbing—the box cutter. She struggled to get it out of her pocket. Then she sat there, perched on the peak of the roof, her right arm around Brian, her left hand holding the box cutter. She held it before her, as if it were a talisman to ward off death.

And now Christine was directly below them.

"Here, Timothy," she said, and reached for Brian's foot.

"NO!"

Sarah lashed out with the box cutter. Its tiny, sharp blade touched Christine's forehead, making her jerk back. A thin line appeared above her eyebrows and began to ooze shiny black droplets.

Christine's face twisted in pain and rage. She raised up on her knees and brought the butcher knife high above her head.

Sarah let go of Brian, desperate now to save him, and threw herself at Christine just as the knife came slashing downward. Sarah drove her shoulder into Christine's chest, knocking her over backward, feeling the knife blade nip her side. The larger woman landed flat on her back with Sarah on top. Sarah heard the knife rattle down the tiles and over the edge. And now they were both tumbling down the roof—Sarah's fingers scraping the roofing tiles, wildly trying to stop her fall, and Christine flailing and clawing at Sarah. Sarah managed to momentarily kick free from Christine, then twisted onto her stomach, spread her arms, and dug the edges of her rubber-soled boots into the roof. Christine rolled and slid down the entire slope of the roof. When she reached the edge, her back was to the void, and she seemed to hang suspended for a moment. Her eyes were filled with hate, locked on Sarah. And then she tumbled over the edge.

Sarah lay flat on the roof and looked up at Brian, who was still perched on the peak of the roof. She held her breath and waited to hear a distant thump as Christine struck the ground.

But she heard nothing. And she realized now that Christine had gone over the edge in complete silence. She hadn't cried out or even whimpered.

"Don't move," Sarah told Brian.

She edged slowly down the roof and cautiously peeked over the edge.

Christine lay in the snowy yard like a broken doll.

Sarah let out her breath in a long, slow shudder.

It's over, she thought, thank God it's—

And then she saw Christine move.

Sarah stared down in disbelief as Christine slowly got to her feet. She paused before straightening up and picked something off the ground—the butcher knife.

Then Sarah heard a voice below her and to her left. Another figure had entered the yard, a figure whose blond hair was visible behind her cap. Officer Pearl was crouching with her hands together and her arms extended in a "V" toward Christine. She said something that Sarah couldn't understand.

Suddenly Christine raised the knife and lurched toward Pearl. Sarah saw the flash and heard the dull snap of Pearl's gun.

Christine continued to stumble forward.

Pearl fired again.

Christine fell and lay still in the snow.

37

SARAH BARELY HEARD THE doorbell through the loud conversation and laughter.

"Excuse me," she said to Jack Dahlquist. She'd been talking to her neighbor and a man named Arthur—she'd forgotten his last name—who taught math at Jefferson High. The two men had just discovered that they were both enthusiastic fly fishermen, so Sarah thought that the doorbell had come at a most opportune moment.

She set her glass of champagne on an end table and nudged her way through the crowded living room to the foyer. From here the dominant sounds came from her left: Jefferson High's stodgy vice-principal, Ralph Anderson, banging out a Golden Oldie on the piano to accompany the singing of his wife and Denise Dahlquist and several other unidentified voices—all a bit off-key but making up for it in volume.

She opened the door to a wave of cold December air.

"Happy New Year," Kay Nealy said. "Sorry we're late."

"Don't worry, there's plenty of party left."

Sarah held the door for them, and Rick kissed her on the cheek.

"Nice to see you again. How's everything?"

"Everything's great. And it's good to see you, too."

Sarah took their coats and squeezed both garments into the overfull hall closet.

"God, Sarah," Kay said, reaching out to touch her neck. "Where did you get *that*?"

Sarah fingered her gold necklace. "Alex gave it to me for Christmas."

"It's beautiful," Kay said, then jammed Rick in the side with her elbow. "He gave me a food processor."

"Hey, it's what you wanted, right?"

Kay rolled her eyes, making Sarah laugh.

"Which way to the bar?" Kay asked.

"Follow me."

Sarah led them to the kitchen. It didn't look as if it would hold another person, but Kay grabbed Rick by the hand and pulled him into the crowd. Sarah stood for a moment in the doorway. She saw Alex getting ice from the refrigerator. After he closed the door, he touched his hand to his neck, making Sarah wonder if the area around his scar was still causing him discomfort—after all, it had been little more than two weeks since his injury. She watched him until he turned her way. He saw her and smiled. She smiled back, and he blew her a kiss.

Sarah felt someone tap her on the arm—Martha Kellog, glass in hand.

"Sorry," Sarah said, moving aside. "I guess I'm blocking the way to the bar."

"No, I'm fine." Martha held up her half-full glass of ginger ale. "It's your son. He's awake, and I think he wants you."

"Thanks, Martha."

"Maybe he was having a nightmare."

"Let's hope not," Sarah said, and walked toward the foyer.

Sarah had worried about Brian's bad dreams, the ones he'd suffered for the first few nights after Christine Helstrum's death. She'd suffered a few of her own, but they had soon faded as her life began to slowly re-form into familiar patterns. In fact, her clearest memory of the ordeal was not being chased by Christine, when her adrenaline had been flowing and her mind had been desperate for survival, but of the time immediately after the danger, when Officer Maestas had sat on the roof with her and Brian and wrapped a blanket around them and waited for the firemen to safely walk them down a ladder.

She'd also had a few nightmares about the basement. These dreams usually didn't involve things that she'd seen but things she'd been told by Officer Pearl and others. Clothing and food scraps had been found stuffed in the furnace ducts. Apparently Christine had been living down there for many days, opening outside doors to confuse them, hiding, laughing, playing her insane game.

What was it like for her, Sarah wondered, squeezed into that furnace duct? Alone, waiting in the dark, pressed in on all sides by cold metal, smelling her own stench.

Sarah found Brian standing on the stairs in his pajamas, two steps from the bottom, looking a bit perplexed by all the commotion.

"I can't sleep, Mom."

"It is pretty loud, isn't it?" She put her hand gently on his head. "Come on, I'll read you a story."

She took him upstairs to his room and closed the door. The sounds from below were no more than a muffled hum. She tucked Brian under the covers without disturbing Patches, who was curled up at the foot of the bed. The big cat blinked once at Sarah, then closed his sleepy green eyes. She tried to remember what he'd looked like with a long tail. It was difficult, because he seemed so normal with his furry stub.

Sarah took down the nearest book at hand from the shelf above Brian's desk. She glanced at the cover—a boy and a girl and a dog riding a flying carpet—then sat on the edge of the bed and began reading.

She was up to page six when the door opened and Alex walked softly in.

"Our son needed to be entertained, too," Sarah said.

Alex held his finger to his lips. "Looks like he's had enough for tonight," he whispered.

Only now did Sarah notice that Brian's eyes were closed. She bent over and kissed him lightly on the forehead, then stood and put the book on his desk. When she turned, she saw Alex pulling the blanket up to Brian's chin. It was a simple act, and she'd seen him do it many times before, but something about it touched her now—as if it were not just an act but a symbol. Safety and comfort, perhaps. Family.

Then she had a grim thought, one she'd had before: Christine had been partly responsible for creating this family. Her vicious acts had resulted in love. And in a way, Sarah realized, Christine's acts had been motivated by love. She'd wanted to get back her son.

What if for some reason they'd taken away *my* son? Sarah thought. What would I have done to get him back? How desperately would I have tried?

Alex looked at her and frowned.

"Are you all right?" He spoke softly, careful not to wake Brian.

"Yes," Sarah said quietly. She smiled and reached out for his hand. "Come on, our friends are waiting."

About the Author

Michael Allegretto is the author of *Death on the Rocks* (which won the Shamus Award for best first private eye novel and was nominated for the Anthony Award for best first mystery novel), *Blood Stone*, and *The Dead of Winter.* He lives in Denver.